LESSER LIVES

The True History
of the First
Mrs. Meredith
and Other

Lesser
Lives

Diane Johnson

Alfred A. Knopf   New York   1972

Library of Congress Cataloging in Publication Data
Johnson, Diane.   The true history of the first Mrs. Meredith
and other lesser lives.
Running title: Lesser lives.
1. Meredith, Mary Ellen, 1821–1861. 2. Meredith, George, 1828–1909.
3. Wallis, Henry, b. 1830.
I. Title. II. Title: Lesser lives.
CT788.M378J64   823'.8 [B]   72–2227
ISBN 0–394–48034–1

Manufactured in the United States of America
First Edition

for Kevin, Darcy, Amanda, and Simon

CONTENTS

ILLUSTRATIONS

ACKNOWLEDGMENTS

I would like to express my grateful thanks to the many people who have helped me with this book: To the librarians of the Huntington Library, the Victoria and Albert and British Museum and Bodleian Libraries, the Carl H. Pforzheimer Library, the Widener Library of Harvard University, the Beinecke Library of Yale University, the Berg Collection of the New York Public Library, to the Royal Marines Historian in England, and to Miss Rose Lambert of the Louisiana State Museum Library in New Orleans. I am grateful also to Professors Ada B. Nisbet and John Espey for their advice and encouragement, to Lionel Stevenson, C. L. Cline, Eleanor L. Nicholes, and Phyllis Bartlett for their kindness in responding to my queries with expert knowledge and assistance, and to Mrs. Elizabeth David, for graciously sending me a copy of a cookbook of Edith Nicolls's. Thanks are also owing to the American Association of University Women, to the Woodrow Wilson Foundation, and to the University of California, Davis and Los Angeles campuses, for financial assistance. I am grateful to Mr. and Mrs. Roberts, present owners of Peacock House, and to Peter Hawkins for his invaluable research assistance and photographs, to Robert Hopkins; to Lady de Montmorency, and to Mr. and Mrs. C. A. Whiting, without whom much of this book could not have been written at all, and to Dan Wickenden for his helpful suggestions; to Toni Roby for her translations from the French; to Betty Kimura, Judy Kalivas, and to my patient family.

Reference to and quotations from the following documents are given with the permission of The Carl and Lily Pforzheimer

Foundation, Inc.: letters to "My own darling Eddy" and to "My kind dear father" from Mary Ellen Peacock. Letters to Henry Wallis are given with the kind cooperation of the Wallis estate, and selections from the Commonplace Book of Mary Ellen Meredith are given with permission of the Beinecke Rare Book and Manuscript Library, Yale University.

Many people have described the Famous Writer presiding at his dinner table, in a clean neckcloth. He is famous; everybody remembers his remarks. He remembers his own remarks, being a writer, and notes them in his diary. We forget that there were other people at the table — a quiet person, now muffled by time, shadowy, whose heart pounded with love, perhaps, or rage, or fear when our writer shuffled in from his study; whose hands, white knuckled, twisted an apron, whose thoughts raced. Or someone who left the room with a full throat of sobs. Of course there is no way really to know the minds of Lizzie Rossetti, or the first Mrs. Milton, or all those silent Dickens children suffering the mad unkindness, the delirious pleasures of their terrifying father's company — with little places of their own to put their small things away in, with small, terrified thoughts.

But we know a lesser life does not seem lesser to the person who leads one. His life is very real to him; he is not a minor figure in it. He looks out of his eyes at our poet, our chronicled statesman; he feels the tears within himself and down his cheeks. All the days of his life we do not know about but he was doing something, anyway — something happy or bitter or merely dull. And he is our real brother.

It was sympathy, then, and curiosity that first sent me looking into the life of Mrs. Meredith. Subsequently I found a number of other, more respectable, historiographical, literary, even culinary reasons, to justify looking into her life, the people she and George Meredith knew, the things they did and thought.

I mean, of course, the first Mrs. Meredith, Mary Ellen, the

daughter of Thomas Love Peacock. The second Mrs. Meredith was a plain, quiet woman, evidently even-tempered, because Meredith said that to argue with her was like "firing broadsides into a mud fort." The first Mrs. Meredith was argumentative and beautiful, and never let loose her hold on the imagination of the great novelist—even though she died early, and he had come to hate her, and rarely spoke of her after her death, and then told people she was mad.

The life of Mary Ellen is always treated, in a paragraph or a page, as an episode in the lives of Peacock or Meredith. It was treated with a certain reserve in early biographies because it involves adultery and recrimination, and makes all the parties look ugly. More recent biographies of Meredith repeat the received version of the story with a certain brisk determination, a kind of feigned acceptance: we know that these things, regrettably, do indeed happen.

Mrs. Meredith's life can be looked upon, of course, as an episode in the lives of Meredith or Peacock, but it cannot have seemed that way to her.

Real creatures exquisitely fantastical

strangely exposed to the world

by a lurid catastrophe. . . .

George Meredith,
preface to THE TRAGIC COMEDIANS

LESSER LIVES

THE NICOLLS

General Sir Edward *m.* Lady Nicolls

| M. | Richard | Jenny | Ellen | Bessie | Edwina | Alicia | Edward |

THE MEREDITHS

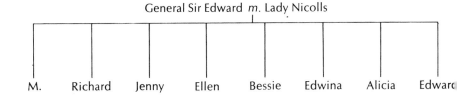

The Great Mel

Augustus *m.* Jane

George Meredith *m.* Mary Ellen Peacock Nico
m.
Marie Vulliamy

| William Maxse | Marie Eveleen (*Riette*) | Arthur |

THE PEACOCKS

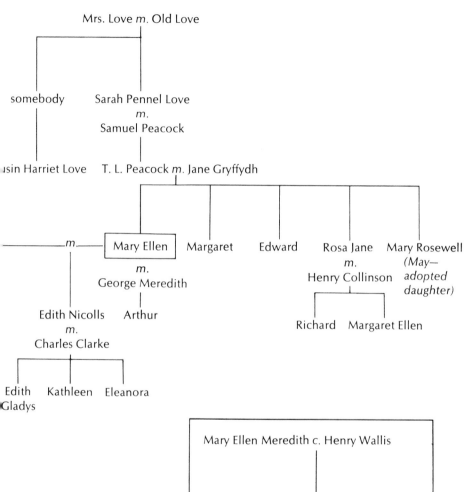

Mrs. Love *m.* Old Love

somebody   Sarah Pennel Love
m.
Samuel Peacock

...sin Harriet Love   T. L. Peacock *m.* Jane Gryffydh

————— *m.* ————— Mary Ellen   Margaret   Edward   Rosa Jane   Mary Rosewell
m.   *m.*   *(May—*
George Meredith   Henry Collinson   *adopted*
daughter)

Edith Nicolls   Arthur
m.
Charles Clarke   Richard   Margaret Ellen

Edith   Kathleen   Eleanora
Gladys

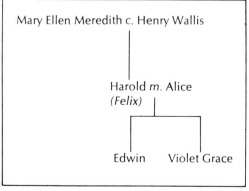

Mary Ellen Meredith *c.* Henry Wallis

Harold *m.* Alice
(Felix)

Edwin   Violet Grace

$\mathcal{W}$e have stopped, or we have pretended to stop, the flow of time, and all the lesser lives with which we are here concerned are collected for introduction. We must try to imagine an occasion, perhaps a ceremonial occasion, some one moment in which we can catch them all in characteristic attitudes. It is a fine autumn day in October 1861. The leaves are turning, smoke hangs in the air from bonfires somewhere. Little beech leaves lie like yellow coins over the dappled graves, over the browned grass and dried creepers. The tall headstones all around are banked with dead leaves but a few roses still blow in the hedge; the yew and cedar, of course, always are green. It is chilly except when you stand in the sun.

The coffin, a plain one, has now been screwed down and lies in the grave. The sexton stands nearby with his shovel and an expression of most perfect rectitude: exactly combining in even proportion his decorous regret that a beautiful woman has died so young, his pious satisfaction that a sinful woman has been taken (one hopes) to a Better Home before she could sink any lower, and a professional impassivity calculated to speed the proceedings along. The young vicar of St. James's, Weybridge, is reading from the book with congruent haste.

It is a funeral. George Meredith's first wife has died. No one is there.

This embarrasses the young vicar. It is awkward to be saying these "comfortable words" in a loud, deep, feeling voice when nobody is there but two drab servant women and a middle-aged man not of this parish, and so doubtless connected with the sinful, London part of her life. This man, who has a military air, peers into the open grave. His head is bowed but his eyes are open. The two women have eyes decently closed and they press handkerchiefs to their noses. Their faces are sorrowful but not surprised. Each has fixed opinions about the human condition and finds nothing here to surprise her. The open eyes of the big, military gentleman do not seem to accept explanation. His glances press the open grave for clues.

"Man, that is born of a woman, hath but a short time to live, and is full of misery. He cometh up, and is cut down, like a flower; he fleeth as it were a shadow, and never continueth in one stay," the vicar reads, and reads a little more and steps back. The sexton steps forward. The ladies walk away together up the path past the church, talking to each other in their high, unpleasant, servants' voices. The middle-aged man lingers, hoping perhaps to pronounce or to hear some reliable summation, hears or delivers none, shakes the vicar's hand, and strides off. Surely a military man, by his walk.

We do not need to attend much further to these few mourners. The first of the two women is Jane Wells, Mary Ellen's maid. She will find another place, a good one, with Lady Blessington of Tunbridge Wells, and will marry a man named Purdue. We do not know if she was fond of Mary Ellen but she was faithful, and conventional about funerals; it was "a blessing someone was, poor creature, for all that her family turned up to lay her to rest." That was Mrs. Bennet's view too, and they exchanged this opinion as they walked. Mrs. Bennet would have brought her charge, little Felix, to see his mother off to her reward, but the father, an Atheist, wouldn't hear of it, and maybe it was just as well (she remarks to Jane Wells), for the sight of his mama's open grave and no one there to mourn her could not help but be a sorrow to him when he was old enough to understand why.

The military gentleman is Captain Henry Howes, just someone she used to know. He is of no importance, except, of course, to himself. We do not know why he turned up at the funeral of this forlorn lady: some remembered affection, some prompting of propriety, some promise to her father, perhaps. He was remembering, as he looked upon the coffin, as people will on such occasions, happier days, when she and her brother, and Hilary St. Croix, and Peter Daniel, and George Meredith—all of them so anxiously literary—all lived in London and were happy. And of them, only Meredith was going to make his mark, that seemed certain already. Well, well. Off he walks, and whether he lives or dies, a matter of utmost consequence to him, we cannot say.

As for the others, since they did not come to her funeral, we shall have to look around for them. Mary Ann Rosewell, called May, is on her way home after making the last of the funeral arrangements. She always gets stuck with attending to these family things, funerals and lyings-in, as though the rest of them thought that because she was of peasant stock her sensibilities were cruder and better able to bear up. She is the adopted daughter of Thomas Love Peacock.

Peacock himself, and his granddaughter, Mary Ellen's oldest child Edith, a girl of seventeen, have stayed at home in Lower Halliford, only a few miles from the churchyard. Edith is with her grandfather when May arrives. Peacock likes to have her near; she is his pet, student, confidante, even allowed in his library. May goes directly to the kitchen to attend to something there, thinking, with a certain hardness of heart, about Edith and about the dead Mary Ellen. Well, she is sorry for them all. May is nearly forty, an aging Cinderella; her emotions are complex but she does not discuss them.

Little Edith inherits Grandpapa's prejudice against funerals and stays home from Mama's funeral out of principle, not because she is unfeeling. And Grandpapa needs her more now than poor Mama can. Edith, born a Victorian, is intensely sad, and weeps more easily than anyone we have yet met, but she weeps secretly, where Grandpapa and May do not see. In their company she is quiet and staunch. She will get a medal from the Queen when she grows up.

Grandpapa is seventy-six, an old man, and his health has suffered through the long weeks since August. He is exhausted from watching his most beloved child, Mary Ellen, slowly die. Now he sits weakly grieving, and in his soul the iron, always present, has seized such hold there is no expression for it. The iron seizes his whole being. He cannot write it off or walk it off. He has about him a kind of pale glitter, mounds of silver hair, sad pallor, still-blue eyes that reveal a bitter, bitter knowledge. The world praises him for his sweet mockery, his charm, his witty books, his well-mannered classicism, his *joie de vivre*. But he has lived for thirty years with a madwoman for a wife. He has seen all his daughters die, and some of their children, and his friends. He is a tall man, sitting very straight in his chair. He looks out over the river, the beautiful Thames that runs in front of his house, on whose banks his children played. He never goes to funerals.

It is possible that Mr. Wallis calls. Mr. Wallis has acted rather well; the family do not think as ill of him as the world does, or at least as the Meredith half of the world does. The Meredith half sees him as a seducer and a villain. It will suppress him; it will pretend he does not exist and though it will continue to admire his paintings, it will leave him out of biographical dictionaries. Poor Mr. Wallis is left with the baby to raise, dear little Felix, christened Harold Meredith, despite Mr. Wallis being his father. Awkward.

May Rosewell, now or some time, gives Mr. Wallis some of Mary Ellen's clothes, and a watch, and some jewelry and her books, and a little picture of her. They had decided it was fitting that he have these things to pass down to Harold. (Somehow, something would have to be done about changing Harold's last name.)

Mr. Wallis goes for a walk in Oatlands Park, past the cottage where she died. Oatlands is beautiful and somber in autumn. Mr. Wallis is sad and a little bewildered. He is young, and he still hopes to become a great painter, and now he has a baby to raise.

Her husband, George Meredith, we see vacationing over in Suffolk, in "a dumpling state," doing some reading and taking brisk walks. He is eating a cold steak-and-kidney pie, but we must not think him insensitive. It is just that he has not yet heard the news of his wife's death. When he does he will be sad; he will be more than sensitive. He will never be free of her. In later years the memory will become so burdensome that he will strike out. "She was mad," he will say, and, "she was nine years older than I" (though she was but six-and-a-half). Surlily, he will refuse to discuss her at all. But now he is cheerful, drinking ale in a public house on the wayside.

Their son Arthur, a small, pale, frightened boy, has been pulled here and put there, and wept over by his dying mother to whom he was carried by excited ladies in carriages in the night, and taken from by his angry, tight-lipped father, and left with all manner of people — friends, publishers, Edith's grandmama in her big mansion. Now he does not know what to think at all. It is Meredith's belief that Arthur does "not feel the blow," but Arthur, of course, feels it, though he has not seen much of his beautiful Mama for several years; she was ill, she was confined, she was ill again, had fled the country. Arthur was not sure where she had been. He was not allowed to speak of Mama. She could not be thought of. She was cloaked, she was shrouded, something awful, shame, disgrace. Arthur, a polite little boy, is given cake by Mrs. Parker, who marvels at his solemn good manners.

Peacock's cousin, Harriet Love, is cheerfully rocking and chatting to her old brother, knowing she is boring him, but enjoying one of the privileges of being an old maid sister; it is a kind of revenge. They have not heard of Mary Ellen's death, so they do not have to decide how to feel. If they did know, they would not mention the matter to their neighbor, Lord Tennyson, who pays them a call and leaves them a Review, as is his habit. How Lord Tennyson felt about such subjects as adultery is very clear. He would have regarded Mary Ellen's death as quite just.

Old Thomas Jefferson Hogg, Peacock's friend from the Shelley days, hears the news from someone in London, but he is too old and near death to care; dying seems suitable to him now. No one tells Claire Clairmont. She would have been interested. She had always been interested in the Peacocks, and sometimes wished she had married Tom Peacock. The fleeting embraces of Lord Byron, whose memory had seemed urgent and ineradicable in her youth, were now so distant they were almost indistinguishable from the embraces of Peacock, which she (perhaps) had never experienced. Claire Clairmont had nearly twenty more years to live, and people would think her an incredible anachronism, though it cannot have seemed so to her.

Lord Broughton, Peacock's dear friend, does not notice the brief note on the back of a letter Peacock had written before the death, so he does not know that Mary Ellen is finally gone, and he sends no comforting words. He could have helped, as Peacock helped him when poor Julia died.

At St. James's, Weybridge, the vicar has gone into the room where the register is kept and enters the burial in form, but he does not, for some reason, mark on the chart the spot where Mary Ellen was buried. In a few years no one will be able to find her grave.

He has left the churchyard, taking his Holy Bible with him, the thud of the shovel has ceased, and Mrs. Wells and Mrs. Bennet have been grandly taken away in a carriage arranged by someone. No sound in the chill autumn air, not even of birds, for the summer birds have mostly gone. A bluish haze of smoke from someone's bonfire, and from sunlight and dust too — an autumn haze settles over the graves in the late afternoon. Now the ghosts approach, curious, a bit cautious, none of them much at home in churchyards. But they have always been interested in Mary Ellen.

Mindful of decorum they first lead up to look upon the grave an old witless woman, who is weeping. She is glad, she sniffles, that her child is at least laid in holy ground. An older, taller woman compresses her lips, nods, leads her away with a backward glance, intelligent and sad. These are Mary Ellen's mother, Jane, and her grandmother, Thomas's mother, old Sarah Peacock, who raised Tom's children and cared for their mother, too. Old Sarah, something of a literary woman herself, once wrote a poem for Mary Ellen's birthday. It ended:

> And may thy later years be blest
> As thy sweet infancy has been.

She is thinking of this now.

Next, some grislier shades appear, wet, dripping, adorned with seaweed and starfish and other regalia of the drowned. Two are young men whose permanently resentful expressions, fixed so at their deaths, are mitigated here by looks of sorrow and of cosmic anger in their glaring dead eyes. The first is young Lieutenant Nicolls, Mary Ellen's husband when she was twenty-two. They were married for three months before his drowning. For him she remains his beautiful bride. He weeps.

The other is the poet Shelley. He had told Peacock that the "little stranger" was "introduced into a rough world." He shrugs but his eyes sting. This Mary Ellen had been brave, but she was born in the wrong time. Like his contemporary, Poe, Shelley thought there was nothing in the world so sad as the death of a young and beautiful woman. He grasps the arm of Edward Nicolls. They had not known each other in life but they find a certain camaraderie now.

Of no importance to Mary Ellen but of interest to us are two other drowned and ghastly figures, a discreet distance away, diffidently attending Shelley and Nicolls. The one, pale and bloated, is Harriet Shelley, and the other is a one-armed sailor whose name is not known. Seaweed decorates his dripping hair.

Shrill and scolding voices, female voices, rustle of petticoats, brisk feet. Mary Shelley is the one in the wide skirt, and the woman in the high-waisted regency gown is her mother, Mary Wollstonecraft. They have pretty, pointed faces and thin lips. They are angry on Mary Ellen's behalf. Their impatient feet tap, they pace over the grave. Must it always be this way for women? Here was one they thought might persevere in woman's name. She had promise. She had courage.

The illness was just bad luck, Mary Shelley thinks, or maybe divine retribution. She had never been entirely sure there was no divine retribution; the facts of her life, indeed, had suggested otherwise.

Men's fault, and intolerable it is, too, her mother thinks. Mary Wollstonecraft, the great feminist, died of childbearing, with puppies sucking at her breasts to draw off the milk.

Mary Shelley had known Mary Ellen Peacock since she was a

tiny girl, and is thinking sentimentally of the child with long gold curls. Mary Wollstonecraft sniffs and sweeps away across the grass.

The shades departed, evening settles, then night. The grave is indistinguishable in darkness from all the other graves. In their different nurseries, her two little sad-eyed boys, Arthur and Felix, are tucked in by their respective nurses. They wonder at the silence. Henry Wallis comes in to kiss Felix. Arthur must go to bed alone. We do not know if they ever met each other, or whether, if they did, they spoke of this day to each other. Their sister Edith has tried to get Grandpapa to go to bed but he only sits, staring, in his armchair. George Meredith cheerfully jokes with some fellows at an inn, and Henry Wallis has a serious discussion with his mother about his new responsibility for Felix. To Mary Ellen, being dead, all this makes no difference, anyway. And now they are *all* dead and to the world they have made little difference.

つ.

The owner of a lesser life does not much survive a century of time, especially when the life was embarrassing to a major life or two. We can imagine the little fires in the various grates, the fervid comminution scenes as bits of paper—letters, recipes— turn to ash at the patient, feeding hands of shocked persons. Mary Ellen Peacock Nicolls Meredith, dead now one hundred and eleven years, survives materially in a lock of hair, a book she owned *(The Arabian Nights),* a green satin dress, another of ecru embroidery, two parasols to match, a dozen letters, a few articles and poems she wrote, and a book of Extracts in which she copied out things that struck her as she read. She survives immaterially but somehow more vividly as a spirited, faithless kind of heroine who turns up in poems and novels by her husband George Meredith. She is remembered in a line here and there in occasional Victorian memoirs by serious gentlemen, who say she was a dashing horsewoman, or whom she teased about their stuffy taste in poetry, for she also had a reputation as a wit.[1] A drawing by her lover shows a calm lady with great almond eyes, in a demure bonnet. Somewhere, in some British parlor, she looks out of a painting called *Fireside Reverie,* and the people who see her every day may wonder—or perhaps it has never occurred to them to wonder—whether the lady over the mantel was ever anyone real. A picture, some old dresses, and a few lines from her pen—from these some things can be known and some things can never be. We know where she got her book ("To Mary Peacock from her Father"). It is not known on what occasion she wore the green satin dress.[2]

It is usual in biographies to trace a family as far back as possible, to discern what is inevitable about the subject because of his forebears: the shape of his nose, say. Biographers of Shelley are fond of pointing out that an ancestor of Shelley's was sent down from Oxford in 1567 for atheism; some fellow two centuries before can always be discovered by our genealogist aunt to have been just like us—same turn for music or thievery.

We can trace Mary Ellen's family for only a few generations, but from these generations alone we can infer that the Peacock women were forceful and literary, and that the men were forceful, literary, and nautical. These tendencies will affect Mary Ellen in unfortunate ways.

It is hard to decide just where to begin a history. Can Shelley's troubles be said to have started in 1567? If we can for a minute imagine a historical personage—Mary Ellen or ourselves, say—as a kind of puppet activated by a skein of threads, thousands and thousands of little strings of complicated determinism stretching off into an invisible infinity, held on the far ends by an infinitude of ancestors and unknown persons who, tugging them, account for our fondness for blackberry jam, or cause our hair to curl—we can see how complicated a proposition it is to try to disentangle one special, shining thread that will carry us back to the beginning. It is all a hopeless web.

And since the beginning is arbitrary, we will arbitrarily begin in the year 1788 when a woman named Sarah Peacock left her husband, Samuel, a glassmaker in London, took her little boy Thomas, and went home to her own mother and father, a Mr. and Mrs. Love, who lived in the small village of Chertsey, south of the river Thames in Surrey. No one knows what caused Sarah Peacock to do this. Wives did not leave their husbands in those days. It betokens, perhaps, a sinister strain of independence, a want of docility.

No doubt there was gossip in the village of Chertsey. Perhaps you would have expected this kind of unbecoming behavior from a daughter of the Loves, nice enough people in their way but eccentric and bookish. Another sort of family might have in-sisted Sarah uphold her duty to her husband Samuel and stay with him in London. Sarah Peacock, it is said, read Gibbon and other such highbrow books.

The Loves *were* nice enough in their way. Old Love had a lot of interesting sea stories. He was retired, and liked to sit around with the other old sailors and swap stories. Old Love had been a Master in the Royal Navy, and had lost his leg on board the ship *Prothee* in the vigorous action of the 12th of April, 1772. That was under Lord Rodney. And old Love's son was beside him during the whole thing.

Of the Loves not much else is known, except they were long-lived. Old Love lived to be eighty-one, and his wife outlived him. Their daughter Sarah had come home from London and looked after them. It is said she had been married in London, and she had a son Tom, a smart little fellow.

Samuel Peacock, glass merchant, whom nobody could ever quite remember, was left by his wife, a termagant and too clever by half; she took their little boy Tom and went to live with her parents. Her mother, old Mrs. Love, was too clever by half, too. Samuel Peacock glass merchant had done the best he could. Sarah was nice enough about it—just up and went—but it is bad when your wife leaves you; it reflects on a man.

Or perhaps Samuel was of a bookish nature too, like his wife and son, and got a lot of reading done, or perhaps he took up with London wenches, what with the wife and boy out of the way down there in Chertsey.

Besides her real grandmothers, Mary Ellen had some spiritual grandmothers, whose influence was, if anything, destructive. Both her biological and spiritual ancestresses were eighteenth-century women and Mary Ellen was a Victorian.[3] Victorians did not like or approve of such redoubtable eighteenth-century types as Mary Shelley, or her mother, the great feminist, Mary Wollstonecraft—immoral, intellectual, blue-stocking ladies, who had lovers and illegitimate babies, wrote novels and held strong beliefs. Mary Wollstonecraft, for example, did not believe in marriage.

It was somehow more possible to be a clever, strong-minded woman with beliefs in the eighteenth century than it was in the nineteenth; the stabler, eighteenth-century society was not so threatened by the notion, and the economics were different; wives were useful and pulled their weight. Unfortunately for Mary Ellen, her father, used to his mother, grandmother, and other intellectual ladies, grew up preferring their sort—grew up to become friends with Mary Shelley and with Claire Clairmont, the mistress of Byron. These women were well-intentioned godmothers whose influence was as destructive as a curse upon the cradle of an infant female born in a time when women had scarcely ever in history been more silly, passive, uninstructed, and suppressed.

Mary Ellen's father, Thomas Love Peacock, was a beautiful little boy, so beautiful with his "mass of flaxen curls" that the queen, Queen Charlotte, once stopped her carriage to hold and kiss him. Only a very pessimistic mother would fail to take this as a fine omen for her boy: power, fame, art, love, perhaps. We may suppose that Sarah often told Thomas of it; his fortune sanctioned by the highest authority, and it came true, too, or most of it. Thomas Peacock grew up to be a writer of "minor classics," and a powerful man of commerce, and he was popular and dined out; if he was cheated in one or two little respects, he had to remember that fortune is relative, and he was more fortunate than most.

Peacock was a Victorian man but an eighteenth-century child, born just at the exciting part of the eighteenth century, when all manner of new, bad things had come into the world and were changing it in strange ways that at the time seemed to promise new, good things for mankind. "Bliss was it in that dawn to be alive, but to be young was very heaven," Wordsworth said of it. Much good would come, it was felt, of the steam engine, invented ten years before Peacock's birth, and the use of it in factories in 1785, the year of his birth. The factories grew, the economy grew, the cities, the middle classes, the number of pounds of cotton brought into England's mills each year grew, and the population and the speed of travel and the wealth of England grew. It might have been the greatest time in history for England.

But at the same time, off the farms the workers went, into the cities, into the factories, and grew wretched, more wretched than ever: poor, starved, crowded, dying, while merchants and industrialists got rich. British ships went forth in new numbers — now to India to conquer there — and the daughters of rich, middle class people learned to read and to grow idle, grew genteel; and Richard Arkwright discovered that little children, being suited in size to his machines, made fine workers for his steam-engined factories, and he filled his factories with little doomed children.

In France, knowing that they could not prosper while the landed aristocracy held power, the people rose up and slaughtered the rich aristocrats, slaughtered priests, kings, queens, little children, each other. Out of this turmoil, twenty-six miles off England's shores, nearly visible from England, the mighty Napoleon rose up to frighten everyone in his bed, and to jeopardize seriously that English money, and those English markets, the whole mercantile Empire; and he might have succeeded, but for Nelson, but for Wellington. It was a strange time to grow up, during twenty years of war with France, with the threat of "Boney" lurking off-shore the whole time, and a lot of people in

England itself thinking that the Revolution ought to come to England on account of the little doomed children. Rich Englishmen made their money right along, of course. In Russia, 50,000 French soldiers—England's enemies—marched to Moscow in British overcoats and British-made boots.

Little Peacock would come to understand all that when he grew up, since he became a lord of commerce as well as a famous writer, but as a little boy he rejoiced in the glorious aspects of the war, like all stout-hearted English boys who grew up with it. He talked with his grandfather (the old, one-legged sailor), and sat at the feet of his uncle and their friends, and listened to stories of naval battles and ships, though he lived near the banks of the river Thames he dreamed about the open sea, and "our brave Nelson" and the odious French.

He wrote about them to amuse his grandfather:

> There is one thing indeed, it has always been held
> In which British sailors by French are excelled: —
> Their skill in *this instance* their *valourous* Fleet
> Never fail to display when our squadrons they meet: —
> And Justice must surely compel us to say
> They are far our superiors in—*running away!!!*—

It was apparently an idyllic childhood. Its documents—letters, poems—emanate affection, humor, security. Though the big world was changing and there were wars, his was a little world at home in Chertsey, at school in Englefield Green, with kind Mama, kind Grandmother, kind, romantic, old sea-going Grandfather, the good schoolmaster, John Wicks, and his sovereign, who kissed him.

Little Tom seems to have had a lively sense of professionalism about his writing from an early age. When he was nine, for instance, he wrote a verse letter to his mother from school:

> So doleful's the news, I am going to tell ye:
> Poor Wade! my schoolfellow, lies low in the gravel;
> One month ere fifteen, put an end to his travel:

> Harmless, and mild, and remark'd for goodnature:
> The cause of his death, was his overgrown stature:
> His epitaph I wrote, as inserted below;
> What tribute more friendly, could I on him bestow.
> The bard craves one shilling, of his own dear Mother;
> And if you think proper, add to it another.

Thomas was not allowed a very long childhood, as we count childhoods. He was sent away to school when he was six, and stayed away for about six years, but when he was not yet thirteen he left school and moved with Sarah to London (Samuel Peacock now being dead), for it was time for him to begin work. It was now nearly the nineteenth century, and he became, of course, that ubiquitous nineteenth-century figure: a clerk. He and his mother lived at 4 Angel Court, Throgmorton Street, which for some reason sounds peculiarly awful, but if it was there is no way to tell. Peacock, a dutiful boy, worked like a man at a job, studied in his spare time, and, remembering that his queen had kissed him, worked hard on the poetry that was, they were all sure, to make him famous. Either at the British Museum, or perhaps at the library of the India House where he would later rule, he "commenced a line of study . . . where he devoted his whole time to reading the authors of ancient Greece and Rome, studying at the same time the architectural remains — the statues, bas reliefs, etc." He won a prize at the age of fifteen for an essay in verse on the subject, "Is History or Biography the more Improving Study?"

Before he was twenty he had published, probably at his own expense, a pamphlet poem, and in 1805, a book of poems — romantic poems, since this was the fashion in the first decade of the nineteenth century. Back in Chertsey in the same year, 1805, his grandfather, Old Love, died, and Sarah left London to look after Mrs. Love. Thomas must have felt that his poetical career was well launched because soon after this he left his job to roam around and write poems, and to absorb life as a man of letters should. He was working on what he hoped would be a great poem about the beautiful river Thames that had run through his childhood. He seems to have roamed for about five years, so we must suppose that Sarah was an indulgent mother.

$\gamma_{\prime\prime}$

On December 27th 1810 Departed this Life Mrs Love of Chertsey (Widow of the late respectable Captain Thomas Love who was formerly in the Holy Land) — This aged Lady had arrived at the great Age of 83. She died in the full assurance of Faith of a Blessed Immortality — For Some time past a visible & gradual Decay of Nature had appeared in her, though not to impair her Memory or Mental Faculties which were Naturally Strong & vigorous.

During a long Life, She had experienced very great troubles & difficulties. But the Mercy of Providence in Supporting Under them was deeply Engraved upon her Mind, & That Mercy was Evident in Sparing her, to the Last, the kind & dutiful attention of a Daughter who devoted her time & Care & thoughts, to the Comfort of this Aged Parent. — If her attention Can be Equalld, it Cannot be Exceeded! . . .

Sometimes She would lament her Coldness & Languor in Devotion, & was anxious for Spiritual Fervour & freedom in Prayer. — As her illness increased & She beheld the affliction of her Daughter, She tenderly desired her to be Comforted, & to put her Trust in God, Saying He would not forsake her but that He had Blessings in Store for her upon Account of her filial kindness, & two nights before her decease She felt Sweetly Composed while Mrs P. was repeating some Hymns to her & began one herself

God moves in a Mysterious Way &c
Cowper

The Night before her Death, it Seem'd as if her Soul was Strengthend & invigorated, as the moment of its Departure approached from its feeble & oppressive Tenement. — *She Conversed for an Hour & an Half, with astonishing Clearness and Energy, & the powers of Speech Seem'd to be restored for that purpose, that She might give Glory to God & begin His Praises while She was Yet upon Earth. She Said* — *"Had I not put Trust in God What Should I have done?* — *what wou'd have become of me?* — *He Comforted & Supported me when my husband & Children were exposed to dangerous Climates Tempests & Battles & brought them home in Safety that we might Enjoy Comfort & Happiness together! God Supported me thro Life in all my troubles and "He promised never to Leave nor forsake me, and Shall I doubt His Goodness in my dying Moments?"* . . .

. . . *Here her powers of utterance were Suspended* — *& Mrs P. Supplied the Last Line [of a hymn]* — *And Very Soon after the impatient & fervent Spirit was released* — *It winged its flight without my apprehension from a Scene of Weakness & Infirmity, from its Earthly perishing Tabernacle"* — *to Immortal Happiness* — *Doubtless to be Re-united Again in the Joyful Morning of the Resurrection* — *when Pain and Infirmity Shall be known No more for Ever* — [4]

Peacock's grandmother died in Chertsey with his mother beside her. Peacock, meantime, had come to a time of life when, besides making himself a famous poet, he began to find himself falling in love. This is an important time for Mary Ellen, for in Peacock's young manhood, how it was spent or misspent — in the parlors of young ladies he was courting, in the beds of mistresses of a worldly sort, in the company of unconventional and intellectual women — he developed or confirmed a view of women rather peculiar for a man of his time. That is why, most

Victorians would have agreed, he did not bring up Mary Ellen as he ought.

Peacock was amorous. It is really better not to look at old pictures at all, and surely not at those that show the subjects of sympathetic biographies as old, portly people. But some drawings of the young Peacock survive, and are fairly satisfying. It is just possible to imagine the young man animate; tall and very slim, strong because of much walking and rowing, with a pretty V-shaped mouth, its expression somewhat arch, and large, bright blue eyes looking right past you. The golden curls are darker now, growing every which way; the skin is very fair, and he has a long, slim nose for looking down.

When he was old a lady wrote to him of himself: "I never can think of you otherwise than as that young and brilliant personage we used to know . . . when you used to repeat poetry, drink champagne, and seem not to have a single link to heavy earth."

This letter is signed by "ever your affectionate Clarinda Atkyns," who had caught a glimpse of him in Grosvenor Square, now white-haired but not "looking any older—and your voice and laugh were still the same." Who, poor lady, was she, and what had her life been, to write so wistfully to this old man, from Ombersly Vicarage, Droitwich?

꙳.

Peacock fell in love a lot. Cousin Harriet remembered "once saying to him 'if ever I write a book it shall be on the plan of the Arabian Nights.—The thousand and one loves of Thomas Love Peacock.'—He laughed most heartily and replied 'Well, I don't think you would be very far out!'" (The Biographer wondered about leaving this out.[5] Victorians minded, in their delicate way, the notion that people might have fallen in love with anyone but the one they married. If your early love had died, and you remained sentimentally single, they would put it in your biography.)[6]

Peacock himself, and Cousin Harriet too, seemed to relish his role of Romantic roué. Cousin Harriet proudly says he was very like the description he makes Miss Ilex give of her lover in *Gryll Grange*: ". . . he was very much of an universal lover, and was always overcome by the smiles of present beauty. He was of a romantic turn of mind: he disliked and avoided the ordinary pursuits of young men: he delighted in the society of accomplished young women, and in that alone."

It was really only his friend Shelley, ardent and excitable, who, when piqued a time or two, referred to Peacock as "cold," or "sensible," and fixed as cold and sensible a disposition that was quixotic and impulsive. Though not as dashing as Shelley — which few people could be—Peacock was dashing, even dissolute, in a sentimental, Romantic way, and was not at all the dispassionate exponent of pure reason we think him. He had, for example, a picturesque, hopeless love, for a maiden named Fanny whom he would meet in secret by some ruins, in the best fashion of his day, and to whom he was engaged until she Married Another, also in the best fashion of the day—after which she died. Little Edith maintained that, until his death, Grandpapa wore a locket of Fanny's hair next to his bosom. One wonders how he explained this to his wife. And there were Lucindas, Clarindas, Matildas, and Mariannes besides.

In those days one of the things it was necessary to do, to make yourself a Romantic Poet, was to travel and look at beautiful scenery. It was therefore Thomas's custom, like that of Miss Ilex's lover, to "disappear for weeks at a time, wandering in forests,

climbing mountains, and descending into the dingles of mountain-streams, with no other companion than a Newfoundland
dog; a large, black dog, with a white breast, four white paws, and
a white tip to his tail." Peacock was captivated by the country
around Maentwrog, in Wales, and went there, as he wrote to a
friend, "resolved to devote the whole interval to exploring the
vicinity, and . . . climbing about the rocks and mountains, by
the rivers and the sea, with indefatigable zeal, carrying in my
mind the bardic triad, that a poet should have an eye that can
see nature, a heart that can feel nature, and a resolution that
dares follow nature; in obedience to which latter injunction I
have nearly broken my neck."[7] In 1811 he settled in one of the
cottages in a tiny village, writing poems and affecting a Romantic,
hermitlike life of study, scenery, and seclusion. A lady who
knew him then told Shelley, "Ah! . . . there Mr. Peacock lived
in a cottage near Tan y bwylch, associating with no one, and
hiding his head like a murderer. . . . But, he was *worse than
that,* he was an *Atheist.*" Small wonder if the daughter of the
local parson fell in love with him, though there is no evidence that she did. It was she who would become Mary Ellen's
mother.

This girl was Jane Gryffydh, and her father, whom Peacock
described as a "dumpy, drunken, mountain-goat," was the rector
of the local parish, a man of some learning and called "Doctor"
by courtesy, having taken an Oxford B.A. Peacock was very
glad to have met him, for in spite of his hermitish intentions
he was secretly glad of company out there in the wilds. He
saw Dr. Gryffydh occasionally, and he must have become
acquainted with Jane, but how well it is difficult to tell. His
only surviving mention of her from this time describes their
parting.

Suddenly one morning he resolved to leave Wales, and he
strolled up to the parsonage ("I could not leave the Vale without
taking leave of Jane Gryffydh,—the most innocent, the most amiable, the most beautiful girl in existence") and asked her to walk
with him to his rooms. "The old lady being in the way, I could
not speak to her there: asked her to walk with me to the Lodge.

She was obliged to dress for church immediately: but promised to call on her way. She did so. I told her my intention of departing that day, and gave her my last remaining copy of the *Genius*," his poem. Jane, with whatever feelings of relief or regret, walked on to church, and that was the last she saw of the handsome poet for eight years. Thomas made another trip to Wales in 1813, but does not seem to have looked her up.

It was the year after his first Wales trip, 1812, that Peacock, now back in London, met Percy Bysshe Shelley, through their mutual friends, the Hookhams. Shelley knew Peacock's poetry. He didn't like it—he had trouble feeling as Peacock did that "the glory of the British Flag is the Happiness of the British People" —but he admired it, and felt at least "the conclusion of *Palmyra* to be the finest piece of poetry I ever read." People have always felt that the friendship of Shelley and Peacock was an odd one between men of most dissimilar temperaments, but they were probably not so dissimilar at this point in time. More is known about this period of Shelley's life than of Peacock's, but they were together a lot. Shelley's life was a harried one of bailiffs, angry parents, elopements, death, delusion, passion, semi-madness, wife-sharing, and suicides. Almost anybody else's life would have seemed tame by comparison, but Peacock, on his own account, at least had an affair with an heiress whom he lived with and who turned out to have no money, got thrown into prison for debt, and fell seriously in love with a lady who refused him.

The affair with the heiress and his subsequent imprisonment for debt are known only through laconic entries in Mary Shelley's diary: "a rich heiress has fallen in love with Peacock and lives with him—she is very miserable—God knows why—P. is on her account & that of M. St. C. & M. is miserable on her own account."

Then, a couple of weeks later: "Letter from Peacock to say that he is in prison—the foolish man lived up to Charlottes expectancies who turns out to have nothing—her behavior is inexplicable—there is a terrible mystery in the affair—his debt is £40—a letter also from Gray who knows nothing about her—this is a funny man also—write to Peacock & send him £2."

The other terrible mystery in the affair is "M. St. C.," or Marianne de St. Croix of Homerton, a shadowy young woman whose family Peacock had known for many years and whom Peacock had evidently planned to marry as early as 1814. Their courtship was interrupted by the escapade with the "heiress," but later, after he had been out of jail awhile, he discussed with the Shelleys his plan of taking Marianne to Canada, so their engagement must have been on again.

His friends were diverted by the off-again, on-again marital plans of Peacock; they were dumfounded, and perhaps secretly impressed, when to everybody's surprise he procured a probationary training period with the East India Company, with a view to taking an examination and, possibly, a job. His friends, and he, had thought of him as an *homme de lettres;* now he was to be a bureaucrat. Would he find time to write his charming novels under the press of heavy responsibilities? they must have asked him. (By now he had almost abandoned poetry and had already written *Nightmare Abbey, Melincourt,* and *Maid Marian.*)[8] After six weeks of study, and after a period of consideration, the East India Company appointed four new officials: an Examiner, Edward Strachey; and three assistants, James Mill, Peacock, and a J. J. Harcourt. Leigh Hunt writes to Mary Shelley: "You have heard, of course, of Peacock's appointment in the India House; we joke him upon his new Oriental grandeur, his Brahminical learning, and his inevitable tendencies to be one of the corrupt; upon which he seems to apprehend Shelleian objurgation. It is an honour to him that 'prosperity' sits on him well. He is very pleasant and hospitable." And Thomas Jefferson Hogg writes to Shelley that Peacock "is well pleased with his change of fortune, and has taken a house in Stamford Street, which, as you might expect from a Republican, he has furnished very handsomely."

He was now well settled, and thirty-four years old, and, very naturally, began to think of marriage, a matter of utmost consequence to Mary Ellen.

We can see that Thomas, with a clever mother and grandmother, and friends like Mary Shelley, who wrote books, and like Claire Clairmont, Byron's mistress, and like Percy Shelley and Hogg and Hookham and Hunt—was part of the kind of set that preferred advanced females; these were by no means the sort of female recommended for marriage in those days. "I own I often feel uneasy," wrote his family minister to young Hogg just after he and Shelley were sent down from Oxford, "at the thoughts of the set to whom your new opinions will introduce you. Many of these women of *Genius* as they wish to be thought are entertaining and fascinating to a young man—Of the sect of Shellyites you must have several—but I think if you compare them with the women with whom you were bred up—your mother & etc., you will own that a man's conjugal happiness is much more likely to be preserved in the old school than the new."[9]

Perhaps Thomas Hogg passed along this advice to Thomas Peacock, and Peacock bore it in mind. In any case he first proposed to Marianne and she, after all those years, refused him. It is a great puzzle. And so Peacock turned around and dashed off a letter of proposal to that Welsh girl he hadn't seen in eight years but remembered thinking of as "the most innocent, amiable girl in existence,"—a nice, old-fashioned girl.

Cousin Harriet was living with Thomas and Sarah in Stamford Street at the time, and remembers that this letter was written under a "feeling of bitter disappointment," whose causes after an "unlooked-for call at the East India House from an old acquaint-ance who suggested it, are *now* known only to myself." Well, Thomas was nothing if not resourceful, and you can't go wrong with a nice, old-fashioned girl.

Of Mary Ellen's mother there remains only one of her letters, so we may imagine her how we please. She was a little Welsh vil-lage girl, the daughter of a parson (like everyone else then, it seems), the child of her father's second wife, who, having mar-ried in 1783, produced five children by 1789, when Jane was born, and another after. Because her father was called "Dr." Gryffydh (for he had taken a bachelor's degree), Jane may have thought herself a little better than the other villagers, or at least more privileged.

Dr. Gryffydh held the parish living in the tiny village of Maentwrog (pronounced Mantoorog), which Peacock had described to a friend as "a delightful spot, enchanting even in the gloom of winter: in summer it must be a terrestrial paradise. It is a beautiful narrow vale, several miles in length, extending in one direction to the sea, and totally embosomed in mountains, the sides of which are covered, in many parts, with large woods of oak." Eight years before his letter of proposal, Peacock had taken a sitting room in a lodging that was too expensive, looking out on a "lovely river, which flows through the vale. In the vicin-ity are many deep glens,—along which copious mountain-streams, of inconceivable clearness, roar over rocky channels, —and numerous waterfalls. . . ." The handsome, visiting poet, who had stayed in the area for fifteen months or so, was a great addition to the neighborhood. Jane had talked to him of Scipio and Hannibal, though she did not apparently talk well enough, because one day he paid that final call, settled with the inn-keeper, and walked back to London, which was the last anybody in Maentwrog had seen of him for eight years.

How Jane spent those eight years we do not know. Perhaps she had suitors—but we do not know about them. Her mind, in any case, cannot have been much occupied with Peacock, because she was beset by misfortunes. Her father died in August 1812, and another minister came to live at the parsonage at Maentwrog. Jane and her mother had to go to live nearby in Tan y bwylch, where their hopes and circumstances were straitened next by the death of the oldest brother, a medical doctor, in February 1813. The only remaining sister, Anne, married and moved off, and the younger brother, David, was probably still at Oxford, and certainly more of a liability than a help. Whatever small resources the family had would have had to be directed to his education; whatever energies Jane had must have partly gone to the care of the "old lady," her mother, nearly seventy by the time Jane hears from Peacock again.

In the eight years since he had left, Jane Gryffydh first of all had become an old maid, aged thirty years and without prospects. Her life may have been rather like that of the old maids in Mrs. Gaskell's village of Cranford a few years later—concerned with daily tasks, with the rituals of visiting, church and charitable activities, all the tasks of a poor household, with "only an occasional little quarrel, spirted [sic] out in a few peppery words and angry jerks of the head; just enough to prevent the even tenor of their lives from becoming too flat. Their dress is very independent of fashion; as they observe: 'What does it signify how we dress here in Cranford, where everybody knows us?' And if they go from home, their reason is equally cogent: 'What does it signify how we dress here, where nobody knows us?'"

It was a limited and doubtless tedious little society where Jane Gryffydh lived until she was thirty, with sore troubles and deaths in the family, and about her personal lot her thought was, perhaps, "What does it signify?"

During his stay the young poet Peacock had written rhapsodically of the beauties of Wales in winter: "I wish I could find language sufficiently powerful to convey to you an idea of the sublime magnificence of the waterfalls in the frost—when the old overhanging oaks are spangled with icicles; the rocks sheeted with frozen foam, formed by the flying spray; and the water, that oozes from their sides, congealed into innumerable pillars of crystal. Every season has its charms. The picturesque tourists, those birds of summer, see not half the beauties of nature." These were probably also less apparent to the small cottagers of Wales, worn by many winters of the bitter cold. One cannot know whether Jane Gryffydh had much sympathy for the beauty of her native place. In any case, it was cold, and it was necessary to walk along down the cobbled steep hill between the cottages to the post office. You can imagine a bitter cold morning, late November, ice, perhaps, on the street, all the streams stopped with ice, all the people indoors keeping the fires going, working at their lap-crafts, mending and storing; Jane Gryffydh putting on her heaviest bonnet and warmest boots. A somewhat perilous short walk, slipping on the slick curbings, but bearing this with a mild, customary fortitude, not grimly. At thirty she has waned but is not extinguished, and her life, though she thought of it as "possessing *none* of the good things," has been growing bleaker only gradually, by stages, and she could still redden from a brisk walk, a greeting in the street, or a sense of possibility which only a sterner sense of reality could correct. She was for those days a middle-aged woman.

The post office, then, and a letter from London. Would she have opened it immediately, or borne it home? Opened it, with a reluctant feeling of hopeful curiosity, read it with a sense of stunned wonder, a chilled sensation of the skin, and pounding heart. It would be more a bad than a good feeling, the sickened realization that something had happened, in a life she was mostly used to, to upset it. Something she would have to rise to, deal with. Putting the letter in her basket or pocket, trying not to think about it at all, until she could be at home to sit down by the fire and reread it. Her mother would perhaps remark, when she got home, that she was redder, or paler, than the short walk would warrant.

There is no salutation. "It is more than eight years since I had the happiness of seeing you:" (She may have had to turn to the signature at this point to see who it was from.) Thomas Peacock, whom she had not forgotten, but not thought much about either.

"I can scarcely hope that you have remembered me as I have remembered you: yet I feel confident that the simplicity and ingenuousness of your disposition will prompt you to answer me with the same candor with which I write to you."

Is this complimentary or not? In any case, she is not so simple and ingenuous at thirty as she was at twenty-one. She reads on.

"I have long entertained the hope of returning to Merionethshire under better auspices than those under which I left it: but fortune always disappointed me, continually offering me prospects which receded as I approached them." Is not, she must have wondered, is not that a fair description of life as it always is?

"Recently she has made me amends for her past unkindness, and has given me much present good, and much promise of progressive prosperity, which leaves me nothing to desire in worldly advantage but to participate it with you. The greatest blessing this world could bestow on me would be to make you my wife: consider if your own feelings will allow you to constitute my happiness." Her ears hum. She looks again at the signature. If she is still at the post office, she here puts the letter away and leaves so that she will not have to reply to anyone who remarks on her strange look. Walks along home with a feeling of suspendedness, and thinks about not slipping on the ice. Thomas Peacock, the atheist poet!

He speaks of happiness. "I desire only to promote yours: and I desire only you: for your value is beyond fortune, of which I want no more than I have. The same circumstances which have given me prosperity confine me to London, and to the duties of the department with which the East India Company has entrusted me: yet I can absent myself for a few days once in every year: if you sanction my wishes, with what delight should I employ them in bringing you to my home! If this be but a baseless dream—if I am even no more in your estimation than the sands on the sea shore—yet I am sure, as I have already said, that you will answer me with the same candor with which I have written." She is uncertain of the tone of this, especially the part about the sand on the shore—the only romantically dashed-off clause in a composition of colons: but one expects some rhetoric in a love letter; perhaps it is only that he is not good at it.

The next part too is strangely ambiguous. "Whatever may be your sentiments, the feelings with which I now write to you, and which more than eight years of absence and silence have neither obliterated nor diminished, will convince you that I never can be otherwise than most sincerely and most affectionately your friend." No rhetoric there at least—only negatives, and the neat avoidance of rhetoric, and the clever guardedness of feelings unspecified, which have been "neither obliterated nor diminished." I think exactly as much of you now as I ever did. But it was a proposal of marriage. It must be entertained.

Jane had read some history, and Scipio, and could talk about Hannibal and the Emperor Otho, but we do not know if theirs was a novel-reading parsonage. We do not know if she had read Mr. Peacock's novels—it would seem she hadn't—or if she had read Miss Austen's novels, but if she had, then Charlotte Lucas might have come to Jane's mind as she does to ours, not then but during the next agitated days. Charlotte agreed to marry the appalling Mr. Collins, though she knew that only a few days before he had proposed for and been rejected by Elizabeth Bennet. Elizabeth was astonished, but "Charlotte herself was tolerably composed . . . his attachment to her must be imaginary. But still he would be her husband. Without thinking highly either of men or of matrimony, marriage had always been her object; it was the only honourable provision for well-educated young women of small fortune, and however uncertain of giving happiness, must be their pleasantest preservative from want." No doubt Jane Gryffydh must have entertained the eligible Mr.

Peacock's proposal more cheerfully, and been thankful that at least Mr. Peacock had not wound up his proposal with "and now nothing remains for me but to assure you in the most animated language of the violence of my affection." But in other respects, a comparison of Mr. Peacock's declaration with that of Mr. Collins shows a few uneasy parallels from which we learn what a decent proposal, in form, was supposed to contain. You begin by alluding to your circumstances in life, then to your wish to marry, then to your indifference to any money your prospective bride may or may not have, and finally you refer to your feelings. Altogether, Mr. Peacock's proposal is more like Mr. Collins's than one could wish.

It must be entertained. Peacock had been, perhaps still was, a dashing and handsome man, full of wit and talent and ambition, a good catch—so in the days that followed the agitated Jane was compelled to think upon herself: what she had become, what the handsome man from London was expecting and would find. Peacock's letter is dated November 20, 1819, and hers in reply, November 30th, though it was not mailed until the fourth of December. Allowing for several days in the mails each way, we may infer that Jane took her time about composing her letter. She may have composed a number of them. And then one sat four days on the mantelpiece before she took it up, boots and bonnet again, and with whatever feeling of trepidation or relief, consigned it to the post. On his side, Peacock had nearly two weeks to consider his hasty epistle, or reconsider, or to wait expectantly, or to put the whole thing out of his mind on the chance that his letter was misdirected, before receiving her reply.

Jane Gryffydh was now thirty, poor, a disappointed provincial person, alone with her old mother, and the brother off at Oxford. She could now relieve them "from their apprehension of [her] dying an old maid," as Charlotte Lucas had relieved her family. People who belittle Jane Austen's preoccupation with husband-catching forget the realities of nineteenth-century life, in which a young woman's marriage search was not only a metaphorical but an actual exercise in survival. She must marry. If she had money there was no question but what she would; if she had no money the case was more desperate. If her father was poor, the peril was boundless, and it was greater in proportion as her father was also genteel. The daughter of a working man could go into "service," could take some kind of job, could even, stereotypes notwithstanding, go on the streets, and retain a certain rough-and-ready expectation of some day settling down with a sturdy husband or a steady job.

But if you were educated, you would have to become a governess, or an old maid aunt, and in either case that would mean living off the charity of others, at the chilliest perimeter of somebody else's family circle: diffident and neglected, unpaid, marginally appreciated, sewing patiently for other people's children. You could never go anywhere, you had no money or station; as time went on, the old maid aunt just dwindled into nothing, and the governess was dispatched to some pensioner's cottage when her usefulness in the schoolroom was over. It was with customary British calculation that the first university for women was opened in the nineteenth century, to assure a gentleman that the Miss Jones (or Miss Eyre) who came to teach his children would be worth the fifty pounds or so he would pay her each year. And there were even Homes for old, failing ones, whose charges were grown up.

If you could not become a governess, things went very hard with you indeed, so that anticipating and preventing this calamity was the major concern of nineteenth-century mothers and their daughters. And a lot of women had rather marry anyone than no one—even a Mr. Collins. Even Elizabeth Bennet might have married him (though we cannot feel she would), had she been older with a few disappointments behind her, and her father dead.

To marry well and go to live in London had long been beyond Jane's expectations but it cannot have been beyond her hopes. She must surely have nursed some "baseless dreams" of her own. But when a wish is granted long after it is conceived, the wisher gains a certain perspective on it, and on himself. The wish is still there, witnessed by the stir of blood, the quickened breath, and mocked too by the intervention of reality—the mirror, the years spent sitting at genteel tasks in the small parlor, self-knowledge. One thinks of the faded Laetitia Dale, in Meredith's *The Egoist*, when her great girlhood passion, Sir Willoughby, finally proposes: " 'I am tired,' she said. 'It is late, I would rather not hear more. I am sorry if I have caused you pain. I suppose you to have spoken with candor. I defend neither my sex nor myself. I can only say, I am a woman as good as dead—happy to be made happy in my way, but so little alive that I cannot realize any other way. As for love, I am thankful to have broken a spell. You have a younger woman in your mind, I am an old one. I have a purely physical desire of life, I have no strength to swim. Such a woman is not the wife for you. . . .' "

Jane Gryffydh wrote to Peacock with more irony, but the sadness, the fatigue underneath are the same:

My dear Sir.

The gratification to hear of your Welfare has very often since you left Merionethshire been <u>much</u> my Wish. But I cannot say I have remembered you as I feel gratified to find you have re-membered me—for I could not flatter myself that <u>your</u> Senti-ments warranted such a remembrance on my part—which knowledge, as well as every expression of generosity your very handsome Epistle contains, claims my highest gratitude. I fear you <u>very</u> much over-rate my worth, and I must tell you that I am less calculated to be <u>your</u> Companion than I <u>even</u> was at the period you knew me: Fortune pouring on my defenceless head an unceasing succession of her Evils, thereby enervating my *mind and disabling it from receiving its due cultivation: this consideration will I <u>hope</u> dispose <u>you</u> to pardon want of presicion [<u>sic</u>] of style <u>and</u> <u>all</u> imperfections.*

I will not, <u>however,</u> <u>disappoint</u> <u>you</u> <u>in</u> <u>Truth</u> and <u>Candor.</u> Your Sentiments on the awful subject of Religion I trust are changed; that is, if they required that change, which I understood you induced some of your acquaintance here to suppose they did, but which was never my <u>firm</u> opinion.

I possess <u>none</u> of the good things of this World. I shall say no more at present than beg you will believe me, with every sentiment of Esteem and a most grateful sense of your good opinion, etc.,

Yours with the greatest sincerity
Jane Gryffydh.

The irony is gentle, the underscorings breathe the faintest hopefulness, the remark about religion warns of the ingenuousness Peacock had remembered. But we do not see, Peacock could not have seen—there is nothing in it to warn us—that within six years this woman will be mad.

Family tradition had it that Peacock expended a few days of his vacation on a trip to Wales to have a look at the lady. She was persuaded.

They were married nearly four months later in Eglwysfach Chapel, Cardiganshire, and Peacock took his bride back to his handsome house in Stamford Street, where he and his mother and Cousin Harriet had been living since his prosperous appointment with the East India Company.

Peacock had not mentioned his coming marriage to his friends, and wrote to Shelley only when it was done. Shelley replied, "I was very much amused by your laconic account of the affair. It is altogether extremely like the *dénouement* of one of your own novels." We do not know if for Jane Gryffydh it was an awkward or a pleasant time, or how she liked the house on Stamford Street, or her mother-in-law, or Peacock's real views on religion when she discovered them, or his clever friends.

His clever friends were not impressed, but neither were they hostile. "Mrs. Peacock seems to be a very good-natured, simple, unaffected, untaught, prettyish Welsh girl," Maria Gisbourne wrote to Mary Shelley, who was still in Italy and hadn't had a look at her yet. Thomas Jefferson Hogg told Shelley that Peacock had married "judiciously."

What, besides pique, Peacock's motive can have been for his impulsive proposal to an almost unknown person, is very hard to say. And it is hard to infer from his books his real attitudes to things. On the one hand, Anthelia, a character in *Melincourt,* says to Mrs. Pinmoney, who had married Mr. Pinmoney with less than seven weeks' acquaintance, "'I should have been afraid that so short an acquaintance would scarcely have been sufficient to acquire that mutual knowledge of each other's tastes, feelings and character, which I should think the only sure basis of matrimonial happiness.'"

And on the other hand, Mr. Glowry says, in *Nightmare Abbey,* that marriage is a lottery, "'and the less choice and selection a man bestows on his ticket the better; for, if he has incurred considerable pains and expense to obtain a lucky number, and his lucky number proves a blank, he experiences not a simple, but a complicated disappointment; the loss of labour and money being superadded to the disappointment of drawing a blank, which, constituting simply and entirely the grievance of him who has chosen his ticket at random, is, from its simplicity, the more endurable.'"

Things must have gone along well enough with the newlyweds at first, though Peacock's behavior confirmed the old saying about bachelors getting set in their ways and never giving up their old friends and habits. In May, just two months after the wedding, when Hogg wrote Shelley that Peacock had married "judiciously," we learn that "notwithstanding his *various* occupations, we sometimes find time for *noctes atticae;* or long walks." About a year later they were taking such long walks that they would be gone for days at a time, without premeditation, which may have been trying to his wife. On June 15, 1821, Peacock and Hogg began a "little stroll" that lasted three days and took them eighty miles.

The next month, July 1821, Mary Ellen was born, at home in Stamford Street. Peacock had wanted to let the house and take his wife to the country, where the atmosphere was less "fumose and cinereous," but he did not, and so Mary Ellen was born in summer, in London, and all went well anyway. Sarah Peacock was there to help, as was a doctor or midwife. Everyone was pleased that Mary Ellen was a girl; no one minded that she was not a boy; there were no dynastic considerations, fortunes or titles to prejudice the arrival of a female child, and Peacock, anyway, liked females.

Shelley, with horrid, prophetic gift, wrote from Italy, about the time he knew the baby was to arrive, "I congratulate you—I hope I ought to do so—on your expected stranger. He is introduced into a rough world." Shelley had reason to know this with three dead children and the drowned Harriet to remind him.

"And how is your little star?" he writes another day. "Our little star is cloudless," Peacock replies. It was an auspicious beginning, but, as in the fairy tale, a glance at the characters of the grandmother Sarah, and the spiritual godmothers, Mary Shelley and Claire Clairmont—restless, intellectual women—might give the thoughtful observer some pause.

A new baby, certain to be the first of many, was a pleasant but not remarkable event; Peacock went on his usual vacation in September, without Jane. He wrote to Shelley, "we have a charming little girl, now eleven weeks old, who grows and flourishes delightfully. . . . She prevented Jane from accompanying me in my rustication." That is, he went off by himself, but he wrote Jane some pleasant letters, which have struck everybody by their affectionate tone, vastly unlike the correct address Victorian husbands would employ. "My dearest love," they all begin, and say such things as, "I think of you night and day and long so much to be with you that I do not think I shall ever pass three weeks from you again. I shall be home either on Saturday Sunday or Monday: on which day I cannot exactly say: it will depend on weather and the opportunities of conveyance,"—in which one may hear both a fond husband and a slightly guilty one. "Love to Mother and Darling," he unfailingly adds. Darling was Mary Ellen.

The next year, Jane and Darling went on the summer rustication with Peacock to a cottage in the Chiltern Hills. Mary Ellen's first sister, Margaret, was born the following March, when Mary Ellen was twenty months old. In that same year the family moved to Lower Halliford, a charming village on the Thames in Surrey, south of London. Here Peacock had taken a cottage first for his mother, then, with the family growing, he took the adjoining cottage; the two were made into one house, a rambling, two-story affair with French doors opening onto the Thames, a low, eighteenth-century kitchen (where Mary Ellen and Peacock would later oversee their cookery experiments), and deep casements to gaze out of upon the lawns and across the river and into the tall shady trees that grow there. None of the Peacocks ever liked to leave this beautiful place for very long.

The little family grew. Margaret was followed by Edward, in 1824 or 1825. Peacock was working hard, both at his job at India House, where he was rising, and at his writing. Like a modern executive, he stayed in town at Stamford Street during the week and joined his wife and children at the suburban establishment on weekends. Sometimes he would bring famous people home: Coulson, the editor of *The Traveller,* or Jeremy Bentham or one of his associates at work, James Mill perhaps, or Edward Strachey.

At first Mary Ellen had, we suppose, a happy and uneventful infancy, a happy childhood in a devoted and successful family in a beautiful place by the river. But then, in 1826 sorrow came to the family, a usual sort of sorrow that Victorians often had to bear—more often than we—and while they undoubtedly never got used to it, they do seem to have had a sort of fatalistic expectation of blows of this kind; death was a part of life. The deaths of little children were commonplace. Little Margaret died.

It was on Sunday. Margaret was ill, a trifling illness that had caused them some anxious moments, but she seemed to be getting better. Peacock had brought Edward Strachey and one or two other men home for the weekend, one of those weekends of walking and talking and good eating he was fond of providing for them. They went out in high spirits for a walk, Peacock and his friends, and when they came back Peacock was told that Margaret was dead.

Peacock, stunned, who had just been laughing and joking with his friends, told Edward Strachey that he saw, he saw now, there were times the world could not be made fun of. It was the first time, or almost the first time, that the world had treated Peacock in this unkind way, but it was to keep after him, the way it will keep after good-natured people, to try them.

Peacock wrote a little epitaph for Margaret:

> Long night succeeds thy little day;
>   O blighted blossom! can it be,
> That this gray stone and grassy clay
>   Have closed our anxious care of thee?
>
> The half-form'd speech of artless thought,
>   That spoke a mind beyond thy years;
> The song, the dance, by nature taught;
>   The sunny smiles, the transient tears;
>
> The symmetry of face and form,
>   The eye with light and life replete;
> The little heart so fondly warm,
>   The voice so musically sweet.
>
> These lost to hope, in memory yet
>   Around the hearts that lov'd thee cling,
> Shadowing, with long and vain regret,
>   The too fair promise of thy spring.

The vicar of Shepperton Church objected to the line "Long night succeeds thy little day." It made no provision for immortal life. It was not suitable to be carved upon a stone in a churchyard. They quarreled bitterly—it was perhaps a diversion for Peacock's grief, which was also bitter; he had no belief in immortality—had only poetry to console him.

Jane had, apparently, a belief in immortality, but she had no poetry to console her, and no resilience. A strangeness came over her. It must have been a bewildering and sad time for Mary Ellen, who was five. The little sister as if asleep, over whom everyone wept, whom she had never seen before so still and white—and then carried away in a tiny coffin, and no one laughing. Papa never laughed any more, and such a strangeness had come over Mama. Mama sat alone in her room; Grandmama dressed and fed them. Mama was never the same after this.

⁊⁊.

"My grandmother was inconsolable for the death of this little child, Margaret; she fell into a bad health, and until her death . . . she was a complete invalid," Edith wrote. Edith means "nervous invalid," which in itself was a euphemism, of course, for something worse. Mary Shelley, for all her faults, was not one for euphemism: "Peacock's wife," she wrote to Maria Gisbourne, "lives in town, quite mad."

As to the origin or the nature of Jane's illness — we can only guess. Perhaps she raved, like Mrs. Rochester, and blamed Peacock for her agonies of spirit. More likely she suffered from one of those long, household forms of madness, or severe neurosis, to which ladies in those days seemed especially prone: they languished with enormous patience, dreadfully hysterical and morbid, unfit for any real task, and were borne by their families with a certain rather creditable fortitude whereas nowadays they would be packed off to an institution. It was not uncommon for the Victorian family to have an "ill" relative upstairs. But what hideous torment for everyone this "illness" meant. Children motherless, prodigious chastity and sublimation for the young father (or the furtive embraces of opera dancers?), the burden of a large household fallen upon an old woman, Sarah Peacock, seventy-two years old. And Jane, in her madness, lived on after this, a burden to everybody for twenty-six more years.

Peacock biographers, as a group, have not had much sense about the human plausibilities of this situation, or perhaps they have been constrained by Peacock's own theories about unintrusive biography. But it seems odd that they could go on for a hundred years blandly referring to Jane's "bad health," and maintaining that Peacock was devoted to her nonetheless, and grief-stricken when she died. Can the several years of happiness — well enough attested to by his fond letters to the bride — possibly sustain a man through twenty-six years of caring for a woman hopelessly insane? At the best his feelings could only have been those of bitter disappointment, masked perhaps by resignation. At the worst, hatred, bitterness. Peacock was not much over forty when all this happened to him: his child died, and then the woman he had embraced so fondly turned in his arms to someone, something else.

And how the twenty-six years passed for Jane we cannot say. Madness is not a happy condition; it is a painful one, tormented, despairing, haunted by alien presences, surrounded by strangers (her husband, her children, the old woman), people who did not know her. They did not understand how she suffered.

Margaret died, and Jane fell ill with grieving over it, and so the next strange thing happened, in that same year, 1826.

Imagine a child playing on the step before a cottage. She has a little game with sticks. She draws the stick through the dust and it makes a trail with a tiny ridge on either side, like the track of a caterpillar. She draws a windy trail and then — this is the principal joy — she stamps it all out with her dirty, bare little feet. Nice dry dust between the toes. She has forgotten her tears that her brothers went off to the river without her. Ma, busy within, will call her soon for she is to be given a lump of the bread dough to play with when Ma is ready. It is warm in the sun.

The mad lady comes. She comes slipping around the hedge and through the low gate. The little girl knows it is the mad lady because they have seen her on her way to church, and Ma said. But the little girl does not know what it means to be mad, and she smiles. The lady is smiling too. Her eyes are great and dark and shining. She whispers softly like Ma when it is time for bed; the lowest whisper, and puts out her hand, and she has cake! So much nicer than bread dough, though not as nice to squeeze. The lady holds the cake out and then she pulls it away again. The little girl watches her and waves her stick. The lady whispers. The little girl is very young, but she understands that the mad lady will give her the cake a little later. She is gathered up, and quickly, very quickly the mad lady, who smells sweet with perfume, carries her off down the street, pressing a bit of cake into her mouth so she will not call out.

The mad lady carries her into a house by the river, and sets her down while she pulls out from a trunk all manner of lovely things: dolls, ribbons, little lace caps. The child clasps a stuffed doll. Eagerly the lady undoes her simple muslin dress and pulls it off, and draws her little arms through a different dress of shiny silk. Her eyes on the doll, the child does not protest.

Later a gentleman comes. His voice is loud, his face very pale. The lady holds the child tightly in her arms, as if she will not let her go, and weeps all over the violet silk.

Edith tells the story as if it were not peculiar: "Very soon after Margaret's death, my grandmother noticed a little girl in its mother's arms, at the door of a cottage on Halliford Green; she was much taken with the child, seeing in it a strong likeness to the little one she was so sorely grieving after; she coaxed the little girl, Mary Rosewell, into her own house by a promise of some cake, and dressed it in her lost child's clothes. My grandfather, on his return from town, looked in through the dining room window as he passed round to the door of his house, and seeing the child standing on the hearth-rug in the room, he was so struck by its likeness to Margaret, that he afterwards declared that he felt quite stunned, for the moment believing that he really saw her again before him. My grandparents finally adopted the child, Mary Rosewell, whose family had lived for generations much respected in the neighborhood, and a most devoted and unselfish adopted daughter she always proved to be.''

That is how the family acquired Mary Rosewell. It cannot have been so easy, of course: Peacock's hope—vain—that the new little Margaretlike child would fill some place in Jane, would help her to be herself again; visiting the Rosewells, simple poor people, making his strange proposal; their anguish, or perhaps relief, depending on how poor they were; his pleas. (Boys, of course, were not given away so easily.) But Mary Anne, whom they called ''May,'' was no cure.

Perhaps a new baby of their own? One more, the last, was born to them the next year. This was Rosa Jane, and she too had to be raised by Sarah Peacock. There were no more children after that.

The little family was complete—the beautiful and complex father, with his laconic manner, his ambition and great energy. The faded and mad mother, who, having been able to adjust to life as a spinster in a little Welsh village, could not adjust to married life, to her brisk husband, to her noisy children or to the loss of one in a real world where mothers lost many of their many children, bore others, managed big households, endured. Sarah Peacock, an old, strong, intellectual woman, who had devoted her life to her one brilliant son, now found herself in her seventies with a large household and four little grandchildren to rear. The children: Mary Ellen, the most brilliant and promising, little Edward, the baby Rosa Jane, and the fisherman's child, May Rosewell, beloved for her face of Margaret who died, taken from her own mother, her own cottage, to grow up a lady at the Peacock's, like a changeling.

So from then on it was not the usual sort of childhood. The children were left, at first, in the complete care of their grandmother, while their father continued to live in town during the week, attending to his India House and becoming involved in the intellectual life of London. He wrote on various topics for the *Westminster Review,* the periodical identified with his colleagues, the Mills; later he reviewed operas and musical events for the *Examiner,* the *Globe,* and the *London Review.* During this period he wrote two novels *(Misfortunes of Elphin* and *Crotchet Castle)*. It may be supposed he did not spend a lot of time at home.

Yet he was a fond father; his children were his emotional realities, for he had no wife. Mary Ellen was his favorite child, perhaps because she was the first, born in a happy time, and she seemed to justify his convictions that girls could be as strong, as spirited, as intelligent and learned as men.

In the nineteenth century this was by no means universally admitted. It was felt by many that women were in fact inferior. Daring thinkers, progressives, later in the century, held the more controversial view that women were not inferior, exactly: they were different. But just as good in their way. Not as smart, perhaps, but more intuitive; especially gifted with moral intuition, which made them the natural tutors of men, who, liable as they were to error, especially sexual error, were taught to look for moral and spiritual guidance to the naturally pure-minded females of their families — first to mother, later to wife. And it was thought better not to tamper with the naturally pure, intuitive moral faculties of girls and women by cluttering their heads with a lot of dangerous, even corrupting, knowledge — like certain passages of Shakespeare or, certainly, the wicked classics of Greece and Rome.

Of course no woman was ever so ideal as the ideal Victorian woman, but it was an age when you tried very hard; you heard lectures and wrote notes to yourself, and read improving volumes on the subject. It was an age that assumed a standard of moral perfection that under the right circumstances could in fact be achieved in this world. There was little indulgence for folly; a severe but rather optimistic view of human nature.

The education of girls and women was mostly directed at preserving them the way society — that is, Victorian fathers and husbands — thought they ought to be. Victorian women knew a little geography and how to add and subtract; they read the cleaner classics and literature of a spiritually improving nature. If you drew and painted and played the piano a little, you were "accomplished." You sewed, perhaps you understood about cooking and domestic management. You were an influence for purity and religiousness in your family; you endured but did not enjoy sex (like the famous lady who confided her secret for getting through it: "I just lie on my back and think of England"). And there was a whole lot about the world you did not know or think of, because you did not want to know, and your husband and brothers did not want you to know, and if you found out, you pretended not to know just the same. You did not know, for example, exactly what happened to any poor girl who was "ruined," although whatever it was, you knew, was dreadful. The ideal Victorian woman was innocent, unlearned, motherly, and, though devoutly worshipped, she was also notoriously dull company both at the dinner table and in bed.

One is tempted to suppose that she must have been encountered more often in the breach than in the observance. The picture that comes down to us of the ideal or even the typical woman is so constrained, so exploited, so ignorant, so dull, that it could not be borne; yet millions of women bore their lives with cheerfulness, or at least fortitude, shored up, it is true, by ramparts of fear (fear of disgrace, shame, and starvation) and of sentiment (motherhood, wifehood, an angel in the house) — and by the preoccupying rigors of relentless childbearing (the average number was nine). Common sense urges us to suppose that beneath the Victorians' public postures of rectitude, formality, and reserve, beneath the bustles and beards, lurked beings much like ourselves. But closer inspection (books, letters, statistics) suggests that our sympathy is misplaced. They were *not* like us. People's psyches conformed, as much as their manners did, to the peculiar notions they had created. Women did loathe sex, and they did call their husbands by their surnames.[10] Husbands did suffer to feel base sexual impulses toward the pure creatures they married; and they did creep ashamedly off to prostitutes, or became impotent — another widespread affliction of the time. (Regarding the incidence of both impotence and large families in the Victorian age, we can only suppose the former intermittent, and the latter, perhaps, a function of anxiety over the former.)

Everyone had headache, and lay about on sofas. Many households, like the Peacocks', had someone crazy or invalid upstairs, as often a victim of the bizarre psychological patterns as of the pitiable medical ignorance then abounding.

༝༞.

Peacock, an affectionate father, a warmhearted man, gazes upon his first-born, a little girl: a cheerful little thing who ran and shouted, and learned to read precociously. Was she to grow up to do nothing better than gossip, have headache, faint? Was she never to know about good books, running, port wine, physical love as a pleasure? As the Chinese bound the feet of their women, Englishmen bound their minds. Peacock determined that this should not happen to his girl. She would be educated, free of cant, self-respecting.

Whether Peacock was right to bring up Mary Ellen as he did is hard to say; it is the old problem of the happy swineherd and the discontented philosopher. Perhaps — people must have often made this remark to one another — perhaps Mary Ellen Peacock would have been better off if she had not been so clever and educated.

Peacock has often aired his views on female education in his books. Even before he created the real Mary Ellen, he had created the fictional Anthelia (the heroine of *Melincourt*). Now that Peacock, Mary Ellen, and Anthelia are all just people in books, perhaps we may say Anthelia is someone Peacock used to know.

Although he created her in 1817, before his marriage, her situation oddly prefigures his own and Mary Ellen's. Anthelia was raised by her father: a "man of great requirements, and of a retired disposition, devoted himself in solitude to the cultivation of his daughter's understanding; for he was one of those who maintained the heretical notion that women are, or at least may be, rational beings; though, from the great pains usually taken in what is called education to make them otherwise, there are unfortunately very few examples to warrant the truth of the theory."

Victorian society amply attested to this. Anthelia, owing to the care of her father, was like Mary Ellen, an exception — studious, sincere, direct, thoughtful. In the book she is admired by an idealistic young man named Forester, who realizes before he has even seen her that she is a rare creature — because he learns that she occasionally locks herself up in her library, something which astonishes his sensible friends Mr. Fax and Mr. Hippy.

"'Locks herself up in a library!' said Mr. Fax: 'a young lady, a beauty and an heiress, in the nineteenth century, thinks of cultivating her understanding!'

"'Strange but true,' said Mr. Hippy."

Mr. Forester is fascinated; later, when he meets her, he is ecstatic to discover she has a taste for Italian poetry, and praises her effusively.

Anthelia: You have a better opinion of the understandings of women, Sir, than the generality of your lordly sex seems disposed to entertain.

Mr. Forester: The conduct of men, in this respect, is much like that of a gardener who should plant a plot of ground with merely ornamental flowers, and then pass sentence on the soil for not bearing substantial fruit. If women are treated only as pretty dolls, and dressed in all the fripperies of irrational education; if the vanity of personal adornment and superficial accomplishments be made from their very earliest years to suppress all mental aspirations, and to supersede all thoughts of intellectual beauty, is it to be inferred that they are incapable of better things? But such is the usual logic of tyranny, which first places its extinguisher on the flame, and then argues that it cannot burn. . . .

The only points practically enforced in female education are sound, colour, and form, — music, dress, drawing, and dancing. The mind is left to take care of itself.

Mr. Fax: And has as much chance of doing so as a horse in a pound, circumscribed in the narrowest limits, and studiously deprived of nourishment.

Anthelia: The simile is, I fear, too just. To think is one of the most unpardonable errors a woman can commit in the eyes of society. In our sex a taste for intellectual pleasures is almost equivalent to taking the veil; and though not absolutely a vow of perpetual celibacy, it has almost always the same practical tendency. . . .

Also, it must be kept in mind at all times that the women we are concerned with conducted their lives, had thoughts, went traveling, ate dinner, and fell in love while entirely encased beneath their gowns in the following articles of clothing: a

chemise, a corset, a camisole over the corset, up to six petticoats—beginning with a short, stiff one, one or two flannel
ones for warmth, a plain one and then some embroidered ones—
a vest or undershirt, stockings, garters, and, depending on the
decade, a whalebone crinoline or bustle. And all of these things
were held on and together with strings, and tapes, and innumerable buttons and hooks.[11]

Whatever we are able to make of Mary Ellen's adulterous
behavior, we will not be able to excuse it on the grounds of
impulse; there could hardly have been such a thing as an impulsive sexual irregularity for women so encumbered.

⌐⁊.

Real records of Mary Ellen's childhood are few, but much may be
inferred. Like Anthelia, Mary Ellen learned to read; she was allowed to read widely, pretty much what she wanted. Probably
she was not started on Latin and Greek so early as Mill had
started that boy of his, the impressive but peculiar John Stuart.
And unlike John Stuart, Mary Ellen was given fiction and poetry,
to develop the heart as well as the head. And Mary Ellen messed
around in boats, like a boy, and learned to row and sail and
swim. She grew up to be a fearless horsewoman, so she was
probably given a pony early. The Peacock children spent most
of their time outdoors.

When Mary Ellen was seven, a precocious, active little
beauty, she would not have been a bit interested in the tailor's
baby born in this year, 1828, at Portsmouth. This was George
Meredith, whom she would marry.

Little George's parents were Welsh like Mary's, and gave
themselves airs about it. Like many Welshmen they thought
themselves descended from kings, and they knew they were
clever and beautiful. But George's father and grandfather before

him were tailors, and a tailor is a particularly ludicrous thing
to an Englishman. This must have been confusing to the little,
only child, George—to be simultaneously better and worse than
other people in the town of Portsmouth. His mother dressed him
in white dresses with blue ribbons, and he had splendid toys,
and fifty people in to a "Tea and Ball" for his fourth or fifth
birthday party. Inside, he was little and afraid. His nursemaid
told him that the sound of the wind whistling through the key-
hole was the ghosts of starved people. Ghosts dwelt right in his
room, too, in the dark, everywhere.

George's mother was also named Jane, like Mary's, and
when George was five she died. It was as if she suddenly went
away. George "merely wondered" at the time, but when he
grew up he wrote a lot of books in which women run away, or
die, or otherwise desert little boys and leave them sad, as if
women inevitably did that. And of course this happened all
over again to George when he grew up, confirming his view.
Whether by thinking that things will happen, you make them
happen is a great question.

When Mary Ellen is ten she takes a trip with Papa to Wales. The
other children have to stay at home with Grandmama. In Wales
they get a letter from Grandmama. She sends her love to "dearest
Ellen," and feels "great happiness in knowing that she is happy."
It was Peacock's birthday. "We are all well—and the whole
family with the addition of little Betty drank health and happiness to you yesterday nor was dear Ellen forgotten." Grandmama has a suggestion for something he should talk over with
Mary Ellen: "I wish you could persuade her to love her Brother
better, poor little boy he has had none of the advantages she

has had—and therefore she should make allowance—he is a very amiable little fellow and would be very fond of her—if she would like him." Mary Ellen, we see, is a real little girl, jealous of her next youngest sibling, impatient of his slowness, and Grandmama had to contend with the normal number of family squabbles and outbursts of temperament; perhaps with more than the usual number of outbursts from Mary Ellen, who was demanding, quick, hot-tempered.

"No Mama yet," Sarah adds. Perhaps they still had some hopes for Mama, that she would one day miraculously come back to her senses. Sarah Peacock hopes that Thomas will return from his trip to Wales "in better health and spirits," suggesting that he had set out in ill health, ill spirits—and no wonder.

Peacock's lot was worsened when Sarah died in 1833. His oldest child was only twelve, and there were three littler ones to manage, but beyond the practical disadvantages, Sarah's death was a devastating personal blow to Thomas, who had been extraordinarily close to his mother in a way that would now occasion remark, but which presented to the Victorian eye only a charming record of unexceptionable sentiment. Peacock had found in his mother his best critic, encourager, and, of course, housekeeper and surrogate Mama to his motherless children.

Now Peacock did not write anything for a long time. He was busier than ever at India House, where he was rising, and he had to oversee his children, hire governesses and servants, commute from Lower Halliford to London daily by rail and cab. He seems to have moved Jane up to London, at least part of the time, possibly to spare the children the sight or care of her. Mary Ellen came to London often, too, and went to operas and plays and museums with Papa. "She is said often to have sat beside him in his usual place, the middle of the front row of the pit," while he wrote operatic reviews, the Biographer tells us.

In 1835, when Mary Ellen was fourteen, Mary Shelley reports to Maria Gisbourne how things went with the Peacock ménage: "I have not seen Peacock for some time. His wife lives in town—she is quite mad—his children in the country all by themselves except for his weekly visits—his eldest girl educates herself and reads Paul de Kock's novels in all innocence."

Mary Ellen seems to have been given considerably more responsibility than most fourteen-year-old girls. For instance, when Peacock was ill that spring, it is to Mary that Mary Shelley writes:

I am much grieved to learn from Mr. Hogg that he had heard that your dear Papa was not quite so well again—the weather being unfavorable—You have been very good to answer my enquiries—but do, Dear Ellen, write by the earliest post—& tell me how he is now—I should be so glad to hear that he is again better—so be a good dear girl & let me know as soon as you can—& forgive me for troubling you—but I am sure you will—as your Papa is almost my oldest friend—and I cannot hear of his illness without feeling very unhappy—

I hope you & your brother & sister are well—

> *Ever affectionately yours*
> *MW Shelley*

Write me rather a longer note & tell me what the doctor says—

Later letters show that by 1839, Mary Ellen often stayed in London with her Papa in Stamford Street, and that she acted rather as his secretary or agent in routine matters. "This letter is more for your Papa than you—but I want an answer and that is not to be hoped for from him and so I trespass on your good nature to make you read my letter and get you to answer me," Mary Shelley, who was always after Peacock about matters relating to his administration of Shelley's affairs, wrote to Mary Ellen. Mary Ellen is eighteen now, and goes out to dine at Mrs. Shelley's, and visits with Thomas Jefferson Hogg—she is "in society." Papa has risen to the post of Examiner, the highest position of the East India Company, which, since by then it was rather like a Department of Indian Affairs in the British govern-ment, made Peacock something like a highly-paid government official—a governor, perhaps, or a Secretary of Commerce.

(Peacock succeeded the philosopher James Mill at this position and, when he retired twenty years later, was succeeded by John Stuart Mill.)

We do not know what sort of childhood Rosa Jane and Edward and May had—a different childhood, no doubt, for it is surely true that every child in a family has a different environment. Apparently they did not get to go to London with Papa; they did not travel to Wales with him. Perhaps they minded. Perhaps Mary Ellen was a kind big sister and perhaps not. We do not know if little May slipped off across the green to see her real mother, her real brothers, or whether she thought herself, when she was young, a spot too grand.

George Meredith's grandfather had been a good tailor and a great character, but George's father was neither good nor great. He went bankrupt in the tailoring business and took up with the servant girl, Matilda Bucket (how one longs to know more about Matilda Bucket), and finally, because he could not support his son, made George a "ward in Chancery," a Dickensian-sounding fate that got him sent by dispassionate people to the sort of schools a person with only sixty-six pounds a year gets sent to— an English boarding school so *déclassé* that the grown-up George would never reveal its name. And when he was fourteen he was sent to a pleasant kind of school in Germany which seems to have combined piety with the inculcation of manly virtues in a more humane way than English schools usually did. So while Mary Ellen lay about reading French novels and "educating" herself, her future husband was being filled with outdoorsy German folk tales and a love of long walks. Later he was sent home to England again and his Guardians in Chancery worried over what to do with him. About the time of Mary Ellen's first marriage, the Guardians decided to send the Meredith boy off to Hong Kong to learn to take daguerreotypes, and though we cannot feel it would have benefited English letters if they had carried through with this plan, things might have gone better for Mary Ellen.

A teenage Mary Ellen, Papa's favorite, spirited, beautiful, well-educated, and well-off, brought up along the sparkling Thames in a prosperous, big Victorian family, with famous men to dinner and Papa a lord of commerce, and everybody (Mama excepted) happy and prosperous. Was Mary Ellen happy? But adolescents are never happy. Mary Ellen, who loved to lie on the grass along the river with Italian poetry and French novels, now discovers her life to be like a French novel, full of love and hate and drama and death. Her own death, even. How sad not to be going to live to grow up. How everyone would miss her. How treacherous she felt herself to be, to die and make everyone sad. But she feels the end is near (she has a pneumonia, perhaps, or the impulse to hurl herself dramatically into the Thames). She writes a farewell epistle to Papa:[12]

My kind dear father

I cannot tell what I wish to say to you and My dear Mama — forget me, I will not speak of myself. Dear Rosa is very delicate, her cough is very very bad and if not looked to at once may become fatal, and dearest Papa, pray place her with Mrs. Jenkins, it is an unfortunate trial to leave a girl by herself. And now dear Papa you will I hope believe me, now when I can have no motive for deceit. Mary Ann has been the evil genius of my existence, do not let her be so to dear Rosa. Dearest Papa, pray let my Eddy have the letter I have written him by a safe channel, and dearest Papa do do pray promote him, get him on for my sake—you will dear Papa I know you will. God bless you My dear dear father—May Rosa and Edward render you that happiness I have taken.

Your unhappy
Mary

Papa keeps these letters; perhaps he will show Mary Ellen these letters when she grows older, and she will laugh and blush at what a silly child she had been. Darling May an evil genius? What a horrid, jealous child she had been. It is not known whether Peacock attended, then, to Rosa's cough—dear Rosa, coughing patiently in some corner, seems to have needed her dying older sister as advocate. Mary has instructions for Eddy, too:

My own darling Eddy

You will grieve for me I know, but do not curse the memory of your Mary by leading a dissipated life, Eddy, dearest Eddy, do not, oh do not, do that. If spirits in the other world feel love and human feelings towards those whom they have left on earth, think dearest Eddy what mine must [be] feeling to know that I have been the wilful cause of your deriliction [sic] from the path of happiness and honour. I know your spirit and your heart my own best love, and I know that I cannot give you a greater proof of my confidence in your fond love for me than in entreating you, as I do darling Eddy, to bear my death as becomes a man.

I know not what more I would say, you will be happy with

another partner, more worthy than I God bless you dearest be happy dearest and do not hate my memory.

Mary Peacock

Eddy one more request and I have done, if you would have my bones rest in peace, oh for the sake of all you hold dearest, do not quarrel or fight duels with any creature. I die in the hope your kindness will grant my soul felt request.

Mary

The phrasing and tone of this letter to Darling Eddy come from the lending-library fiction which her too-indulgent Papa had permitted her to read, but that was the Victorian style for these great occasions—deathbed requests and the like. When Mary Ellen grew older and learned to distinguish life from fiction her style became laconic, ironic, lifelike.

Were Eddy's great vices—a propensity to quarrel and fight duels, to deviation from the path of happiness and honor, and (great heavens!) to dissipation—also drawn from a lending-library conception of young men, or was this really a wild young man whom Mary Ellen loved? Anyway, who *was* darling Eddy?

If we have heard of Mary Ellen at all, we have heard of her as the first wife of George Meredith, briefly adorning those pages of his autobiograhical works that treat his youth. As if she were formed for George's youth by some vaguely malign spirit seeking to try him—the Comic Spirit, perhaps, whose sole interest lay in providing George with those formative experiences so essential to a coming great writer. As if *she* had no past worth speaking of—was, perhaps, created simply for the occasion. But of course Mary Ellen, when she married George Meredith, had had a past already. Had already fallen in love, had already been married, had given birth to a child — all those life experiences that we normally expect to take place after the close of a Victorian novel, had taken place for Mary Ellen before the story with George began. The real drama of her life may have seemed to her to have nothing to do with George Meredith at all.

⁀⁊.

When Mary Ellen was about twelve, Papa became involved in a new venture. Always interested in ships, he now became interested in steamships. The Russians, rivals of the East India Company in some areas of Asia, had used steamships to navigate the Volga and the Caspian Sea, but Englishmen did not think them practical either for river navigation or for the long trip between England and India, and also did not think the Russians would bring steamships to the Euphrates and Tigris Rivers if the English did not. Peacock thought otherwise on all of these points.

Accordingly, he began to organize, to prove, approve, testify, correspond, converse, write articles, first in support of steam communication with India and secondarily to promote the exploration of the Indian rivers. These matters were somewhat controversial, and they were expensive. The East India Company was now effectively a department of the British Government, so there were parliamentary committees, secret and select, for him to convince. He collected a great scrapbook about the Euphrates, in which, characteristically, he had entered every notice, from Gibbon and everywhere, from which he would quote. He talked to people like the explorer F. R. Chesney and corresponded with him. A stream of inventors with gadgets for steamships beat a path to his door, knowing it would be Peacock who would approve or disapprove all steamship gadget patents. Papa went on little steam voyages in the Channel, trying out his "iron chickens." Possibly the children went along.

Peacock's interest may have arisen as a consequence of his friendship with Macgregor Laird, or possibly the other way round. Macgregor Laird had married Ellen Nicolls, whose father, then Captain Edward Nicolls of the Royal Marines, was in the middle of a distinguished career of exploring and island-governing. Captain (later General) Nicolls was at this time interested in the control of slave trading on the African coasts, and was active in promoting the use of steamships there. Laird manufactured steamships. It was all very tidy. How pleased everyone must have been when Mary Ellen and Captain Nicolls's elder boy, Edward, took to each other, making even tidier the correspondence among interests—interest and profit all round.

If Darling Eddy was a wild young man, he got it from his fierce father, who was known as "fighting Nicolls." *The Globe and Laurel,* a journal of the Royal Marines, summarizes his career as follows:

Sir Edward Nicolls was in action with the enemies of his country 107 times, and it is not too much to say of him "a more distinguished soldier never lived," for certainly no man ever saw more service than he did, and he has left behind him a name and a fame unequalled in the page of history. . . . He was constantly employed in boat and battery actions, and in most desperate cutting out expeditions. . . . He commanded the Royal Marines at the siege of Curaçao, in February, 1804, where he stormed and took Fort Piscadero of 10 guns, and drove the Dutch troops from the heights. He served also in the trenches, and for 28 consecutive days had to repel three or four attacks of the enemy daily. He also defeated an allied force of 500 men, and destroyed Fort Piscadero. He served at the forcing of the Dardanelles in 1807, when he captured the Turkish commodore's flag, and assisted in the destruction of his ship. He also captured and destroyed the redoubt on Point Pesquies and spiked the guns therein. He was present at the blockade of Corfu in 1807, and with the expedition to Egypt in the same year, when he rendered very important services in charge of a station in the desert, and was taken prisoner. On the 26th June, 1808, with a boat's crew only, he boarded and captured the Italian gunboat <u>Volpe</u>, near Corfu, after a chase of two hours. On the 18th May, 1809, he landed with two lieutenants and 120 Royal Marines on the Island of Anholt, defeated with the bayonet a force of 200 Danish troops, captured the island, and took upwards of 500 prisoners; for this service he received a letter of thanks, and was appointed governor of the island. He served in North America during the war in that country, and raised and commanded a large force of Indians, rendering incalculable service to the British arms by continually harassing the United States army. He co-operated in the siege of Fort Bowyer in 1814 in command of a regiment of Greek Indians [<u>sic</u>], and was three times wounded during the bombardment, he having insisted on being carried to the post of honour, although unable from sickness to walk. He was the senior major of all the force before New Orleans in 1815, and as such urged his right to lead the battalion of Royal Marines in the assault; this honour was refused him on the ground that if he fell, there would be no officer competent to command his army of Indians. He also performed other very important services during the war, and was specially mentioned in the gazette in 1807, 1808, and 1809. During the above brilliant career he had his left leg broken, his right leg severely wounded, was shot through the body and right arm, received a terrible sabre cut on the head, was bayonetted in the chest, and lost the sight of an eye in his last, or 107th action. In December, 1815, he was awarded a pension of £250 a year for these wounds, and received a second sword of honour. He retired on full pay 15th May, 1835; was awarded a good service pension of £150 a year on 30th June, 1842; and was made a K.C.B. on the 5th July, 1855. The heart of every member of the corps may well glow with pride when he claims Sir Edward Nicolls as a brother in arms, for had the Royal Marines no other hero to boast of, his career alone might well suffice to entitle them to a world-wide reputation for gallantry. No better history of the corps — during the half century of his service — can be found than

*the glorious record of his brilliant exploits, and in the long cata-
logue of its achievements it is impossible to read a nobler page.*

The Marines' journal finishes with a remark to its readers
which is not beside the point of this work: "The memory of Sir
Edward Nicolls will ever be cherished and regarded with pride
by the officers and men of the corps in which he so nobly served.
They will remember too, that though 'Fighting Nicolls' was
ever in the front in all his splendid actions, he was backed up by
the strong arms and the dauntless hearts of his soldiers, and the
Royal Marines can never forget that the laurels now encircling
their badge (the finest in the Service) owed the growth to the
torrents of blood shed by those brave men."

It is hard to know what Darling Eddy was like, for he did not
live long enough to leave much record of himself, but we hope
he was like his father, who left bits and records of great enthusiastic schemes, full of the indignant ring of principles unusual
in a military man, and a manly humanitarianism not often found
in them either, especially in the nineteenth century. Once he
wrote to Lord Bathhurst with a fine scheme for colonizing New
Zealand:

*The New Zealanders are represented as a brave and warlike
race of Men, with the important addition to their characters of
being as affectionate, intelligent and industrious, as they are
hardy, active, and ingenious; possessing minds capable of receiving and profiting by instruction, and hearts that bear a grateful sense of any kindness they receive. It must however be admitted that great odium attaches to them in consequence of the
abhorrent custom of eating their war victoms [sic], and of the
commission of other acts of cruelty, practised on the crews of
some of the European ships which have touched on their coasts;
but your Memorialist is confident that the plan which he is
about to propose for the colonization of the Island would (by
removing the causes of these evils) entirely put a stop to such
ferocious acts.*[13]

He has someone in mind for the job, too: "It is his anxious wish to be considered by your Lordship, as eligible and competent to be intrusted with the Colonization of New Zealand, . . . your memorialist trusts that 30 years Services will be a sufficient warrant, for his future Zeal and activity in promoting any undertaking which may conduce to the welfare of his Country." In this, as in most of his schemes, he had little luck.

Peacock, fond from boyhood of hearing sea adventures, as he had done from his Grandfather Love, was fond of them in manhood too, and he must have gotten on well with Mary Ellen's father-in-law, the fiery old Marine.

How pleased everyone was when Eddy and Mary Ellen fell in love. Even though their marriage must wait for Edward's prospects to straighten out, and for Mary Ellen to grow a little older, their engagement had very general approval. Some stuffier relatives might perhaps have echoed Sir William Elliot's objections to the naval profession in Jane Austen's *Persuasion:* "I have two strong grounds of objection to it. First, as being the means of bringing persons of obscure birth into undue distinction, and raising men to honours which their fathers and grandfathers never dreamt of; and, secondly, as it cuts up a man's youth and vigour most horribly; a sailor grows old sooner than any other man. . . . They are all knocked about, and exposed to every climate, and every weather, till they are not fit to be seen. It is a pity they are not knocked on the head at once, before they reach Admiral Baldwin's age."

But now Eddy was young and fair, with good family and every good prospect, and with the high temper needed to manage the temperamental Mary Ellen, too. Most of the family friends took, as Hogg did, a congratulatory tone (the marriage of a daughter in any family was a matter for relieved celebration in those days):

Dear Peacock,

Receive my congratulations on Your Daughter's marriage. I earnestly hope, that the union may prove an auspicious one in all respects.

I shall always feel a most lively interest in the welfare of Mary Ellen. I expect to hear soon, that Mr. N. has been appointed an Admiral of the Bed Squadron; & has become as illustrious in his profession, as the conjoint Glory of Cornelius van Tromp & Horatio Nelson co(d) make him. And I wo(d), that all this sh(d) be, if it were possible, without so much as taking the trouble (& as it is the pleasantest mode of going to the stars), to uncross his legs, or take his hands out of his pockets once!—

With kind regards & good wishes to the Bride, I am

> *Dear P.—*
> *Yours truly,*
> *T Jeffn Hogg*

3 Plowden Bgs
Temple, 17th Jan'y. 1844

So Edward and Mary Ellen were married amid very general approval, at Shepperton, Surrey, and Mary Ellen put up her hair, which she had worn until now in long pale curls, and became a young wife, and went off with Edward to Ireland, where Edward had command of a ship. A steamship, of course, quite in the family line. Perhaps they took a cottage—Mary had a fondness for cottages and for housekeeping. Perhaps they had a nice Irish cow. Or most likely—for surely they would not be in Ireland for long—they were still in lodgings, with a few things of their own, bride-presents and hand-me-downs to make the place seem theirs. Mary, with years of managing the Peacock household behind her, was already an accomplished cook, so that Eddy fared better in this respect than many young husbands.

Eddy was wild and brave and fearless, as a son must be who has such a fearless father if he is not to disgrace the family — an option, of course, seized by many Victorian sons. But not Eddy. And Eddy had a beautiful bride, herself fearless, who liked to go on board ship; would come up on deck in a gale; Eddy and Mary would laugh at a gale. Eddy had command of a steam vessel — a circumstance in which the family connections may be discerned — but it was his own ship, and he and Mary were in Ireland, here to start their new grownup life, newly wed and with a ship to command. Fine prospects. They had been married about two months and then one morning, in a gale, Mary and Eddy on board the *Dwarf* observed a yacht anchored nearby begin to drag its moorings, and Eddy with a few of his men put off in two little boats to help. One capsized and Eddy and some others went to rescue a one-armed sailor — but their little boat was swept over in the gale and something hit Eddy on the head and that was the end of him. They took Mary Ellen below, perhaps; or perhaps she remained standing at the rail, staring into the black water for Eddy, but they did not find him then.

They had been married in January 1844. In March, Mary was already pregnant. One day Edward went out in his ship, in a storm, and was drowned while trying to rescue someone. These things are certain. Of the actual circumstance of Eddy's death, accounts differ. Edith wrote of the father she never saw: "He was lost at sea at Tarbert, in Kerry, at the mouth of the Shannon, the March of that same year, while endeavoring to save the life of a poor one-armed man." This has remained the received account.

But the most unexpected pitfalls beset the Biographer. A descendant of the Nicolls family, looking after Eddy's memory, is anxious that it be correct in all accounts, and writes a cautionary letter: "I expect that by now you have got details about Lieut. Edward from the various record offices but of course I would answer any questions about him which I knew — there is one small detail which occurs to me. He did not go to try & save a 'one armed member of the crew.' This should be 'a member of the crew who was single-handed in a boat.' When this boat capsized in the Shannon Estuary, E. N. & 5 others went to help in a 'gig,' which was itself swept over by the Gale — E. N. & one other man being lost.

"I do hope that E. N.'s death will not be sentimentalized since he died in pursuit of his duties, & it would be so unlike any of the Nicolls family to treat it as high tragedy." And indeed darling Eddy did not live long enough, or die to sufficient purpose, to be called tragic, though the young bride and widow, alone in her lodgings in Tarbert, might, of course, have felt this death to be something in the tragic vein.

Everyone was horrified by the shocking news: Mary Shelley wrote to Claire Clairmont: "I am sorry to have to report an event which will distress you, tho it does not touch you nearly — poor Mary has lost her husband. They were stationed you know, in the south of Ireland — going out on some act of duty in an open boat, during one of the late terrible storms — on the 11th of this month, the boat upset & he & another were drowned. — Peacock I believe has set off for his unfortunate daughter — It is most sad! — " Mary Shelley was better able than most, no doubt, to guess how Mary Ellen must be feeling.

T. J. Hogg writes:

Dear Peacock,

We were All much Shocked & distressed at your severe domestic affliction; it is so heavy a blow indeed, that I know not what to say about it.

As for the unhappy young Lady, I sincerely hope & trust, that, in due time, she may meet with some person worthy to supply the cruel loss; & indeed I scarcely know anyone more likely to attract the regards of an intelligent & estimable young man.

I hope, that, not withstanding your sorrows, we may still contrive to be together during the fine weather sometimes.

I go on Monday to join the Circuit at Liverpool

> *Your's truly,*
> *T Jeffn Hogg*

23 March 1844

And Mary Shelley to Claire: "I have no news of poor Mary— except that she begged her father not to go over to her—but leave her to manage everything herself—this was at first—I should think that by this time [?] She is over—some day soon I shall go by steamer and pay Peacock a visit at the I[ndia] H[ouse]."

But in June: "Mrs. Nicolls is still in Ireland." So we do not know if Peacock went to help her or not, or why she stayed there alone so long, or why she wanted to manage by herself. But she was to be like this through other trials—would withdraw, would cope, would persevere with tight-lipped practicality. Her later trials were to be worse but she cut her teeth on trouble here.

In the autumn Edith was born at the Nicolls's family home at Shooter's Hill, in Kent. She was fatherless, but she had fond grandparents, a devoted mother, aunts, uncles. She had an odd life. History, with its eyes fixed on Grandpapa, has looked right past Edith, with only brief thanks to her for writing her memoir of Peacock, for remembering things that no one else could, and for putting together, from personal knowledge and recollection, explanations and dates for her grandfather's work. Scholars have been a little condescending, though, because she made some mistakes a careful male scholar would not have made. Helpful male scholars oversaw her little undertakings and made suggestions. No one has ever said if Edith grew up beautiful like her mother, and, in truth, her tone is not that of a beautiful woman, but of a wise, strong, and interesting one who became a Remarkable Woman in a logical direction, gotten from Mama and Grandpapa. We shall want to watch little Edith.

But in 1844 she was only just born, and taken to Lower Halliford. A little later she lived with Mama in London, and again at Lower Halliford, when Mama married That Man, and she was sent off to school, and stayed with her dead Papa's family sometimes, and visited Mama in her cheap lodgings here and there, sat by her dying Mama, perhaps, and certainly by her dying Grandpapa, and learned very early to cope with people's vagaries, the way they had of running off, and dying, and being sad. Little Edith kept to her own way and remembered everything that she had learned.

Mary Ellen was now twenty-three years old, a widow and a mother. It is a wonder that nobody came and married her immediately, for she must have presented to the Victorian eye a sight more affecting than any other: a young woman, having "acquired the endearing name of Mother," was obliged by custom to wear a little cap; and Mary's cap—how tragic, how lovely—must be of black. It is the situation of Thackeray's Amelia. Thackeray tells us we "must draw back in the presence of the cruel grief under which [she] is bleeding. Tread silently round the hapless couch of the poor prostrate soul. Shut gently the door of the dark chamber wherein she suffers, as those kind people did who nursed her through the first months of her pain, and never left her until heaven had sent her consolation. A day came—of almost terrified delight and wonder—when the poor widowed girl pressed a child upon her breast—a child, with the eyes of [him] who was gone—a little boy, as beautiful as a cherub. What a miracle it was to hear its first cry! How she laughed and wept over it—how love, and hope, and prayer woke again in her bosom as the baby nestled there. . . ." All England wept, and Thackeray finally rivaled Dickens.

ス.

But Mary Ellen does not seem to have been like Amelia—not at *all*—and was perhaps even more dashing than Becky. If she was unfortunate in meeting up with George Meredith, we, at least, are fortunate that George was a novelist and left some heroines in books who reputedly owe a lot to Mary. There is one special type of ironic, fascinating, and sophisticated *femme du monde* who keeps recurring: named, unflatteringly, "Mrs. Mount" in the first book George wrote after their separation: later, in *Rhoda Fleming*, after the sting had worn off, "Mrs. Lovell," which is kinder. Mrs. Lovell had gone off very young with a military husband who was killed in a duel, in defense of her reputation, and now was back in England, very much the queenly hostess of a place on a river that sounds exactly like Peacock's: "A white mansion among great oaks, in view of the summer sails and winter masts of the yachting squadron. The house was ruled, during the congregation of Christmas guests, by charming Mrs. Lovell, who relieved the invalid Lady of the house of the many serious cares attending the reception of visitors, and did it all with ease. Under her sovereignty the place was delightful, and if it was by repute pleasanter to young men than to any other class, it will be admitted that she satisfied those who are loudest in giving tongue to praise." And also: "The lady had a small jointure, and lived partly with her uncle, Lord Elling, partly with Squire Blancove, her aunt's husband, and a little by herself, which was when she counted money in her purse, and chose to assert her independence," which may give us some clue as to Mary Ellen's mode of life after Eddy's death.[14]

And, if Mary Ellen was like Mrs. Lovell, what was Mrs. Lovell like?: "She was golden and white, like an autumnal birch-tree, —yellow hair, with warm-toned streaks in it, shading a fabulously fair skin. Then, too, she was tall, of a nervous build, supple and proud in motion, a brilliant horsewoman, and a most distinguished sitter in an easy drawing-room chair, which is, let me impress upon you, no mean quality. After riding out for hours with a sweet comrade, who has thrown the mantle of dignity half-way off her shoulders, it is perplexing, and mixed strangely of humiliation and ecstasy, to come upon her clouded majesty where she reclines as upon rose-hued clouds, in a mystic circle of restriction (she who laughed at your jokes, and capped them, two hours ago) a queen."

This is very like the "dashing horsewoman who attracted

much attention from the young men of the day," as Holman Hunt described Mary Ellen.

Mrs. Lovell was something of a gambler; and though there is no trace of a taste in Mary Ellen for wagers or cards, she was a gambler too, in the important ways:

The thirst for shows of valour and wit was insane with her, but she asked for nothing that she herself did not give in abundance, and with beauty superadded. Her propensity to bet sprang of her passion for combat; she was not greedy of money, or reckless in using it; but with a difference of opinion arising, her instinct forcibly prompted her to back her own. If the stake was the risk of a lover's life, she was ready to put down the stake, and would have marvelled contemptuously at the lover complaining. "Sheep! sheep!" she thought of those who dared not fight, and had a wavering tendency to affix the epithet to those who simply did not fight.

Withal, Mrs. Lovell was a sensible person; clear-headed and shrewd; logical, too, more than the run of her sex: I may say, profoundly practical. So much so, that she systematically reserved the after-years for enlightenment upon two or three doubts of herself, which struck her in the calm of her spirit, from time to time.

Although Eddy was drowned in 1844, and we do not hear of Mary Ellen again until 1848, we may conclude she was up to something in the interval.

She seems, after leaving the Nicolls's, to have gone with her new baby back to Lower Halliford at first, to Papa, where fond Rosa Jane and May could help with Baby, and the quiet Thames could ease her memory of the turbulent Shannon and restore her confidence in rivers. The flow of time—she read, sewed, chatted, went to parties at the houses of their neighbors, sparkled wittily at her own table with the great men Papa brought down from London. Took up writing during this time. Healed. Sometimes went with Edith to visit the Nicolls. Rode horses; maybe bet.

She was not happy. At times great bitterness, great melancholy, would overwhelm her. In a day when resignation was the approved posture against adversity, Mary Ellen was not good at resignation.

She would fling herself into things. Sometimes she would go to London, where Papa was Somebody, and the conversation was good and people were amusing. She would visit and gossip with their friends. Old Hogg amused her with his stories—she was a married woman now, and had a certain license to listen to racy stories, even to tell them, or to read French novels. She was beautiful and witty. She was not happy. She did not soon forget Edward; on the other hand she would think twice before sacrificing this freedom for another marriage.

She kept busy. Here as in other things she was not typical of the female half of mankind in her time, for women then were fascinating in their indolence. Indeed, they had to be specially trained to endure it. But Mary Ellen had her child, her writing, her cookery experiments, good company.

Sometimes in London she stayed with her brother Edward, who, after several unsuccessful attempts at this and that—school, the Navy—had gotten an appointment at India House, no doubt through the offices of Peacock, who had also found places for the sons of scores (it seems) of other old friends; Hilary St. Croix, for example, one of the St. Croix family whose Marianne had refused Peacock thirty years before.

Ned Peacock and Hilary had a lot of lively friends, among them a Bohemian solicitor named Charnock and an artist, Peter Austin Daniel (who also worked at India House), and a young clerk in Charnock's offices—George Meredith.

Mary was 27. George Meredith was then 20; by all accounts

handsome, demonstrably brilliant, and charming. Mary did not fall in love with him at once.

⌐⊃.

George fell in love with Mary Ellen at once. Like the young hero of *Rhoda Fleming*, "He lost altogether his right judgement; even the cooler afterthoughts were lost. What sort of man had Harry been, her first husband? A dashing soldier, a quarrelsome duelist, a dull dog. But, dull to her? She, at least, was reverential to the memory of him.

"She lisped now and then of 'my husband,' very prettily and with intense provocation; and yet she worshipped brains. Evidently she thirsted for that rare union of brains and bravery in a man, and would never surrender till she had discovered it. Perhaps she fancied it did not exist. It might be that she took Edward [read George] as the type of brains, and Harry [read Edward] as of bravery, and supposed that the two qualities were not to be had actually in conjunction."

As wicked Bella Mount seduced Richard Feverel, so Mary Ellen (or so George implies by his vivid recollection of the process) ensnares George:[15]

Though this lady never expressed an idea, Richard was not mistaken in her cleverness. She could make evenings pass gaily, and one was not the fellow to the other. She could make you forget she was a woman, and then bring the fact startlingly home to you. She could read men with one quiver of her half-closed eye-lashes. She could catch the coming mood in a man, and fit herself to it. What does a woman want with ideas, who can do thus much? Keenness of perception, conformity, delicacy of handling, these be all the qualities necessary to parasites.

Love would have scared the youth: she banished it from her tongue. It may also have been true that it sickened her. She played on his higher nature. She understood spontaneously what would be most strange and taking to him. . . . She had opened a wider view of the world to him, and a colder. He thought poorly of girls. A woman—a sensible, brave, beautiful woman seemed, on comparison, infinitely nobler than those weak creatures.

George and Mary Ellen and Hilary and Peter Daniel occupied themselves with a literary project, a little magazine they took turns editing. *The Monthly Observer.* This magazine has been of great interest to Meredith scholars because it contains his earliest known work, but we see Mary here too, in her role of noble, melancholy woman, writing in a *philosophe* frame of mind about death. Here it is in English; see pages 204–5 for the original French text—mistakes and all.

DEATH[16]

What is death? A passage, a strange grief we live in the middle of, which we all fear. And where does this fear come from? for we find it in everybody's heart—even those who most want to die; they want to be dead, but they fear dying. Isn't this fear a sort of guard which God has placed at the door of the afterlife, or as we call it, the "other world"; it is there to forbid us entrance until our time comes. When one presents a ticket signed by the Eternal, perhaps the sentinel will depart from the door.

We usually see death as final, as the end of life, the end of all we have known and felt, followed by a new state where we have none of the things which made us happy or sad here below. But it cannot be that. We see that in nature, all death is birth. Even the most dreadful corruptions — are they finished when they are finished on earth? No. One sees on the contrary that the earth benevolently changes them into new life. Do not the petals of the pretty flower fall in order to provide for the new fruit? and does not the fruit yield its rich juices so that the seed may take root. And doesn't it, when it falls, fall in order to create a new life? For nature, which so often through its beautiful analogies reveals the supernatural to us, does it not show us the infallibility of this principle, that death is also birth. When our souls are ripe, when they have gained from the passions and indifferences of this world all that can either sustain or destroy them, do they not break the bonds which can no longer contain them? Death is only a crossing, a moment, but it is followed by eternity! And in this eternity there is as much joy for him who has just been born as there is sadness here below for him who has died.

But there is much that is unknown and mysterious for us in this crossing. Who knows what change, what division, it puts between us and those whom we have lost sight of through this strange procedure. Are they carried off forever? Do they follow with the same affection they did here below? We know nothing about it, but though we want certainty we have the spirit of Faith, that tells us that God never created anything in vain, and assures us that He has not given us the capacity to love only for a moment, only as a joke.

> Mary Nicolls
> *Monthly Observer* #11, Jan. 1849

Young George was very enthusiastic about Mary Ellen's writing. He was already smitten with this beautiful lady, her tragic past, her good literary connections, and her intellect, too, for he had the old Romantic notion, as Shelley had, of a spiritual and intellectual, as well as a physical mate, or thought he had. This was about the time that everybody was reading Tennyson's poem, *The Princess,* which had as its subject the education of women, and as its heroine, a beautiful bluestocking princess named Ida. The admiring young man gave Mary Ellen a copy, dedicated "To Cornelia,"—another famous lady intellectual— "as the Lady most ambitious and best endowed to take fair Ida for a prototype, this volume from One who trusts some day to sing her praises/Albeit in humbler measures." Of brains in a lady, he was later to write, "we are to learn the nature of this possession in the lady who is our wife." But now, though he was not called upon to comment on Mary Ellen's essay on death, his French being, perhaps, not so good as his German, he waxes ecstatic about a little sad and not very good poem she had written about a Blackbird, perhaps with poor drowned Edward still in mind:

THE BLACKBIRD

Being the true history of a blackbird known to me.

> Rains of sorrow, fruitful showers,
> Calling forth the leaves and flowers
>   Of holy charity,
> That unwept from ductless eyes,
> In the spirit do surprise
>   Germs of mystery;
>
> Not alone in human bosoms
> Flourish the immortal blossoms
>   Of divinity,
> But in earth's most careless creature
> Dwells a link or blooms a feature,
>   Of immortality.
>
> They shot the happy blackbird's mate,
> Long rose the heart cry, desolate,
>   From his golden bill;

Dimly an angel voice is heard
In the bosom of the bird, —
    "There are sadder still,"

"Of love, and liberty that be
"Chief blessings unto thine and thee
    "One leaveth thee,
"Look down, where hung by yonder cot,
"A caged brother knoweth not
    "What either be,

"To him the pulse of love doth seem
"The vision of a hopeless dream
    "And mockery,
"That sea of air where others sport
"To him a mist where shadows float
    "No verity."

Whisper of the viewless angel,
Uttered he in clear evangel,
    From his quiv'ring throat,
And ever round the caged bird
His legendary song is heard
    On the breeze to float,

And to the loveless prisoner
Choice blackbird dainties, quaint, and rare,
    He with care doth bring;
Sorrow from his heart departeth
At each solace he imparted
    In his communing.

The enamored young man is rapturous in his praises:

This is a beautiful Poem. A melancholy subject touched by a loving hand and were it not for a slight mysticism in the opening verse — would be throughout delicious. It is true also! — A blackbird is called by the Poetess from the mourning for his mate, to behold another imprisoned bird of his own species, whose heart has never known the Divinity of Love—whose wing has long ceased to feel the liberty to which it was born—whose song is a blind song—a fluting of notes and nothing more— "There are sadder still." He can instantly comprehend the weight of these words when he sees the poor blackbird in the Cage—O not to have loved, never to have Loved! That must be infinitely worse than but to mourn the absence of a mate—for it is but absence. He flies down from his Liberty to console the unhappy bird, bringing her choice "blackbird dainties." Does the Prisoner repay the bereaved bird with her Love? It will suggest itself. The second verse is lovely. . . .—Yes! The Universe is but a succession of links and we are all united—in nobility—and gentleness and Love. All that is brutish is alien of kin—but gentle Love uniteth all. And this the Poet hath sung and sung most worthily and well—We hope for more of these <u>*true*</u> *touches of Beauty from the Lady lyrist. And tho' we cannot say that she eclipses her prose articles thereby, at all events she refreshes her mind and feathers her genius at the same time that to us she "imparteth true solace in her communing."*

The direction of George's praise is clear enough. "Does the Prisoner repay the bereaved bird with her love? It will suggest itself." In a few years George rewrites this poem and publishes it as his own.

But now he was in love, and meant to be taken seriously. "A brilliant, witty, beautiful woman," says Cousin Stewart Ellis, George's first biographer (and second cousin). "Meredith was immediately attracted by Mrs. Nicolls and she to him, but the mutual attraction was probably only of a physical nature." Unhallowed attractions of this kind were, as every Victorian knew, doomed to failure. Years later a little acrimonious debate sprang up over the circumstances surrounding the engagement of Mary Ellen and George. Little Edith remembered that the voluble young poet proposed six times before Mary Ellen could conquer her wary sense of the unlikeliness of the whole thing—he so much younger, unsettled, she a mother, a widow—and her love of freedom, for she had apparently come to enjoy the freedoms that having been married conferred upon a female and that being a widow enhanced.

But George in later years was given to ungenerous remarks about the entire affair—if he spoke of it at all, and he almost never did; he hinted that he had been ensnared in some way he could not honorably escape from.

In any case, 1849 was an exciting year for both of them. In June, George sent a poem, "Chillianwallah," which he had contributed to the *Monthly Observer,* to a real magazine and it was accepted! *Chamber's Edinburgh Magazine* had recognized him as a genuine poet! and this must have lent force to his conviction—perhaps to Mary Ellen's too—that his literary career was launched. His fame would be only a matter of time, and they hoped not too long in coming. High hopes. In July, Mary Ellen went to France on an unknown errand—probably to visit the Nicolls, who lived at times in Normandy, and there to discuss with them her remarriage. She had remained close to Lady Nicolls and "Fighting Nicolls," and they were fond of her and loved their granddaughter Edith.

When Mary returned she took Meredith to Lower Halliford to get acquainted with Papa. It was here, Edith remembered, that she ran into the drawing room and caught George and Mama in a passionate embrace. "Mama," she wailed afterward, "I don't like that man."

Neither did Thomas Love Peacock, but then he didn't like anyone his children married, except, presumably, Eddy Nicolls. He came to the wedding, though: at St. George's, Hanover Square, on August 9th, 1849. Meredith's father, the tailor, had left England a few months before to settle in Cape Town, so the groom gratefully identified himself, without fear of contradiction, as the son of Augustus Meredith, "Esq.," and now that he had freed himself from his article to Charnock, he was free of all taint of trade and of any profession but letters.

The young couple went on a honeymoon to Germany, where George wrote rhapsodical poems; the marriage was clearly a success:

RHINE-LAND

We lean'd beneath the purple vine,
  In Andernach, the hoary;
And at our elbows ran the Rhine
  In rosy twilight glory.

Athwart the Seven-hills far seen
  The sun had fail'd to broaden;
Above us stream'd in fading sheen
  The highway he had trodden.

        .   .   .

No longer severing our embrace
  Was Night a sword between us;
But richest mystery robed in grace
  To lock us close, and screen us.

Five years later he would write:

Like sculptured effigies they might be seen
Upon their marriage-tomb, the sword between.

After the wedding trip, George and Mary Ellen came back to take up their respective literary careers, or rather, what they thought of as one literary career, in London. The groom was promising, but there was no money, so at first they lived in Peacock's London quarters, and Peacock (probably) commuted to Lower Halliford. And very soon the Merediths moved near Lower Halliford themselves, into a fascinating boardinghouse, The Limes, in Weybridge.

This was a good place for a literary couple. Tom Taylor, a successful dramatist, lived at The Limes too, along with some artists and musicians; there was the good conversation of the landlady, a Mrs. Macirone, the singing of her gifted daughters, Giulia and Emilia, and some aristocratic neighbors, the Duff Gordons, and nearby were Peacock and his important visitors. "Meredith and his talented wife found a congenial link in their literary pursuits. They were both writing a good deal of poetry, and sometimes they collaborated," Cousin Stewart says.

And they had another stroke of luck. George was a particular admirer of an important poet of the time, Richard Henry Horne, who was a great friend of Elizabeth Barrett's, the author of an important critical work, *A New Spirit of the Age,* and of some much admired epic poems — and Horne had been encouraging. Now Charles Dickens was starting his magazine *Household Words,* and Horne recommended George as someone to do some writing for it. Dickens paid hard cash. George also had poems published in *The Leader* in 1850, and possibly in the *Manchester Guardian.* Hopefully, George and Mary Ellen began to think of bringing out a volume of George's poems; they were sure his reputation would soon be made.

Apparently Mary Ellen was launched on a writing career too. She and Papa collaborated on an amusing, long article, "Gastronomy and Civilisation," which appeared in *Fraser's Magazine,* and on a cookery book,[17] for which a publisher had advanced thirty pounds, and Mary Ellen wrote a long review of another contemporary cookery book, *Soyer's Modern Housewife,* for *Fraser's.* Hogg writes to her that he will "be happy to read your next article in *Fraser's Magazine.* . . . When I receive the Laureat's [sic] poems [George's], I will try hard to read myself young again. . . ." by enjoying their praise of Mary Ellen's charms. Mary Ellen was apparently writing poems too, because George published a spate of poems in periodicals about then, which he later repudiated by saying that some had been written by Mary, and moreover that he didn't remember which were which.[18]

His own volume of poetry, *Poems,* appeared in May 1851, a simple little book dedicated to Peacock, whose friend Parker had published it, and, possibly, whose fifty pounds had financed it. The reviews were encouraging. The Reverend Charles Kingsley found it full of health and sweetness; the Church of England thought the "studied and amplified voluptuousness" of two of the poems was worse than anything in Ovid; George Henry Lewes and William Michael Rossetti both praised it, and the real Laureate, Tennyson, wrote to say he wished that *he* had written one of the poems ("Love in the Valley"), and invited George to visit him. No doubt George and Mary's happiness was quite complete in 1851.

But there were ominous notes. Peacock and Mary Ellen were great cooks and great gourmets.[19] George had indigestion. At the age of twenty-two or so he seems rather young to have had indigestion, but he did. "The Dyspeptic," old Hogg called him—surely an unpleasant thing to be, and to be called. Perhaps he was one of those ostentatious sufferers, pointedly refusing rich dishes and leaving the table in obvious pain, since everyone was so aware of his affliction. Or perhaps Mary Ellen had written Hogg bemoaning it, for they were still fast friends and good correspondents. Hogg could be expected to sympathize with a woman who had to cook for a dyspeptic; Hogg was a gourmet too, and Peacock's companion at the glorious annual Whitebait Dinners that Mary Ellen helped with. "The predisposition to indigestion with which all the children of this generation come into the world, and the stomach disease which commercial anxiety, literary irritation and moral vexation are tending to produce in all classes of men, may both be ameliorated or prevented by a true understanding of the principles and applications of diet and cookery," Mary Ellen wrote in her review of Soyer, but she apparently found George a difficult case.[20]

For a dyspeptic to be married to a gourmet — and great cooks were conspicuously rare in England — was surely an ironic thing, but possibly no coincidence. Ill-suited couples often seem to develop these mutually punitive neuroses: the dog-lover's wife is inevitably allergic to dogs. It is perhaps to George's credit that he maintained a lifelong posture of a roistering drinker and diner, when he was really so delicate that he couldn't bear to see Rossetti eat eggs in the morning; and was obliged by the sight to leave off lodging with Rossetti and Swinburne. But this was later.

"The stomach, not the heart, as poets write, is the great centre of existence and feeling," Mary Ellen wrote in her article on Soyer:

It is the first organ to sympathise with an affection of the heart, and the first to endeavour to alleviate it, by reminding the lover, through the pressing admonitions of hunger, of other duties and pleasures. When the stomach receives an antagonistic element, it revenges itself by sending up morbid impressions to the brain. Many are the blue devils which a vulgar rich dinner has raised, and scattered on evil missions amongst the children of men; many a childish disobedience is concocted in a soda-cake; and many a lover's quarrel lies in ambush at the bottom of a tureen of soup, where it jostles with matrimonial squabbles, morbid creeds, and poetic misprisions. Of course these influences are more or less potent according to the strength or weakness of the stomach and the brain.

And babies came, as babies always came, as the natural consequence of marriage, to the Victorian woman. Indeed, the Victorian woman does not seem to question that babies must come. The endless series of confinements she had to expect — twenty was not an uncommon number, though of course very few of this number survived — does much to explain her contentment with the notion that she ought not to like sex. It would certainly explain why that may have actually been the case — a husband's embraces were fraught with consequences. The fecundity of Mrs. Grundy does much to explain her resolute refusal to allow prostitution to be discussed — or abolished.

Little is said about the extraordinary biological martyrs of the Victorian age: Mrs. Dickens comes to mind as one, or Queen Victoria herself, who had nine children. The wonder is that women then were so meek about their burden of relentless childbearing, and that even very nice, sensitive men were notoriously "inconsiderate" about exercising their "marital rights" when it meant an enormous family to support.

In any case, Mary Ellen began to be more or less continuously pregnant, and bore "more than one child" to George between 1850 and 1852. But they were born dead, or died very soon after. This was disheartening but not calamitous, for Victorian women knew that it often happened. Perhaps they did not let their maternal feelings come in with a rush, like milk, but made themselves wait a little while before they allowed themselves to love a new baby. One thinks, for example, of Mary Shelley's pathetic letter to Hogg, years earlier:

My dearest Hogg my baby is dead — will you come to me as soon as you can — I wish to see you — It was perfectly well when I went to bed — I awoke in the night to give it suck it appeared to [be] sleeping so quietly that I would not awake it — it was dead then but we did not find that out till morning — from its appearance it evidently died of convulsions —

Will you come—you are so calm a creature & Shelley is afraid of a fever from the milk—for I am no longer a mother now

Mary

It is probable that these pregnancies caused, or made much worse, Mary Ellen's disease of the kidneys. But Victorians did not make such simple medical connections, or if they did, they did not complain.

Christmas of 1851. Thomas Love Peacock is visiting his friend Lord Broughton—John Cam Hobhouse, who was Byron's friend. Peacock enjoys these visits. He likes Broughton's pretty daughters, and the other people whom he meets here. He is a gay and worldly guest. Another guest, Disraeli, his great admirer, was excited to meet him; Thackeray met him there (and thought Peacock *too* worldly). Between visits, Peacock and Broughton correspond, with family news and scholarly questions, but now Peacock has gotten away from town for a while and is peacefully expansive, and it is Christmas.

Soon after, the news comes that his wife Jane is dead. Poor Jane, who had been crazy for a quarter-century. "It can hardly have been other than a release," remarks the Biographer, "but his care of her throughout had been devoted, and his grief was bitter. He shut himself up in his study, sought consolation from his books, and for some weeks hardly emerged except to attend at the India House." The Biographer is a good man, unwilling to imagine that the bitterness derived from anything but the most exemplary grief, unable to see that an ironical, passionate, gay, and cynical man could feel anything beside grief at being thus tied for a quarter-century to a madwoman.

Then, or some time, Peacock sat in his study and with a bitter heart wrote something very horrid that shocked little Edith, and even, perhaps, the Biographer, who left it out of the collected edition of his works:

TRANSLATION OF AN ANAPESTIC ODE TO CHRIST:
MATTHEW X, 34[21]

Oh! all ye who use your utmost exertions to avoid all false worship, and to hate all teachers of falsehood, if truthlovingly and unremittingly ye lift up your mind to wisdom, come now in a body and dash in pieces, strike, shake, beat, cut down, chop in pieces and overthrow the cursed imposter, the people-destroying son of Erebos, a false prophet, who, a causer of death, like a THIEF at midnight, came to throw on the sad Earth "Not Peace But a Sword"—not peace—but a sword defiled with blood newly shed: and to make hateful what is dearest to all mortals, and to all delights.—Break in pieces, hurl down him who is a seller of marvels, him who is hostile to the Graces, and him who is abominable to Aphrodite, the hater of the marriage-bed, this mischievous wonder-worker, this destroyer of the world, CHRIST.

The parson's daughter and Peacock had been ill-suited, it is easy to see in retrospect.

Other events shadowed the end of 1851. George and Mary Ellen left The Limes for Southend on Sea, where Mary Peacock, Edward's wife, was staying. George and Mary Ellen were very poor, their babies were dead, debt loomed, they were too proud to ask Papa for help. Hogg, with an odd foreboding, wrote Mary Ellen, "I am glad you are so pleasantly landed at the Wharf; but keep the Bunk in repair, or it is all over with you!''

Then Mary Ellen's Mama died, the poor ghost Jane, and they came back to Weybridge, and after the burial settled in a shabby cottage by the Parish Schools. Here George, who had resisted the notion of gainful employment, accepted the notion of putting his pen to something that at least might pay: prose instead of poetry. And he began an ''Arabian Tale,'' which would become *The Shaving of Shagpat.* In September 1852, Mary Ellen became pregnant again. But they were cheerful; they were still cheerful.

MARIAN

> She can be as wise as we,
>   And wiser when she wishes;
> She can knit with cunning wit,
>   And dress her husband's dishes.
> She can flourish staff or pen,
>   And deal a wound that lingers;
> She can talk the talk of men,
>   And touch with thrilling fingers.

~).

1853. By now their financial situation was dire and Papa rescued them. Probably Mary Ellen liked this no better than she had liked everyone's solicitude after Eddy's death. Leave her to manage, she had said. Now they had to move in with Papa.

It was not a success. Papa was sixty-eight, and set in his ways. And he could not stand George — could not stand his smoking, his finicky diet, or his literary talk. George was undeterred — still smoked, and tried earnestly to engage his august parent-in-law in discussions about books: Tennyson, whom he admired and Peacock didn't; German literature which he loved and Peacock didn't.

And Papa was bothered by the baby, when he came, for babies are noisy and attended by a lot of commotion. After Arthur was born, in June, Peacock rented them a cottage, Vine Cottage, across the green from him; moved them out and felt relieved. Is this the cottage "with tiny rooms?" Hogg asks. "May it prove commodious, and above all things, Lucky! And, I hope the dyspepsy is less difficult; I would that the Patient were well placed, in E.I.H. or elsewhere; how can we help him?"

But the patient would not accept the sort of help that meant dull employment at the East India House or elsewhere; this must have been hard for Peacock, and perhaps Mary Ellen too, to understand. There was a strain on this point . . .

Hogg cheers up Mary Ellen, housebound with her new baby, by writing of a French novel they were all reading: "I have heard it discussed formerly, with great vehemence amongst Ladies, whether the Chevalier had ever crossed the Rubicon with her? [The heroine.] The question was to be determined not extrinsically, but by the internal evidence of her letters. Passages were adduced whch were thought to prove the affirmative; others equally decisive were cited to demonstrate the negative. — a man of course can know no more of such matters than what he is told: the poor benighted creature comprehends only so much, as has been revealed to him. When you read the Letters you will decide the vexed Question, without appeal. Unless perchance they shd take it up to the House of Lords, whither Love, doubtless because he is blind sometimes strays; & what the Law-Lords & Bishops will make of it is hard to say: probably what they too often make, a Sad Hash!"

George had published only two or three poems this year. He worked on his "Arabian Tale." They lived in their tiny cottage, and like most couples with a baby they were less cheerful than they had been, though Arthur flourished beautifully, and Hogg writes of him, "I am quite converted by him to babies, that is to all babies like him. He is a wonderfully good and intelligent little mite [?]; and sometimes he looks very pretty:

his mother manages him perfectly!" Of this period George remarked in later years, "When I was young, had there been given me a little sunshine of encouragement, what an impetus to do better work would have been mine. I had thoughts, ideas, ravishment; but all fell on a frosty soil, and a little sunshine would have been so helpful to me." Perhaps he minded that Mary Ellen was busy with the baby.

Mary Ellen took care of the baby, and prepared special diets for George's difficult stomach, and read Constant's *Adolphe*.

Adolphe is about a young man and an older mistress, and it is full of terrible wisdom, things Mary Ellen must have liked, and yet not quite liked, to read. It tells the story, first of the death of love, and then of poor Ellenore, with odd prescience:

The moment some secret exists between two loving hearts, the moment one of them can decide to conceal one single thought from the other, the spell is broken and the bliss destroyed. Anger, injustice, even wandering affections can be put right again, but dissimulation brings into love a foreign element which perverts and withers it even in its own eyes. . . .

It is a dreadful misfortune not to be loved when we are in love, but it is a very great one to be loved passionately when we have ceased to love. . . .

". . . She is ten years older than you, and you are twenty-six; you will look after her another ten years and she will be old whilst you will have reached the prime of life with nothing satisfying either begun or finished. . . ."

And so I watched her slowly moving towards her end; I saw the warning signs of death stamp themselves upon her noble and expressive features. I saw, and what a humiliating and dreadful sight it was, that proud, forceful character of hers suffer a thousand confused and incoherent transformations through bodily pain as though at this awful moment her soul, crushed by her physical being, was changing its shape in count-

less ways in order to adapt itself the less painfully to the dissolu-
tion of her body.

1854. The happy couple—are they still happy?—remained
most of this year in the cottage across from Papa in Lower Halliford. Hogg writes, rather crossly, on the anniversary of their
wedding day, "May it ever be a cause of Joy!—You told me
some time ago that I am not to have the pleasure of visiting you
this summer. The house of Socrates was small, but it was large
enough, he said, he could fill it with friends. You are still more
independent than Socrates, for you are satisfied with a house
that will not admit a single friend. Do you find it pleasant and
commodious for yourselves? How are you? How are the dear
Children? How is George the Fifth; is he less dyspeptic? Not to
digest your delicate meats is to insult your art!"

But they evidently did find room for a friend now and then,
for it was in this year that their friend, the promising young
painter Henry Wallis, painted Mary Ellen in a pensive attitude
before the fire: *Fireside Reverie,* and accompanied it with part
of a little poem of George's:

> is she . . .
> She, . . .
> In evening's lulling stillness, while the ray
> Tints her soft cheek, like sunset on fair streams?
> Is she the star of one that is away;
> She, that by the fire so gravely dreams?

Toward the end of the year they spent some time at Dover,
but Mary Ellen was "unwell, Arthur but poorly," so the visit
was not restorative, and not pleasant for George. He writes

to a friend that he is thinking of going into the East India House the following year. They were more greatly in debt than ever.

1855. They were again at Lower Halliford for most of this year, George still working on his "Arabian Tale," *The Shaving of Shagpat.* They had now been married for seven years; they did not seem to be so often in one another's company. George, desperate for literary recognition, grew more difficult. Mary Ellen grew more independent, or rather fell back into the independent ways of her widowhood — would join George in town or not join him, as she pleased, or take Arthur and go to the seaside. She too busied herself with the launching of *Shagpat,* about which they were hopeful. A successful novel could mitigate their worsening debts. Debts were always a serious worry to Mary Ellen, who did not like them. They did not always like each other's friends. We do not know what they talked of long evenings in the cottage at Lower Halliford, now that Mary Ellen was not so solicitous of George's stomachache, and George less full of effusions of love. One thinks of Colonel De Craye's description of marriage in Meredith's *The Egoist,* in answer to the question, "What is to rescue the pair from a monotony multiplied by two?" "Our poor couple are staring wide awake. All their dreaming's done. They've emptied their bottle of elixir, or broken it; and she has a thirst for the use of the tongue, and he to yawn with a crony. And they may converse, they're not aware of it, more than the desert that has drunk a shower. So as soon as possible she's away to the ladies, and he puts on his Club."

⌒⁊.

The Merediths had a friend named Henry Wallis, a painter. Sometime during 1855, George and Henry went around to Peter Daniel's rooms, where poor Chatterton, it is said, had killed himself; and George posed as Chatterton, lying half off a sofa in a deathly stupor, the poisonous draught nearby. The painting was hung in the Royal Academy Exhibition of 1856, and Ruskin said of it: "Faultless and wonderful: a most noble example of the great school. Examine it well inch by inch, it is one of the pictures which intend, and accomplish, the entire placing before your eyes of an actual fact — and that a solemn one. Give it much time. . . ."

The picture was an enormous success. It was bought by Augustus Egg, another painter, who printed a pamphlet announcing that "The Death of Chatterton painted by H. Wallis, Esq., now the property of Augustus Leopold Egg, Esq., A.R.A. To Be Engraved in the Highest Style of the Art, by T. P. Barlow Esq. (artists proofs 8/8/0: proofs before letters: 6/6/0; proofs 4/4/0 and prints 2/2/0) with etchings and coloured copies, five guineas each." A great commercial success evidently; these same prints would probably not fetch so much today.

Many will rejoice to know that the talented Mr. Barlow is engaged to reproduce an important plate from this picture, which is precisely one of that class of subjects better suited to the engraver than to receive the charm of colour from the painter. Others, no doubt, will suppose that a picture portraying "The Death of Chatterton" will be painful: nothing of the kind; — here the most refined and sensitive cannot be offended. The Artist has invested his subject with a charm, a fascination that binds you to it, and is beyond description. It is the essence of poetry and teaches a moral beyond the power and capabilities of language.

Everyone was sure that Henry Wallis would become a great painter.

XVI

In our old shipwrecked days there was an hour,
When in the firelight steadily aglow,
Joined slackly, we beheld the red chasm grow
Among the clicking coals. Our library-bower
That eve was left to us: and hushed we sat
As lovers to whom Time is whispering.
From sudden-opened doors we hear them sing:
The nodding elders mixed good wine with chat.
Well knew we that Life's greatest treasure lay
With us, and of it was our talk. 'Ah, yes!
Love dies!' I said: I never thought it less.
She yearned to me that sentence to unsay.
Then when the fire domed blackening, I found
Her cheek was salt against my kiss, and swift
Up the sharp scale of sobs her breast did lift: —
Now am I haunted by that taste! that sound!

— from Meredith's *Modern Love*[22]

The Historian cannot capture a process so slow as the death of
a marriage. He would need some other medium than the pen
to do it with — perhaps one of those cameras that photograph
the growing of a plant and the unfolding of its blossoms. With
such a camera we could see the expressions change, telescoping
the imperceptible changes of seven years into a few moments.
We watch the passionate adoring glances glaze to cordiality,
grow expressionless, contract with pain. The once ardent glances

are now averted; fingers disentwine and are folded behind the separate backs. Backs are turned.

"They sharpened their wits on each other," Edith explained it. They had too many debts and miscarriages; their rooms were too dreary and narrow to remain cheerful in. You cannot live on love. Mary Ellen was often ill, pregnancy after pregnancy. George was passionately ambitious for literary fame and would not jeopardize it by everyday work. He could not eat her "delicate meats." They were too clever and high-strung for each other. Mary Ellen supposedly got religious and George made fun of her.[23] Mary Ellen's views on marriage were too "fast" and French for George, who was after all a tailor's son and a Victorian. All these, and other, explanations have been offered. All, no doubt, are partly right and partly wrong.

The Biographer, the Historian, never mentioned a certain side of marriage. We are told that people were "very happy," or that they had "marital difficulties," or that they became "estranged"; not a word about a certain side of marriage, though. It is as if all grownup people knew, and it need be mentioned no further, what marriage is also about, and what it really means to be "very happy," or "estranged." And they do know, no doubt, when it comes to themselves, but it is easy to forget that historical people embrace too. Socrates and his blushing maiden bride, Xantippe.

Certainly nobody mentioned it during the Victorian period, except for nasty people like Rossetti, whose "Nuptial Sleep"[24] is *still* left out of its place in his sonnet sequence when it is printed in college anthologies. And George. George wrote a sonnet sequence that shocked everybody: *Modern Love*. It told

about the end of a marriage, and it began with our couple in
bed:

> By this he knew she wept with waking eyes:
> That, at his hand's light quiver by her head,
> The strange low sobs that shook their common bed
> Were called into her with a sharp surprise,
> And strangled mute, like little gaping snakes,
> Dreadfully venomous to him. She lay
> Stone-still, and the long darkness flowed away
> With muffled pulses. Then, as midnight makes
> Her giant heart of Memory and Tears
> Drink the pale drug of silence, and so beat
> Sleep's heavy measure, they from head to feet
> Were moveless, looking through their dead black years,
> By vain regret scrawled over the blank wall.
> Like sculptured effigies they might be seen
> Upon their marriage-tomb, the sword between;
> Each wishing for the sword that severs all.

A literary description. But for George and Mary Ellen the long,
wakeful nights and cold embraces were real.

Here let us close the curtain. Behind it we hear a scraping of
chairs, the scratch of a pen, feet moving. When the curtain
opens, half a century has passed. George Meredith, the great
man, is gazing off in profile. He is vain of his profile and allows
photographers and official painters only that view of him. It is
handsome, with its white beard and truly chiseled lineaments. In
the gray eyes: wisdom and suffering. Meredith, lion, great
writer, venerable, testy, renowned for the obscurity and im-

penetrability of his works, and his tenacity in keeping to his own line when no one could understand him. Artistic integrity, vision, Meredith had. People sitting at his feet.

1906. A young man is sitting at his feet today, an interviewer, an admirer, the Biographer perhaps. (Though this young man is too timid to make a good biographer.) He has been privileged to chat with Mr. Meredith this afternoon, which means to listen a lot, for Meredith is quite deaf and talks nonstop. The young man hopes to shout a question or two into his ear trumpet. They are in the garden; they have had tea. Other people are present; his daughter Riette, that "frank, cold, spoiled, shallow" girl, as another visitor called her, and his son Will. His poor second wife Marie had been dead a number of years now.[25] People know —remark it in his countenance—that he has suffered. In his youth, the tale was, he suffered neglect and an unhappy marriage. Poor man. But now it is the modern world, and people take him for rides in automobiles. He suffers from deafness and an affliction of the spine, but he has lived to enjoy the fruits of an immense fame.

The young man, seeing his moment—the ladies are taking a turn around the garden—leans forward. An awkward subject; his voice is low and hesitant. The early marriage—the daughter of Thomas Love Peacock—a separation?

A thunderous roar. The voice recovers its modulation. Then it slides up shrilly. The ladies, hearing the shrill cry, come back across the grass with speedy swishes; the daughter's arms are outstretched in an attitude of alarm. The master's glance at her is for an instant imploring. What has been said? What will happen? The heart of the timid visitor pounds in shame. Now Meredith recovers his majesty, except for a slight purple around the wattles. The pursed lips affect a musing expression, the expression of a man who is trying to remember a forgotten and trivial incident of his youth. But the eyes belie him; they have a bitter glint. They have a bitter, bitter glint never unlearned. He picks up his ear trumpet and leans toward the timid interviewer:

"What did you say?"

It is too late to unsay. The Timid rephrases the question. Were you not married once, sir, very young, before you were married to the late Mrs. Meredith?

Ah, yes. Too young. While a mere boy still articled to a solicitor. Entrapped into it, really. A sad affair. She was mad, you know. Madness on her mother's side of the family. And she was nine years — nearly a decade! — older than me. A mistake, a sad mistake. No sun warmed my rooftree.

This is the version the timid interviewer conveyed to the waiting world. The Biographer repeated it. The world is sympathetic. To be married to a madwoman in his youth is just the thing for a writer, though. Formative. A mad *old* woman, think of that. (Someone would eventually figure out that Mary Ellen was only six and a half years older than George.) His exaggeration of her age was certainly ungenerous, but it was whispered that she had run off with a minor Pre-Raphaelite, which proves that George was correct on the detail of her madness. What woman altogether sane would leave a man so clearly destined to be great? A man who would be called the "champion of women," would be considered a great feminist whose ability to understand and portray women — particularly lively, independent ones — suggested a wisdom and maturity almost unrivaled among the dogmatic, insecure males of the nineteenth century. How could anyone leave a man like that?

The sun a half-century before shone as bright, perhaps brighter; the air was less full of soot and railway grime. Women's clothes had not changed much by 1906, so it is not necessary to revise in memory the costumes of the women as they moved gracefully along the Seaford walks. It was as yesterday.

1856. Mary Ellen and her children: Edith, who was twelve,

and three-year-old Arthur in his sailor suit. People no doubt looked at them with pleasure; nothing so pleased the Victorian eye as the sight of a beautiful young matron with her children. The husband was away as usual. Some would have condemned but most would have secretly sympathized with the slight frivolity implied by the French novel in her reticule. Many nice women one knew read French novels, reflecting aloud to their intimate friends their relief that the English were not French. And after all, this lovely, slim young matron did not neglect her children for French novels. The children were cheerful and pretty.

George was away as usual. He had not gotten a position they had been hoping for—what sort of place is not certain—but he had not gotten it, and Mary Ellen was "racking her brain" to see what she could do to get some money. They were as usual low on money.

It was now August. The year 1856 had begun very well. Their dimmed prospects had brightened; they had their fine son, and now they had their book, *The Shaving of Shagpat*, and this book had been received very well; had been reviewed enthusiastically by George Eliot, for example, and by Charles Kent, to whom Mary Ellen writes a thank-you that sounds both strangely proprietary and very proud. Clearly her confidence in George's literary abilities was undiminished—or had revived:

Lower Halliford
January 24 [*1856*]

Dear Mr. Kent,

I was quite sure that I was indebted to your friendly hand for the three <u>Suns</u> and I thought it very kind of you, for the review was so appreciative and full that I was very glad to have so many copies to lend among my friends. I am as much surprised as gratified to find the book so well received, for the work is so unlike modern literature that I expected it would not be understood. The first notice was in the <u>Spectator</u> and just of the kind I had expected from all sides, flippant, disparaging, ignorant, and assuming; I knew it required courage and honesty to review so unusual a book well and to these first favourable reviews I shall always feel it owes the most, whatever subsequent notices may say.

I hope your health is quite restored and that Mrs. Kent has that great reward for her devoted nursing and care of you. Pray remember me very kindly to her and believe me

> Faithfully yours,
> Mary Meredith

P.S. I should have explained that I did not know till Mr. Meredith came down this week where I should write to you.

> M. M.

The postscript is significant: we note that George had been away. In the spring he begins a new work of fiction which they call *The Fair Frankincense,* in whose behalf Mary Ellen writes the publisher Edward Chapman, her friend; this letter too suggests that she and George are not much together:

Dear Mr. Chapman,

On my return yesterday evening I found a letter from George in which he directs me to ask you for the remainder of the money you were so kind as to advance to him.

I am obliged to go to the City this morning and shall not be back in time to see you today, will you therefore be so good as to forward the money to me here, as I am to make a payment, to which George is pledged, with it before 12 tomorrow. If you should find that you know any of the Parthenon Club and can help us with them I think you will not need much asking to do so.

In haste, I am

> Faithfully yours,
> Mary Meredith

In the late spring they moved from Lower Halliford again, first to Felixstowe, and then to Seaford for the summer, where they stayed in cheap lodgings amongst a "straggling row of villas facing a muddy beach." George was enthusiastic for a while. He wrote to their friend Eyre Crowe, inviting him down: "Here is fishing, bathing, rowing, sailing, lounging, running, pic-nicing, and a cook who builds a basis of strength to make us equal to all these superhuman efforts." Their baby Arthur was a wise little fellow, who remarked, "Pussy can sing, but Pussy can't laugh. And the poor old Donkey can't sing and he can't laugh." One day he woke up to see Mary Ellen preparing to go out: "Don't yoo go, Mama, from yoo baby. Yoo bed will cry for yoo, Mama dear," he said.

꿋?·

That spring Mary Ellen fell ill again, perhaps in connection with another pregnancy, and George found a pressing need to go somewhere else.

She convalesced slowly, and wracked her brain for something to do about their financial straits, and wrote sprightly letters to their friends. Henry Wallis writes from Spain, and Mary Ellen, in replying, speaks of his letter: "I cannot help rejoicing to have it, a description written on the spot & impressions noted as they occur are so much more graphic than any after recollection of either can be. Then again your handwriting offers more conclusive evidence of the heat of Bayonne than any after assurance would do. With all my longing for Spain I don't think, with that racked handwriting before me, I would go there in August. In respect of climate Bayonne may be said to have come to England as Birnam Wood came to Dunsidane [sic]. In London on Saturday the thermometer was 84 in the shade, & here the whole town has turned into the sea."

Henry was off painting Montaigne's study among other things, for he was fond of doing the rooms and birthplaces of famous writers, especially after his great success with *The Death of Chatterton.* He evidently had had a problem getting into Montaigne's rooms. Mary Ellen remarks, with characteristic irony, "What a misfortune that Montaigne's tower should have fallen into the hands of such a brute. I am very glad you insisted on having admittance. I have no doubt your moral force controlled the wretched slave into yielding the miserable two hours he dared not withhold."

Because George had not gotten his place, Mary Ellen had been trying to repair the family fortunes by writing, but with little success. She writes disconsolately to Henry: "Whether all the intelligence I ever possessed is quite swallowed up by my long illness, or whether the attempt to begin work in this tremendous heat is the cause of failure I have not yet made up my mind, but I am much discouraged that it is ten days since I began to hunt for an idea and that I have not found one."

George is not there. It is lonely. She invites Wallis to stay with them on his way back—"if you come back by way of Dieppe of course we shall see you." And she sends a message from Arthur which might wistfully echo her own thoughts: "Edith is at a picnic or she would have a message. George [has?] not returned. Arthur sends his love and a kiss," and says "for yoo to come to me when yoos done yoo painting, cos I wants me Wallis." And perhaps Henry did come back by way of Dieppe.

It is not clear when Henry and Mary Ellen reached their "understanding." The autumn passed, and winter. George was now at Seaford, beginning *Richard Feverel,* and Mary Ellen had gone to Blackheath with Arthur and Edith, to visit Lady Nicolls. At Christmas George writes to a friend, "Mrs. Meredith is staying at Blackheath. Don't wait to send by her, as I am anxious she should spend Christmas in town. Dulness [*sic*] will put out the wax lights, increase the weight of the pudding, toughen the turkey, make lead of the beef, turn the entire feast into a nightmare, down here, to one not head and heel at work. . . ."

SONNET XXIII

'Tis Christmas weather, and a country house
Receives us: rooms are full: we can but get
An attic-crib. Such lovers will not fret
At that, it is half-said. The great carouse
Knocks hard upon the midnight's hollow door,
But when I knock at hers, I see the pit.
Why did I come here in that dullard fit?
I enter, and lie couched upon the floor.
Passing, I caught the coverlet's quick beat: —
Come, Shame, burn to my soul! and Pride, and Pain —
Foul demons that have tortured me, enchain!
Out in the freezing darkness the lambs bleat.
The small bird stiffens in the low starlight.
I know not how, but shuddering as I slept,
I dreamed a banished angel to me crept:
My feet were nourished on her breasts all night.

— from Meredith's *Modern Love*

We shall pause here to introduce Henry. He is about to let himself in for a whole lot of trouble. For instance, for his indiscretion, he has been strangely excised from the family photograph of British history, rather as if George Meredith's censorious friends had gone back and cut him out with a pair of scissors, or perhaps it is owing to the gentlemanly reticence of Henry's own friends. He does not appear in the *Dictionary of National Biography* (begun by Meredith's friend Leslie Stephen) for example, although his paintings hang in the Tate and other important galleries, and were twice called "Picture of the Year" by Ruskin; and although he became a major authority on Far Eastern ceramics, and wrote a lot of books about them, and donated heavily from his valuable collection of pieces to the Victoria and Albert Museum (which argued fiercely with the British Museum for the rest at his death), and did a lot of other things that usually get you in the *DNB,* or at least an obituary in *The Times.* Rather, though he was to live beyond the First World War, sixty years longer than the faintly remembered Victorian lady he once loved, his name turns up only briefly, fugitively now, in biographies of Meredith and Peacock, as a treacherous person who appeared at an inopportune moment to seduce Mrs. Meredith, father a child on her, and vanish like an incubus at her death.

Of course it was not like that at all. Literary history and literary convention conspire to project into our minds at the idea of a lover — a painter, a seducer — an unscrupulous and cynical young man, doubtless dark, who took advantage of the wretchedness of Mary Ellen and George to lure her away for his selfish sexual purposes and to discard her when he tired. Literary history and literary convention do Henry Wallis much injustice.

For Henry was a decent fellow who lived sixty more years, devotedly raised their little, illegitimate child in full view of his London acquaintance (which was rather larger than George's), and perhaps raised his hat to George, if they were ever so unlucky as to meet in after-years. When Mary Ellen died, Henry Wallis did not disappear at all, but instead let his apartment to the Burne-Joneses and took the baby to Capri for his health.

And what is Henry like? He has not entered the story like the villain of fiction in any very swashbuckling way, though he may wear a long black cloak, an artist's hat, perhaps. He does not dash; rather, he is small and amiable. He is young, almost nine years younger than Mary Ellen. He cares passionately about the cause of freedom, and about the Worker's Lot, and about Art. In his early twenties, he is already an antiquarian in his soul, likes old houses where the famous dead were born, likes bits of old lace, the feel of velvet. He is attracted to the meticulous medievalizing of the Pre-Raphaelites, and to their ways, and they like him too. He is a Pre-Raphaelite brother in the second degree. He is rich, the son of a successful architect. He has been to Paris and studied art there. He hopes to become a great artist, but he has too much money, is too much the dilettante, too fond of travel and strange sights. Not driven like George by the inner goad of humble origins, or by a need for money, the compulsions that produce greatness. Henry is a charming friend of the family.

And sometime between August 1856 and July 1857, Mary Ellen and Henry began an adulterous affair.[26] We may only guess at the agitation, the confusion, remorse or exultation, furtive, fugitive pleasure or long, languid sensual afternoons, impulse or deliberation that accompanied this desperate action. We can only guess whether it was with happy heedlessness or with a self-justified feeling of bitter rectitude that Mary Ellen removed her camisole, chemise, corset, six petticoats, stockings and garters to make love to Henry.[27]

SONNET XXII

What may the woman labour to confess?
There is about her mouth a nervous twitch.
'Tis something to be told, or hidden:—which?

I get a glimpse of hell in this mild guess.
She has desires of touch, as if to feel
That all the household things are things she knew.
She stops before the glass. What sight in view?
A face that seems the latest to reveal!
For she turns from it hastily, and tossed
Irresolute steals shadow-like to where
I stand; and wavering pale before me there,
Her tears fall still as oak-leaves after frost.
She will not speak. I will not ask. We are
League-sundered by the silent gulf between.
You burly lovers on the village green,
Yours is a lower, and a happier star!

—from Meredith's *Modern Love*

It was a happy time in the spring of 1857 for little Arthur, who was three and a half, and learned to whistle. He can "be a poor moosic man, now."

Mary Ellen became interested in courtesans, "lost women," and the like, and reread Dumas's *La Dame aux Camélias,* and mused about it:

Manon Lescaut is most certainly the most beautiful book of the heart that has ever been written, the most earnest anatomy of passion that has been done. I have said earlier that I have much indulgence for courtesans; this indulgence stems especially from my frequent reading of Manon.

Marguerite, a sinner like Manon, and perhaps converted like her, had died in a sumptuous bed (it seemed, after what I had seen, the bed of her past), but in a desert of the heart, a barren, a vaster, a more pitiless desert than that in which Manon had found her last resting-place.

Is there anything sadder in the world than the old age of vice, especially in a woman? She preserves no dignity, she inspires no interest. . . . What sublime childishness is love.

Do not let us despise the woman who is neither mother, sister, maid, nor wife.

Mary Ellen copied these passages out to remember them.

One of the most interesting of Mary Ellen's surviving documents is her Commonplace Book, which, though it was in no sense a diary, reveals her in many ways. It was her custom, as it was the custom of many Victorians, to keep such a book of "extracts" from things they had been reading. Perhaps their Bible-reading English forefathers had given people the feeling that things written down had a special veracity; a scriptureless generation compiled Bibles of its own: collections of maxims, moving passages, recipes, things "worth copying," as "Henry Ryecroft" put it—things sufficiently true, untrue, or interesting to sanctify them by one's labor and to keep permanently accessible in a day when most books went back to the lending library.

By means of her Commonplace Book, we know what Mary Ellen was reading in 1856, about the time she left George. We know what things particularly struck her, though we cannot know if she agreed or disagreed with the passages she copied out, or if she only meant to use them some way in her own writing. A very brief study of the marginal remarks in the volumes along the shelf at the public library suggests that readers tend to underline or annotate the things they agree with (How true! Well put!) and that is probably true of Mary, too. How Mary Ellen's Commonplace Book survived the subsequent Meredithian bonfires is not clear—it was perhaps in Edith's hands, or some other of the Peacocks.

The themes of Mary Ellen's notes reveal an intellectual woman, with a taste for aphorism, in extreme agitation of mind. In a day when women did not admit such things to themselves, she had admitted that she did not love her husband. In a day when such things were never done, she recognized that she wanted to leave him. That she had been, or wanted to be, unfaithful to him. That their marriage was a mistake. Moreover, a woman struggling with extreme feelings of guilt about these discoveries, struggling to subdue guilt, to feel herself not a victim of the narrow Victorian moral code but somehow above it, observant of a higher morality in which love and independence had a place—in which people were not bound legalistically to other people, in which people were not to be martyrs to other people, or to rules. An educated and witty woman. And yet, withal, a Victorian woman, convinced at heart of the superiority of men, a little ashamed of being prey to powerful emotions and powerful convictions. Mary Ellen sought self-respect and justification, and, perhaps, an ideal of love. The themes of her notes are recurring: a woman having doubts about a man she loves; the nature of marriage; the loss of illusion about love; deceitful women; the necessity of suffering to achieve moral perfection; adultery; courtesans. She reads *Camille, Manon.*

George was evidently around some of the time this book was being filled, for he has copied out a poem in it. Mary Ellen does not care if he reads what she has copied from other people's words: "From her book he gained no insight into herself. There was no character bearing any evidence of self-perturbation, or veiled complaint, or confession. His fancy had run off to a new, untrodden field, there it could gather fresh flowers at its will; only leaving the traces of its whereabouts like the gypsies — You may tell where we have been/By the burnt spot on the green, that is, by quotation and allusion to things he knew she had read of, and studied" — a passage Mary Ellen found in *Mme. Clarinda Singleheart.*

⁇.

EXTRACTS FROM MARY ELLEN'S COMMONPLACE
BOOK OF EXTRACTS

Terrible moment when we first dare to view with feelings of repugnance the being that our soul has long idolised. It is the most awful of revelations; we start back in horror as if in the act of profanation.

"All you value is a slave with no will of her own."
"One who has a will, but knows how to resign it."
"That you may have the victory."
"No, but that you may be greater than he that taketh a city."
He opened "The Baptistry" as it lay on the table, & pointed to the sentence — "If thou refuseth the cross sent thee by an angel, the devil will impose on thee a heavier weight."
'Are humility & submission my cross, asked she?'
If you would only so regard them you would find the secret

*of peace. If you would only tame yourself before trouble is sent
to tame you.*

Charlotte Yonge: Heartsease or The Brother's Wife

*"What good is it?" she says: "You see me dead since you have
spoken to me. I have done everything possible in order to re-
kindle some human feeling within myself, but I find nothing.
Love, oh, it is dead: compassion, dead; between the two ex-
tremes, what scattering of illusions! . . . That's the misfortune of
these kinds of experience."*

Alexandre Dumas: Olympe de Clèves

*I was tired,—mind-weary: the temper is easily irritated in such a
state.*

*What are those political revolutions, whose strange & mighty
vicissitudes we are ever dilating on, compared with the moral
mutations that are passing daily under our own eyes; uprooting
the hearts of families, shattering to pieces domestic circles,
scattering to the winds the plans and prospects of a generation
& blasting as with a mildew the ripening harvest of long cherished affection.*

*"Isn't it a shame that a mature man, as I am at present, submits
like a child to the whim of a woman?" "No, it is not at all a
shame."*

*I, who am used to questioning myself about everything and to
governing myself, how can you want me to take as a master a
man who submits to instinct and who is guided by chance?*

George Sand: Roman de Mauprat

*Say what they like, there is a pang in balked affection, for which
no wealth, power, or place, watchful indulgence, or sedulous
kindness, can compensate.*

*William represented the woman of Endor an awful sybil—a
woman endowed, perhaps, at first, with all that could endear
her to others, and make her happy in herself; but severed, it
might be, by some disappointed affection or evil passion, from*

communion and sympathy with her kind, & impelled her by her own disordered longings, to penetrate into the unknown.

In circumstances of difficulty of any kind the advance always comes from the woman. Because she is naturally more ingenuous, courageous & generous than the man.

Weary-Foot Common

"Only a little headache." How often the heart lays its griefs upon the head.

Give unto me, made lowly wise
The spirit of self-sacrifice.
Charlotte Yonge: Heartsease

The intimacy between Claudia & Robert seemed at first to be merely a contact of the two intellectual natures; but opinions on the most abstruse subjects; are so much modified by personal character. Literature besides is a sort of freemasonry, which sets aside conventionalities, & brings individuals together on a common ground & more than common sympathy.

Weary-Foot Common

It is seldom sympathy and help go together: those who can give us help often cannot, or will not, give us sympathy; & those who sympathize most with us can frequently help us the least.

Selina Bunbury: "Our Own Story"

Right is right, and wrong is wrong: and right and wrong admit not of either exchange or compromise.

D. Gifford: St. James' Chronicle

. . . I felt at this hour that man was not made for this selfish preservation of despair which we call self-denial or stoicism. No one can abandon the care of his honour without abandoning respect for the principle of honour. If it is noble to sacrifice personal life and glory to the mysterious lapses of the conscience, it is a cowardice to abandon one and the other to the madness of unjust persecution. I felt myself restored again in my own eyes and I passed the rest of this important night seeking ways of re-

Mary Ellen at thirty-seven, drawing by Henry Wallis.

1858

Thomas Love Peacock
at thirty-one and as a boy,
and Sarah Peacock.

Opposite
Peacock at seventy-three,
painting by Henry Wallis.

A previously unknown photograph of Peacock.

"Fighting Nicolls," General Sir Edward Nicolls, K.C.B.

The beautiful three-year-old George Meredith.

Peacock's house along the Thames, where Mary Ellen grew up and Peacock lived till his death.

Vine Cottage, where George Meredith and Mary Ellen lived after moving out of Peacock's.

Opposite
George Meredith with his son Arthur.

D. G. Rossetti's portrait of Arthur Meredith.

Copied from the outline
Engraving in the "Florentine
Gallery" vol of portraits
of painters.
T.L. Peacock stated
this to be the best
portrait of Shelley

Ant. Leisman.   he knew of. the one in
Moxon's "Shelley" being quite unlike.
Peacock's copy of the vol of the Florentine
Gall: containing this portrait is the the

Mary Shelley in 1841, painting by Richard Rothwell.

Henry Wallis in later years.

Opposite
Henry Wallis's
<u>The</u> <u>Death</u> <u>of</u> <u>Chatterton</u>,
for which George Meredith
was the model.

Photograph of Felix
at age four or five.

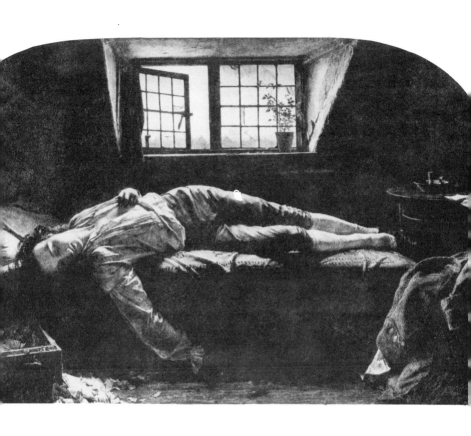

Drawing by Henry Wallis.

Henry Wallis's famous painting
The Dead Stonebreaker.

*habilitating myself—with as much perseverance as I had de-
voted to abandoning myself to fate. With a feeling of strength
I felt the rebirth of hope.*

Translated from George Sand: Roman de Mauprat

*Conventionalism is the slave of the prudent, not the master. It
is for ever crouching in the eye of the world, befits only a timid
spirit, ignorant that the world's applause always waits on noble
action, when justified by the emergency and magnitude of the
stake.*

Weary-Foot Common

*In some things unhappiness is good, for him who knows how to
think; the more I saw how painful and grievous it was to have
severed such ties, the more I felt what had been lacking in the
marriage,—the elements of happiness and equity of a too-
exalted order, so that the real society does not concern itself with
them. Society endeavours, on the contrary, to belittle this
sacred institution, by likening it to a contract which involves
material interests; it attacks it from all sides at once, by the spirit
of its manners, by its prejudices, by its hypocritical disbelief.
The ideal in love is certainly eternal faithfulness. Moral and religious laws have tried to consecrate this ideal: material matters
trouble it, civil laws are created in such a manner that they are
often rendered impossible or illusory.*

George Sand: Roman de Mauprat

*Patience, if you believe it is your duty to denounce me, go ahead,
do it: all that I desire, is that I not be condemned without having
been understood; I prefer a trial by law to one by opinion!*

*The human heart at the best presents a fearful spectacle: & few
suspect the close & sisterly relationship that exists between the
Genii who govern it—Vice and Virtue.*

*He had for some time reconciled his mind to entertain the idea
of Henrietta's treachery to him. Softened by time, atoned for by
long suffering, extenuated by the constant sincerity of his purpose, his original imprudence, to use his own phrase, [?] his*

misconduct, had gradually ceased to figure as a valid & sufficient cause for her behavior to him. . . .

Meadows started with nothing better nor worse than a commonplace conscience. A vicious habit is an iron that soon scars that
sort of article. . . . And one frightful thing in all this was that his
love for Susan was not only strong but in itself a good love. I
mean it was a love founded on esteem; it was a passionate love
and yet a profound and tender affection. It was the love which
under different circumstances has often saved men, aye and
women too, from a frivolous, selfish and sometimes from a vicious life. This love Meadows thought & hoped would hallow
the unlawful means by which he must crown it. In fact he was
mixing vice & virtue. The snow was to whiten the pitch not the
pitch to blacken the snow. Thousands had tried this before him
and will try it after him. Oh, that I could persuade them to mix
fire and gun powder instead!

"Don't talk so, George. True pals like you & me never reproach
one another. They stand & fall together like men."

"It is never too late to mend"

Driftwood's air could never be otherwise than truthful because
when he told a lie he was always the first to believe it.

The parting was not so bad as the anticipation. It never is. The
very effort to conceal the feelings divides them, if the heart is
shared between grief and pride, desolation and triumph.

"I shouldn't like to do anything too bad."
  "What d'ye mean by too bad?"
  "Punishable by law."
  "Is it not your own conscience you fear, then?" asked Mead-
ows gloomily.
  "Oh dear me, Sir, only the Law."

He does not accomplish anything to pry too much into what was
before, in a pretty woman's life: we must take her as we find her,
however we may find her, and never ask her any of those in-
discreet questions which would embarrass her or make her day-

dream. What good would it be? You won't prevent what already has been, and it is a great folly to wish to base the future on the past.

        Paul de Kock: L'amour qui passe et L'amour qui vient

The victim had unwittingly revenged herself. He had stabbed her heart again and again, and drained it. He had battered this poor heart till it had become more like leather than flesh and blood, and now he wanted to nestle in it and be warmed by it: to kill the affections and revive them at will, No!!!!

When the story is blown and laughed over, this man's vanity will keep my name out of it. He won't miss a chance of telling the world how clever he is. My game is to pass for honest, not clever.

The wicked are in earnest and the good are lukewarm.

Marriage was holy. Love was altered by it, for the Victorian, from something a bit nasty to something pure and wonderful. The Victorian anticipated in the state of Holy Matrimony the most serious emotional experience of his life—quite a different attitude from that of casual eighteenth-century people, with their arrangements, contracts, practicalities. Ah, sacred love.

    Adultery was therefore a nearly unspeakable crime, regarded with almost Biblical ferocity. Indeed it was inextricably involved with a Victorian vision of apocalypse. Tennyson's ideal society of the round table, in *Idylls of the King,* was utterly wrecked by adultery, which was the Laureate's serious prediction about his own society too. Love and Marriage and Womanhood and Motherhood and all manner of similar sacred things were invested with sanctity solely in the vain hope of shoring up a morality which was not, as Tennyson and others clearly saw, getting better as mankind progressed but worse. More prostitution. More anxiety. More censorship. More prudery. The closer the awareness of the base desires that prompted man, the more frantic he became to deny them. In the confusion of guilt and shame that engulfed them, good Victorians (like George) clung to the view of Holy Matrimony in the hope it would float them above the danger. The danger was within. They tried to keep their bodies "pure."

The realistic, the ironic, the old-fashioned just shook their heads in wonder and did not understand at all. Like Mary Ellen. She seems to have seen it much as her father's old friend Shelley saw it. Shelley had said, "A husband and wife ought to continue so long united as they love each other: any law which should bind them to cohabitation for one moment after the decay of their affection would be a most intolerable tyranny, and the most unworthy of toleration. . . . Love is free. . . ."

If you do not cherish illusions, you do not suffer when they are blighted. Mary Ellen knew all along that love could die — that physical passion is no respecter of empty vows. That marriage is sometimes a mockery. She copied out a passage that interested her, from Dumas, discussing how the very word "adultery" had come to be used at all only in the nineteenth century — was not even used by, say, Molière, who was merely amused by cuckoldry. "Has society [in the nineteenth century] become more moral? At first glance it would seem so." But no, it is merely a legalistic development: "From the first moment that the husband saw that children had a legal right to his inheritance, he wanted this to be a natural right; and from that moment on the word 'adultery' became a real word, that is to say, synonymous with 'crime' for the wife, with 'flight' for the child. That is how the nineteenth century came to take seriously the word the eighteenth century took as comical." Mary Ellen copied this passage in her book.

The embraces of a new lover in all ages for all women have surely been attended by the same uncertainties and ardor. We may only guess at the mysteries of Mary Ellen's mind now, wherever she and Henry are, in some lodging on a bed, or out of doors behind a hedgerow. Fleeting comparisons to whose advantage we have no way of knowing. A different man will touch you in a different way. A woman near forty must try hard to please.

Perhaps Mary Ellen, a little cynical and thirty-six years old, found the twenty-seven-year-old Henry easy prey for a beautiful and sophisticated woman. Perhaps Henry, though he loved her dearly, found Mary Ellen a little faded. Or perhaps not. Perhaps they thought each other absolutely wonderful. Did Mary Ellen prefer painters to writers after all? Writers to naval lieutenants? It is a question she must have asked herself. Was it not perhaps imprudent to establish a durable relationship with a lady who was someone else's wife? Henry must have asked himself. But no doubt they thought each other absolutely wonderful.

We can only guess, too, at the scene between Mary Ellen and George, at which it was decided that they would separate for a time. Mary Ellen seems to have handled it smoothly. A trial separation. "The parting was not so bad as the anticipation. It never is," Mary Ellen had copied in her book.

"The Separation was her own doing, though not regretted by me, save for my boy's sake. It was not a formal separation, and was not considered to be final, until I had reason for knowing that it must be so," George explained a few years later to a new prospective father-in-law. They were both Victorians; George did not need to elaborate for Mr. Vulliamy the meaning of the last phrase, "it must be so."

⁀⁊·

Whatever happened to the marriage of Mary Ellen and George, it must have been bad indeed, for women did not often leave their husbands in Victorian times. A woman without her natural protector was a woman in peril, devoid of legal rights, money (for that would remain with her husband since a married woman could not hold property on her own), her children (for the law awarded children to even the cruelest of fathers rather than to the mother); she was prey to seducers, scandal, social ostracism. Women, unless they were very independent, aristocratic, and rich, would bear dreadful abuses, would allow themselves to be beaten or starved — even sold, as in Hardy's novel, *The Mayor of Casterbridge* — before they would leave.

The very rich sometimes did divorce. Until 1858 it took an act of Parliament. After 1858 there was Sir Creswell Creswell's divorce court, but that was too late for George and Mary Ellen. George could not charge Mary Ellen with adultery because he had not in fact done so earlier — which, to the British mind, represented a tacit complicity. Adultery was of course the only ground for divorce. Unbearable cruelty, for example, would not count; and of course it was far easier for a man to divorce a woman for infidelity, since infidelity in a woman was utterly reprehensible. The courts were apt to wink if a woman charged her husband with the same thing. A desperate woman had nothing on her side in Victorian England; so, most often, she stuck.

Consequently, either the Meredith marriage was unusually awful, or Mary Ellen was unusually independent. This latter seems to have been it. She had confidence in her own resiliency and gifts of mind. Refused to accept a condition of life that bound people together in loveless chains. She had a little money; she could write; she did not care about public opinion. Mary Ellen thought of herself as a person, as Victorian women often did not.

It was her upbringing. Got it from old Peacock. Fascinating woman; very charming; very brilliant, no doubt — but you're better off with a nice, old-fashioned girl.

1857. Summer again. Mary Ellen alone in Seaford, the break with George complete. She has been ill, has been convalescing slowly in the late spring as the days brighten, but is feeling better now. She and Henry have probably become lovers, but Mary is her own woman, independent. Now that she is feeling better she must think of her living: "I cannot bear my life of illness here and am full of schemes of work that I want your advice and help in," she writes Henry, whom she is expecting for a visit.

Like everyone else in England that summer, Mary had become interested in the murder trial of Madeleine Smith. Mary had perhaps more reason than most Englishwomen to feel a sneaking sympathy for Madeleine, an affinity: sisters under the skin. Madeleine Smith was a high-spirited, young Scottish girl, from a wealthy and utterly respectable, even exemplary, family in Glasgow. Like Mary Ellen, she was the oldest, intelligent and capable, responsible for many matters in their genteel household. Like Mary Ellen, she was passionate. "Madeleine Smith was born before her time," says Madeleine's historian, F. Tennyson Jesse, whose book, *The Trial of Madeleine Smith,* in the series *Notable British Trials,* contains transcripts of the evidence, testimony, and summations. "She had all the profound physical passion . . . which was a thing supposed at that particular date not to exist in a 'nice' woman." And, with a most horrifying singlemindedness, a most shocking unwomanliness, with the most daring abandon of every good principle with which she had undoubtedly been imbued, she had allowed herself to be seduced by a penniless young clerk named Emile L'Angelier, who wanted to marry her. They were in love, they made love, and Madeleine enjoyed it—she said so in her ardent letters to him, which were found and offered in evidence at her trial.

The problem was that Madeleine's parents wanted her to marry a rich neighbor, to whom she was engaged, and they would never have approved of Emile L'Angelier. Would sooner disown her than allow her to marry a penniless young clerk. An old story—with the added difficulty that L'Angelier did not want a disowned Madeleine; he wanted her with her family status and marriage portion intact, the complete package. Would not marry a disowned Madeleine. Emile felt that if Madeleine would just explain to her parents not only that she was in love with him but that she was "spoiled" already, no longer a virgin—they would instantly allow them to be married. Such situations were the continual secret dread of every Victorian parent.

"Think of the consequences if I were never to marry you . . ." he wrote her. (A draft of this letter was found in his rooms after his death.) "Try your friends once more—tell your determination—say nothing will change you, that you have thought seriously of it—and on that I shall fix speaking to Huggins for September. Unless you do something of that sort, Heaven only knows when I shall marry you. Unless you do, dearest, I shall have to leave the country. . . . It is your parents' fault if shame is the result; they are to blame for it all. . . . Mimi, dearest, you must take a bold step to be my wife. I would entreat you, pet, by the love you have for me, Mimi, do speak to your mother. . . . Oh! Mimi, be bold for once, do not fear them—tell them you are my wife before God. Do not let them leave you without being married, for I cannot answer what would happen. My conscience reproaches me of a sin that marriage only can efface. . . . I was not angry at your allowing me, Mimi, but I am sad it happened. You had no resolution. . . . It was very bad indeed. I shall look with regret on that night. No, nothing except our Marriage will efface it from my memory. Mimi, only fancy if it was known." From which it can be seen that Emile was a repulsive little man indeed. But he was right, no doubt, that if her "shame" was known, on one else would have her, and her parents would be obliged to let them marry.

Why, then, did Madeleine not tell her parents? Apparently not from fear of the consequences. The truth was that she had been getting tired of Emile, and was rather disposed to marry the rich neighbor, with whom, after all, she was bound to be more comfortable. She tried to break off the secret affair with

Emile. She tried to get her letters back. But he would not give them back. He grew difficult. And then, to judge by a new flurry of fond letters from Madeleine, the affair was on again, and Madeleine was kind to him again, and then one night poor Emile had a funny attack of something awful — the third such attack — and died in hideous pain and a pile of green vomit, before his landlady could get help for him.

Madeleine, it seems, had bought arsenic three times just about then, quite openly, "for her complexion," and there was quite a lot of arsenic in poor Emile's stomach. And the redhot letters were found in his room from — of all people — little Madeleine Smith.

It is still not known whether Madeleine murdered Emile or not. The evidence was circumstantial but suggestive. People debated it and the related moral problems endlessly, the length and breadth of England.

A lot of people felt that Madeleine should be hanged. This feeling, a very powerful, emotional one, was related to their sense of sexual outrage. A girl of good family who could allow herself to be seduced was clearly capable of doing murder too, and deserved an awful fate in either case. Her poor parents — no wonder they stayed in their sickbeds the whole time; of course they could not have been expected to attend the trial of a daughter who had so disgraced them. Madeleine was a kind of public enemy, for the bad example she set for the daughters of England, if for nothing else. And the worst thing of all was that she had not been seduced out of mere weakmindedness; she was apparently unrepentant about having had sexual relations and even — this was awful — even apparently had enjoyed them. This was a point dwelt upon by the Lord-Justice in the prosecution, with a par-

ticular sense of dazed, bewildered dismay. He says, in his summation: "The letters continued on her part in the same terms of
passionate love for a very considerable time. I say 'passionate
love,' because, unhappily, they are written without any sense of
decency and in most licentious terms." His Lordship then read
one of the letters which ended, "Oh, to be in thy embrace, my
sweet love. Love again to thee from thy ever-loving and ever-
devoted Mimi, thine own wife." "What," asks his Lordship,
"could she expect but sexual intercourse after thus presenting
and inviting it?" His Lordship cannot conceive of a nice girl
wishing sexual intercourse, but she did, of course, and if Emile
had "only let her go when she got tired of him she would probably have never regretted it. . . ." As the Historian of the affair
tells us:

Her candour seemed to the Lord-Justice almost incredible, and
he continues as follows: "Can you be surprised after such
letters . . . that, he got possession of her person? On the 7th of
May she writes to him, and in that letter is there the slightest
appearance of grief or remorse? None whatever. It is the letter
of a girl rejoicing in what had passed, and alluding to it, in one
passage in particular, in terms which I will not read, for perhaps
they were never previously committed to paper as having passed
between a man and a woman. What passed must have passed
out of doors, not in the house, and she talks of the act as hers as
much as his." These remarks, which at that time were considered the most severe condemnation, convey a truth which
was Madeleine's only justification. The act was as much hers
as his, and she never pretended otherwise. As to the satisfaction
of her desire, she probably thought that it made small difference
whether it took place respectably in a bedroom or beneath the
trees at Rowaleyn. "This letter from a girl," continued the
Judge, "written at five in the morning, just after she had sub-
mitted to his embraces. Can you conceive any worse state of
mind than this letter exhibits?"

Many Englishmen could not.

But Madeleine had partisans, too. A lot of people thought her innocent (a woman, an Angel in the House, could not possibly murder someone), or that the evidence was too slight to convict her without injuring irreparably the British system of jurisprudence and the presumed rights of free British subjects. People who thought her *truly* innocent also pointed out that she *seemed* innocent. She was so forthright, her head held so proudly, such an air of honor and rectitude about her. And, too, people of her social class did not commit murder. That she had been seduced — well — that was another matter, and certainly unfortunate; but murder — impossible.

Other people felt that she probably did it but that Emile deserved it — the most unmitigated scoundrel that ever lived. They would not condone murder, of course, but would not be sorry to see Madeleine get off, because the fellow was *so* unspeakable. Seducing above his station was bad enough, but threatening to expose her was dastardly beyond anything. And his letter reproaching *her* for the whole thing was unbelievable: "I was not angry at your allowing me, Mimi, but I am sad it happened. You had no resolution. . . . It was very bad indeed. I shall look with regret on that night." Indeed! (Though these reproaches were probably not so much a function of Emile's unscrupulous calculation as of his own truly Victorian, conflicted sexual values. Still it is hard to sympathize with a fellow who says such things to the maiden he has just "ruined.")

In any case, in a trial that remains a model of scrupulous courtroom procedure, Madeleine won a verdict of "not proven." She was swept off home for a time, later married an artist, became a socialist, and, it is said, went to America. Doubtless she prospered.

If for no other reason, this trial is interesting because it shows how a pleasant, apparently normal girl, weighing the relative consequences of either the exposure of her sexual misbehavior or putting some arsenic in her lover's cocoa might choose to offer the cocoa. The one way lay certain ruin; the other way she merely ran the risk of being hanged and the certainty of a lifetime of bad conscience. Poor ruined Mary

Ellen Meredith must have reflected upon this choice with special interest.

Mary Ellen seems to have looked upon Madeleine as the victim of a male society, and to have identified somewhat with Madeleine's plight, but her comment is not entirely clear. In a letter to Henry she quotes from a newspaper account of the trial which a friend has sent her:[28]

"Madeleine Smith is a very young lady of short stature and slight form, with features sharp and prominent and restless sparkling eye, with keen and animated expression and healthful complexion. She was dressed simply yet elegantly, a small fashionable bonnet exposing the whole front of her head. She also had lavender coloured gloves, a white cambric handkerchief, and a silver-tipped smelling bottle. She was perfectly self-possessed and even sometimes smiled with all the air and grace of a young lady in the drawing room. Altogether she had a most attractive appearance, and her very aspect and demeanor seemed to advocate her cause." [The underlines are Mary Ellen's.] Do all men think a woman's attractiveness lies in her accomplishment in the science of forgetting, even if she be guiltless of crime? My conclusion is very different—but then—,

---

An enigmatic comment. Whether or not she considered herself guiltless of some "crime" or other, her tone is one of tired injury, expressive of something she had not been able to forget. But then . . .

Like Mary Ellen, Miss Smith may have read The Spectator:

Spectator, Feb. 9th, 1856. Arsenic is taken for cosmetic purposes. It is taken at first in very small quantities; the quantity may be increased as is the case with many other poisons, until it reaches an amount that would be dangerous if not fatal to begin with. But the arsenic remains, and it is said that the patient may continue the practice for a lengthened period, though with

certain death at a distant date; but that if he stops short and ab-
stains, the body loses its faculty for resisting the poisonous
agency, and he dies of the arsenic he has left off taking.

Mary Ellen had copied this passage out in her Commonplace Book.

⌒⌒.

1857. Whether or not the connection between Mary Ellen and
Henry was of a "criminal" character yet, it would soon become so. But Mary Ellen thought of herself as an independent
woman. This attitude, unusual in an Englishwoman of her day,
was rather French. In France, women of the *demi-monde,* to
which she apparently thought of herself as now belonging, conducted their own lives, finances, and business affairs with considerably more freedom and practicality than their married
British sisters could imagine doing. Leaving George had been
her notion and she would abide by the consequences; the liaison
with Henry is evidently quite unrelated in her mind.

She needs to earn some money and is trying to think up some
scheme to do so. "Don't be alarmed, it is nothing of the genius
business, I abominate writing and would much rather scrub
floors," she writes to Henry, apropos, evidently, of her attempt
to write something. "But I indulge in visions of 'a cottage near
a wood,' with one north room which I propose to let to 'a Nartis,'
a cow of my own, which will be the terror and pride of my life,
a pig that shall be transformed into strengthening bacon, fowls
that supply the whole household with *New Loid Heggs.*" She
evidently expects to support this bucolic existence, however
ironically described, in part by her own efforts, with a little revenue derived, perhaps, from rent paid by the Nartis.

Henry, off painting as usual, is expected. His painting was

going well. Earlier in the spring he had finished his *Montaigne* picture, begun in the two hours stolen by moral force from the "wretched slave" who guarded Montaigne's room. *Montaigne* had hung in the Royal Academy exhibition, and Ruskin said of it: "Not, I think, quite so successful as the 'Chatterton' of last year; but it contends with greater difficulties, and is full of marvellous painting. It is terribly hurt by its frame, and by the surrounding colours and lights; seen through the hand, the effect is almost like reality. That is a beautifully characteristic fragment of homely French architecture seen through the window. I should think this picture required long looking at, and that it is seen to greater disadvantage by careless passers by than almost any of its neighbors."

"I have laid in *nine gallons of tonic medicine* for you, but such is my good nature that I will help you through with it," Mary Ellen tells him. (Wine?) Mary Ellen was evidently feeling enough better to enjoy the active outdoor things she was accustomed to. "I propose one or two excursions [in a boat, probably], and that we may return safe therefrom I beseech you to invest in a compass."

Henry must have arrived not long after this because before the end of the month she had become pregnant again.

Later in the summer she and Henry go to Wales. Papa writes to her, sends her a *Morning Post* and an answer to something she had asked about a passage in Horace: "*Sat.* L. II. 6. v. 53: *Numquid de Dacis audisti?*" [Have you heard anything about the Dacians?] In the *Morning Post* he recommends an article on Mr. Spurgeon "under the head of *Transpontine Preachments.*"

Mary Ellen is evidently exploring the scenery around her

mother's birthplace. Papa recommends "the finest waterfalls in North Wales are those of Cain, Mawddach, and Dolymelyn-llyn, between Dolgelly, and Maentwrog: the latter five miles from Dolgelly, and close to the road: the two former about two miles further, very near each other, but quite away from the road: Rhaiader Du, two or three miles from Maentwrog towards Harlech: Rhaiader y Wennol, near Capel Curig." Mary Ellen has sent Papa a little Welsh plant which he has set in stonework and hopes will thrive.

Her "affectionate father" continues in this chatty vein, and makes no mention of George. George's new book comes out in this month, August: *Farina, A Legend of Cologne*. Neither a success nor a failure. George has moved to London, and lives at 7 Hobury Street, Chelsea, and is writing *Richard Feverel*. Arthur's whereabouts are not clear, but he is not with George, so he is probably being looked after by Aunt May, while Mama vacations, or perhaps he is with his sister Edith at her Grand-mama Nicolls's in Blackheath.

"Sacred to the most dear and blessed memory of the wife and children of Henry Collinson Esq. Rt. Hon. Sec. of the Middle Temple London. First of Richard Vyse Collinson born 29th May 1856 died 27 March 1857 aged 11 mounthes. Secondly of Margaret Ellen Collinson Born 3rd March 1854, Died 10th June 1857, Aged 3 years and 3 mounthes. Thirdly of Rosa Jane Collinson Mother of the Above. Born 19th September 1827 Died 5th October 1857. Aged 30 years. 'Blessed are the Pure in heart for they shall see God.' Matt. ch 5 v 8. 'But Mary kept all these things and pondered them in her heart.' Luke ch 2 v 19."

From which we see that in this year, 1857, poor little Rosa Jane has died. Of her cough, no doubt. She dies before we have had much time to notice her. Her two little children have died too, and Papa has had them all buried at the cemetery at Shepperton. Why have they come home? What happened to Mr. Collinson, whom Rosa married? Who *was* Mr. Collinson? Had Papa forgiven poor Rosa Jane for marrying him? Her life may have been even more sad and eventful than Mary Ellen's, if we knew about it, but nobody, nobody at all, has kept any track of Rosa Jane. Nobody has mentioned her in letters and she has left nothing behind. Papa has much to grieve for, between Rosa Jane's death and Mary Ellen's carryings-on.

Careful attention to the account on her tombstone reveals that Circumstance, with characteristic malice, preserved Rosa Jane alive long enough to make her endure the deaths of her two babies, before killing her off too.

⁊.

1858. Everyone reassembled at Lower Halliford. Papa seemed to like Henry. In January he sat to him for the little portrait that now hangs in the National Portrait Gallery — a picture that Edith never liked, always feeling that it made his face too red. But those were the days when it was not considered nice to have too red a face. Peacock, bearing in mind Henry's historical inclinations, supplied ideas for paintings. His imagination, as usual, was caught by fathers and daughters. He writes to Henry:

The most illustrious lady of Voltaire's intimacy was La Marquise du Chatelet. It was to her he addressed that beautiful little poem:

"Si vous voulez que j'aime encore:"

and many others. Many of his works have relation to her. Her death was the greatest sorrow of his life.

His latest domestic companion was his niece, Madame Denis.

One of the most striking instances of his kindness of heart was his providing for Mademoiselle Corneille, serving her as a father when she was all but destitute. She was educated at Ferney. He settled an income on her, and gave her a dowry on her marriage: of which he says: *24th Jan 1763: Nous marions Mademoiselle Corneille à un gentilhomme du voisinage, officier de dragons, Sage, doux, brave, d'une jolie figure, aimant la service du roi et sa femme, possédant dix mille livres de rente, à peu près, à la porte de Ferney. Je les loge tous deux. Nous sommes tous heureux. Je finis en patriarche. . . .*

Le nom de notre futur est Dapuits. Frère Thiériot doit être fort aise [?] de la fortune de Mlle. Corneille. Elle la mérite. Savez-vous bien que cette enfant a nourri long-temps son pere et sa mere du travail de ses petites mains? La voilà recompensée. Sa vie est un roman.

I should prefer Mlle. Corneille as the heroine of a picture of Voltaire. She may be associated, in the character of a daughter, with every phase of his domestic life.[29]

In early April, Mary Ellen, her confinement approaching, left Arthur in the care of a Mrs. Chapman, perhaps Mrs. Edward Chapman, wife of the publisher, and, Edith being then away at school, went with her sister May to an Elm Cottage at Clifton, near Bristol, to await the birth of Henry's baby. The baby was born later that month, a little boy, and because the legal format of birth certificates of this period left no space for odd contingencies or embarrassing exactitudes, in the place for "Father," was entered "George Meredith, Author." The baby was called Harold Meredith.

Although the shame of infidelity and seduction and illegiti-macy was powerful in those days, there seems in Mary Ellen's family to have been no particular secrecy, or only a little, surrounding this event. Peacock writes cheerfully to Claire Clairmont: "May has been more than three weeks with Mary Ellen, at a place near Bristol. She comes home tomorrow. Mary Ellen has a fine boy whom she calls Harry Agincourt." Agincourt—a victory, against overwhelming odds, and owing to Henry. "Agincourt" was not really Harold's name, of course, but just a joke Mary Ellen has made up, and Peacock passes it along to Claire.

It is just conceivable, but highly unlikely, that Peacock did not realize that the father was not George; he certainly knew that George and Mary Ellen had not lived together recently enough for this to be possible. It is likely that Peacock regarded Harold as a regrettable but natural consequence of the whole catastrophe that had issued from Mary Ellen's wedding to the Dyspeptic. And Claire, who had had a baby out of wedlock her-self, Lord Byron's child, Allegra, could scarcely have been shocked.

The family may have been a little reticent with some of their more prudish London acquaintance, though. Mary Ellen writes anxiously to Henry from Elm Cottage: "I hear no word of Arthur now—I cannot write to Mrs. Chapman without mentioning Baby. Do you think I may venture to do so? I must have Arthur for Edith's holidays." This also suggests that Arthur had not yet fallen into George's hands.

Henry had remained in London for the opening of the annual Royal Academy Show. He was unhappy that his pictures were badly exhibited. Mary was reassuring: "They are too grand to be much injured by any such stupidity, and will shine like the sun through clouds. Send me Ruskin's pamphlet when you have read it. You see even *The Spectator* speaks of The Stonebreaker as the best of the best." She was right—Ruskin acclaimed *The Stonebreaker*, though in qualified terms, as "Picture of the Year."

---

562. Thou wert our Conscript. (H. Wallis)

On the whole, to my mind, the picture of the year; and but narrowly missing being a first-rate of any year. It is entirely pathetic and beautiful in purpose and colour; its only fault being a somewhat too heavy laying of the body of paint, more especially in the distant sky, which has no joy nor clearness when it is looked close into, and in the blue of the hills that rise against it, which is also too uniform and dead. All perfect painting is light painting—light at some point of the touch at all events; no half inch of a good picture but tells, when it is looked at, "None but my master could have laid me so."

The ivy, ferns, &c., seem to me somewhat hastily painted, but they are lovely in colour, and may pass blameless, as I think it would have been in false taste to elaborate this subject further. The death quietness given by the action of the startled weasel is very striking.

Mary Ellen, who had always been maternal, was delighted with her new little baby, the love-child whom they called Felix, which means happiness.[30] "The darling baby keeps as good as ever, never cries, coos and laughs, sleeps and feeds and so his innocent life flows sweetly on."

She chats of inconsequential things: "Some day when you are passing a silk-shop see if you can match me this. I want two or three yards according to the price — two will do if more than 4^s a yard. . . ."

But there is one ominous note: "I am not suffering from anything and am getting on well but I am very weak, as I have never been before, dragging pains in my limbs, and swelled ancles [*sic*], but I have no doubt caution and rest will remove these, and if it does not I shall apply to Dr. Kidd. Unless Baby and I are quite well when we leave this I shall be afraid to go any very uncivilized place and I positively will not miss strawberries this year." The swelled "ancles" and dragging pains are symptoms of yet another attack of the renal disease she could not really ever recover from.

Hers are on the whole rather laconic and undemanding letters from a Victorian mistress to her lover, especially a mistress who has just given birth to an illegitimate child. She no longer writes like a Victorian heroine, as she had when a girl, in exclamation points and effusions of "Oh." Now her tone is equable and independent, though her position is precarious. Her letters are pleasantly free from any flights of ingratiating tact in a day when the love letters of the securest women were often doubly stifled by decorum and insecurity.

It is probable that Mary Ellen's comfortable tone here, hard to reconcile with Meredith's description of her as a "madwoman," was both a matter of temperament and a consequence of an understanding between herself and Henry, in which they were fond, affectionate, and not bound to each other. They could not marry, and Mary Ellen was too realistic to expect Romantic Adventure; her pleasures were to be in her children, in strawberries, and probably, when she got to feeling better, in her writing.

George, meanwhile, was in lodgings in London, "ill, overworked, vexed," as he wrote to Eyre Crowe. Their friends had strangely polarized since his breakup with Mary Ellen. "I have seen none of the set but Dan, and him not for a fortnight." Dan was Peter Austin Daniel, ultimately *Henry's* oldest friend and executor, just as Eyre Crowe was ultimately to sponsor the new little Harold in his future career. George must have felt uncertain where people's loyalties lay, and he was a man who needed loyalty, "sunshine," bland approval.

George was afraid of the world. He knew he was; he despised in himself this fear of what people, what the World, would say but he could not help fearing it. He dreaded to have the World find out about his humiliation.

The World, of course, found out. It found out about the baby and it found out that Mary Ellen had gone off with Henry Wallis. It gossiped. Dickens, who was down on George anyway for allying himself with a new periodical, *Once a Week*, and deserting the Dickensian camp, writes smugly to his editor Wills the gossip he has heard from the actor Macready:

Friday, Twenty-Second October, 1858

My Dear Wills:

—If you look at the passage in Macready's letter, which refers to Mrs. Meredith, you will see what I mean when I ask you if you will write to him [George], and enquire whether he will receive the money for the paper, or what is to be done with it; telling him at the same time how much the sum is.

This evidently refers to some things Mary Ellen had written; it is typical of the times (as well as of Dickens), that an editor would not dream of asking a woman what she wanted done with her own money, as long as she had a husband. One longs to know whether George accepted the money for Mary Ellen's writing, and how much it was. Dickens adds, "Was she paid for her former paper or papers? That passage in her note looks to me as if she never had been paid."[31]

All this gossip was an unalloyed horror to George, though posterity may feel grateful if his brilliant portrayal of Willoughby Patterne's desperate stratagems to conceal his personal humiliations from the world owe anything to this experience. George's own desperate stratagems now were to plunge into his equally brilliant but face-saving poem *Modern Love*, and to make some new friends who didn't know anything of his "matrimonial antecedents."

The errant lovers, Mary Ellen and Henry, had not, of course, dashed off romantically to Capri, as tradition has held. They did go there, but in quite another spirit.[32] Henry solicitously took Mary Ellen there for the winter, hoping she would regain her still failing health. It is not clear whether little Harold went with them, but probably he did. Henry always felt Capri to be a most salutary place, and good for painting too. Edith was again at school, and Arthur was left with General Sir Edward and Lady Nicolls at Blackheath. They had become nearly as fond of him as they were of their real grandchild, Edith.

How George suffered. Like Willoughby, he "was in the jaws of the world. We have the phrase, that a man is himself, under certain trying circumstances. There is no need to say it of Sir Willoughby: he was thrice himself when danger menaced: himself inspired him. He could read at a single glance the Polyphemus eye in the general head of a company." His whole acquaintance "had a similarity in the variety of their expressions that made up one giant eye for him, perfectly, if awfully, legible. He discerned the fact that his demon secret was abroad, universal. He ascribed it to fate. He was in the jaws of the world, on the world's teeth. . . . His ears tingled. He and his whole story discussed in public! Himself unroofed! And the marvel that he of all men should be in such a tangle, naked and blown on, condemned to use his cunningest arts to unwind and cover himself, struck him as though the lord of his kind were running the gauntlet of a legion of imps. He felt their lashes."

1859. Early in the year Mary Ellen came back from Capri, apparently alone, giving rise to the traditional view that she and

Henry had quarreled and parted or—to put it more strongly—
that he had deserted her. This, it is true, is what inevitably happened to heroines in novels who were imprudent enough to run
away with men. The circumstances are somewhat clouded now,
but it seems more likely that Mary Ellen and Henry did not part
at all. They just went underground, to provide for an undisturbed
and scandal-free future. That this was so is testified to by the
lifelong cordial relations between Henry and the Peacock
family. Mary Ellen's few little things were given to him when
she died. He corresponded with and called upon Edith as long
as he lived, and contributed to the Halliford edition of Peacock's
works. Also, among Henry's things is a packet of letters, replies
to an advertisement placed in *The Times*, Monday, February 14,
1859—about the time he and Mary Ellen were both back in
England:

*WANTED, for a permanency, by a gentleman and his wife,
without children, in a house where there are no other lodgers,
FURNISHED APARTMENTS, consisting of one or two sitting
rooms and two bed rooms, with attendance, &c. Terms not to ex-
ceed £2.5ˢ per week, all extras inclusive. A short distance from
town, and of easy access by rail, not objected to. Address L. M.,
care of Messrs. Davies and Co., advertising agents, Finch-lane,
E.C.*

L. M. would be the agent who then passes replies on to his
client. It all sounds very much as if Henry was setting up that
fine Victorian institution, the Love Nest. Meanwhile, Mary Ellen
went off to spend Easter vacation at Seaford with Edith, and
Henry took rooms at 62 Great Russell Street, in respectable
separation.

Woman's Lot: we learn a little more of it from the replies to the advertisement, dozens of replies from the respectable widows of London, anxious, poor, obliged to let their drawing rooms ("watercloset on the same floor"); obliged to give their tenants "first-rate references" of their respectability. If you were poor it was essential to cling to your respectability; it was also necessary to hope for an extra thirty shillings a week, and if the Gentleman and Lady who came to rent it were not—you suspected— quite what they ought to be—if they *seemed* respectable, that would just have to do:

A gentleman and his Wife only, having a much larger House than they require would be happy to let the Drawing room with 2, 3 or more rooms Well furnished with use of Piano—good cooking and attendance with great attention to cleanliness, and all the comforts of a home can be offered—

Drawing room lofty with 2 Bedrooms and extra room if required 30/ per week Watercloset on same floor—situated most central being

34 King Street
Bloomsbury Square

Can refer to a Lady and Gentleman who occupied the apartments until lately.

Sir

In reply to your Advertisement in the "Times" Paper of this Morning for furnished apartments I beg to offer you the same with every comfort and attention at the sum named should the situation be suitable.

My House is large, airy and genteelly furnished it is close to Lord Hollands Park and Kensington Gardens and the Omnibuses pass the Square to all parts every ten minutes, and having no family enables me to observe the greatest punctality [sic] in my establishment

To L. M.
Davis & Co   Address
Advertising Agents   Mrs Holloway
1 Finch Lane   3 Warwick Square West
                             Kensington
                             Feb 14th

A Lady who is about taking a House in the healthy and really beautiful neighbourhood of Highbury, also but a little distance from the railway which runs from thence to the City, Blackwall [& etc.?] — would be much gratified by an interview on the subject of their advertisement with L M — she thinks a negociation [sic] in the requirement of both parties — (one, wishing a pleasant residence, and the other side desiring to find respectable persons as permanent inmates) might be agreeably entertained; if the short time arrangements would take making would be of no particular object to the Gentleman and Lady seeking a permanent and congenial Home.

For making an appointment to enter into all particulars please address to

Mrs. Newbold
3 St Georges Terrace
Liverpool Road
Islington

Monday
Feb[ry] 14th, 1859

Sir

I beg to say in answer to your advertisement that you can be accomodated [sic] with the apartments you require, in my house which is well and comfortably Furnished There are no children or other Inmates and as I keep two Servants and there are only two in Family you would have very good attendance I am the Widow of an officer and can give first rate references as to my respectability Should the neighbourhood of Kensington suit you I shall be happy to show you the rooms Hoping you will favor me with a line

> I remain
> Sir
> Yours obediently
> Mrs L Hellens   [?]

1 Cambridge Terrace
Holland Road
Kensington

One very bad thing had happened to complicate Mary Ellen's life. When she set out for Capri she had left Arthur with her former mother-in-law, Lady Nicolls. She came back to find that George had got him. There is a scene in Meredith's *Harry Richmond* where a father comes to claim his little son from the aristocratic parents of his former wife. In the book the wife, named Marian, is mad. The father storms up to the door in the night and insists on seeing his little boy. "Some minutes later the boy was taken out of his bed by his aunt Dorothy, who dressed him by the dark window-light, crying bitterly, while she said Hush, hush,: and fastened on his small garments between tender huggings of his body and kissings of his cheek. He was told that he had nothing to be afraid of. A gentleman wanted to see him; nothing more. Whether the gentleman was a good gentleman, and not a robber, he could not learn." The little boy is taken up and shown by his grandpapa to a man whom he hardly knew. "'Kiss the little chap and back to bed with him,'" growled the squire.

"The boy was heartily kissed and asked if he had forgotten his papa. He replied that he had no papa: he had a mama and a grandpapa. The stranger gave a deep groan. 'You see what you have done; you have cut m﹒﹖ off from my own,' he said terribly to the squire; but tried immediately to soothe the urchin with nursery talk and the pats on the shoulder which encourage a little boy to grow fast and tall. . . ."

After further argument the father steals the little boy off into the night. He is a wonderful, fantastic father, with candy and extravagant tales; it has usually been assumed that it was George's own father he was re-creating in his book. But perhaps "The Great Mel" is the sort of father George wished to be, too, wooing with his verbal brilliance the little boy in whom there might just possibly remain some residual affection for his mother.

For George, things were looking up. He had taken Arthur to a place at Esher, near Weybridge, where he and Mary Ellen had lived when they were first married. He had a housekeeper, and an altogether more settled life now, and took up again with their old neighbors, the Duff Gordons, whose sixteen-year-old daughter Janet he was in love with. He was writing a novel, *Evan Harrington,* about a young man with origins in tailordom and how he got on with fancy people (like the Duff Gordons). He made the tailors seem ridiculous and the aristocrats pleasant, so he, Meredith, got on very well. The novel began to run in the February issue of *Once a Week,* and he had gotten a reader's job at the publishing firm of Chapman and Hall, so there was steady money at last.

In fact there was just one problem in his life: Mary Ellen.

Instead of considerately throwing herself into the Thames or coming to some other conclusion, as an erring wife should do—and an old one at that, nearly forty, so different from the blooming Janet—Mary Ellen was around. She even saw people George knew, and they spoke to her, perhaps even called on her at her shabby place at Twickenham, or had she moved to Richmond Hill by now? George hated the idea that for others Mary existed. For him, she did not.

She had the appalling nerve to visit him once, about Arthur, for a brief moment—"the space of two minutes only," he assured his future father-in-law, anxious to convince him of his inflexible rectitude. He must have turned her out. No, she could not have Arthur; she could not even see Arthur. Like the sanctimonious villain in a satire on Victorian life, George knew his moral rights, and he was supported in them—he must have known, must have felt her silent approval and encouragement and support—by Mrs. Grundy, that representative of British mid-Victorian respectability, whom he already affected to despise. Mrs. Grundy and George knew that a woman who left her husband should not even *wish* to corrupt her child by her company. British law took a similar view; mothers were rarely given custody of their children even in cases where it was the father who was the adulterer. George, with the Crown and Mrs. Grundy on his side, was adamant.

The real people they knew, of course, were more graceful. Every Victorian did not behave like Victorians in a play—some conspired to help Mary Ellen. They would sneak Arthur out for little furtive visits with her in London, "or at Petersham, in the avenue leading to Ham House," says the Biographer. Perhaps Mary Ellen would bring him toys; perhaps she brought sweets, or maybe she brought his little brother for him to see. Arthur could not talk about these visits to Papa. Mama could not even be mentioned. It was very strange for Arthur.

1860. Mary Ellen now had a tiny cottage in Oatlands Park, a few miles from Lower Halliford and Papa, and Edith, when she came home on holidays from school. Harold and his nurse, Mrs. Bennet, were with her or nearby, for Mary Ellen was not really strong enough any longer to care for a lively two-year-old by herself. The old illness was worse: she would swell and ache; her head would pound pitilessly. She grew weaker, paler. Then she would feel more herself again, and try to work, and see her friends, and put things in order. She had set her face toward the future with, as it were, existential fortitude, as though there were going to be a future.

In the summer of 1860 she writes a graceful little letter to Edward Chapman, but beneath the surface cordiality there is growing desperation — debt, and her sense that her illness *might* be fatal:

My dear Mr. Chapman,

Can you lend me £10 till Michaelmas. In the event of my death between this and that Papa will repay it to you. I have no other security to you except my own assertion that I have never yet borrowed a penny without returning it at the specified time. If you can oblige me please send me a check here. I have let my house to Parker and taken a little cottage for boating at Weybridge so that what I have had to buy for that and the moving spare things from Richmond has taken up my loose cash and I never get in debt.

I am so vexed that the first letter I greet you with after your perilous journey to 'Foreign Parts' should be about money that I will not write to answer Mrs. Chapman's last kind letter now but shall do so by-and-bye on a sheet unalloyed by Mammon.

I should be glad to hear however how you like the place and how you performed the journey.

And with kindest love to all your family, believe me

Faithfully yours,
Mary Meredith

Evidently Mr. Chapman obliged, because four days later, July 8, 1860, she writes to thank him:

My dear Mr. Chapman,

Many thanks for your kindness: the first two halves came safely. Never having written or seen an I.O.U., I think it better to send it now so that if not right you can send it to me to be corrected with the other half notes.

I am hard at work getting my boating cottage in order, in a few days I shall write to Mrs. Chapman. I am very glad you all like the place.

With love to all, believe me

> *Faithfully yours,*
> *Mary Meredith*

I have said October 1, because though I shall have the money on the 29th of September I may not be able to transfer it to you by that time.

We cannot be sure of the mysteries of Mary Ellen's finances now. Where did she get the Richmond house which she had let to Parker? From whence did she expect the money in September to repay to Chapman?

To her old friend Hogg, who had recently lost an old friend, she wrote a letter of condolence in December, and to him must have allowed a glimpse of her true despair. Hogg replies: "You treat life somewhat cynically as 'une froide plaisanterie': if you are justified by the authority of Voltaire in considering the dispensation of weather as a pleasantry, certainly it is a cold one at present. At this season it is the custom to say to a friend, A Happy New Year!: it is superfluous to offer the accustomed wish to *you*, because you have enough of talent and originality to make for yourself, under any circumstances, Many Happy New Years!"

But of course this was not true. She had talent and originality but could not live to see another New Year. Perhaps life really is *une froide plaisanterie.* She had not liked to worry old Hogg with the news that she was dying, but she seems to have known it herself.

⁓.

Oatlands Park had been the grounds of the house of the Duke of York: beautiful formal gardens, wild woods, ponds. By 1861 the house had been converted into a hotel owned by a Mr. Peppercorn, but the grounds had not changed much. There was a strange grotto made of shells, a broadwater, seventy acres of land and wood. Near the grotto was Grotto Cottage, formerly the home of some retainer, and now of Mary Ellen. Grotto Cottage is tiny, almost like a playhouse, a little pitch-roofed playhouse with mud walls and small windows.[33]

You could not long stay indoors in Grotto Cottage, but Mary Ellen wanted always to be outdoors anyway. And the spring of 1861 was no doubt beautiful, like all English springs. The snow melted in the Oatlands woods, wild flowers sprang up all over the valley of the Thames. There were walks and walls to sit on in the warming sun; you could look at the birds returning, ripples of bud along the twig. Along the walls at Oatlands, urns are positioned, supported by cast nymphs who, with time and hard winters, have lost their arms and heads. Maimed nymphs supporting funereal urns. Perhaps Mary Ellen, accustomed to them, did not think about the maimed nymphs, the mocking gargoyles that served for garden ornament.

Mary Ellen could walk among the beautiful trees, among moss and roses, or sit on a stone bench to do her sewing. She made a little suit of gray flannel for Harold, with braid on the sleeves, and a red cloak lined in oiled cloth for waterproofing. No doubt she read the latest of George's books, *Evan Harrington,* if she had not already read it in serial. Henry hung two lovely pictures, *Gondomar* and *Elaine,* in the Royal Academy Exhibition. Perhaps, as at other times, she tried to do her writing; she had her living to get, if she was to be a long time dying.

In the summer, she spent some time with Papa. Perhaps she spent her birthday there. This was her fortieth birthday, one to cause introspection in the most cheerful of celebrants. She had not had long enough—she must have thought—not nearly long enough to do all the things she had planned to do. She had been true to herself, in a way. "Will that young girl be true to herself?" was a question she had written once in her book.

If she was unhappy now it was because she could not live as long as she had planned, had not been as wise as she ought, or as strong. She and Papa walked along the river, and May and Edith were there; no doubt they did not talk of death. A beautiful, clear summer. Perhaps they had a picnic on her birthday. Perhaps when Papa looked at her, his beautiful Mary Ellen so ill, he would have to look away quickly or she would see his tears.

A few days after her last visit to Papa she fell more ill than she ever had before, more quickly. Intimations of mortality. She sends for Papa, who writes his friend Lord Broughton on August 16: "Day after day, I have tried to [write to?] you, but always in vain. It seemed as if I could not trace the letters for what I had to say. At the same time with your last kind letter, I received a message from my eldest, and only surviving daughter, that she was extremely ill, and earnestly wished to see me. She lives two miles from me in Oatlands Park. She had been here, and had left only three days before: not well, but with no symptoms of serious illness. I have never seen such a fearful change in so short a time. I have been with her every day. She seems to grow rapidly worse. But while there is life, there is hope."

False hope. Mary Ellen was dying. With the scrupulous Victorian sense of decorum about death, her friends worried about Arthur. Arthur ought to see his mother before she was gone. One night, when it seemed nearly too late, Lady Hornby—who used to be little Emilia Macirone, their landlady's daughter at The Limes—came flying to George at Copsham Cottage in Weybridge to beg him to send Arthur now, before it was too late. The hour was inconvenient. George got up and lit the lamp and heard Lady Hornby out and searched his heart and said, No. And returned to bed. Shaken, Lady Hornby went away again.

George must have seen, in the clear autumnal morning, that this was carrying bitterness beyond the bounds of decency. He eventually relented and sent Arthur to Oatlands, but too late to save himself from opprobrium. Even his dear friends were distant and reproachful about this. Janet Duff-Gordon (now Ross), whom he still loved, thought enough of him to write reproachfully, or perhaps inquiringly, hoping it wasn't true that George had been unable to forgive a dying woman.

"Your letter was based on false intelligence, my dear," George replied. "It was perfectly right of you to take up the case as you did. I am glad you like me well enough to do so. Be sure I would not miss your friendship for much; and would stoop my pride for it, even if that stood in the way. As it is there is no feeling of the sort. God bless you. . . . Arthur is now at Weybridge seeing his mother daily."

This hypocritical passage was suppressed by Meredith's first editor, his son Will, except for the last line. Similarly, his first biographer, Cousin Stewart, was at a loss to excuse George's behavior in refusing to go, or to allow Arthur to go, to Mary Ellen: "He had that horror of illness and the circumstances of death which is generally found in a man of imaginative temperament: that is the only excuse that can be offered in mitigation of censure."

Early October. Mary Ellen seems for a while to be getting better, and Papa writes to Lord Broughton that, "Yesterday gave the first ray of hope I have seen for many days. It may be fallacious:

but it enables me to write under something like a cheerful influence. Still there neither is, nor has been since the beginning of August, a day on which I could say to myself 'I can now leave home with a quiet mind.'"

And George writes to Maxse, "My darling boy is quite well. He has cried a little, I am told. I am afraid his feelings have been a trifle worked on, though not by his mother so much as the servants and friends in her house."

Were little boys then not supposed to cry—Arthur was just eight—when their mamas were dying?

It is nice to know that Mary Ellen did not try to sentimentalize the forthcoming event—though she did send a lock of her hair, a long, shining, light-brown tress; to Harold's nurse, for Harold to keep as he grew up. It is the hair of a young woman, with no trace of gray.

We are startled at George's allusion to servants and friends in Mary Ellen's house. The earliest and widely accepted account is that she died quite alone. For a long time people said that Papa—even Papa—had never laid eyes on her since her dereliction with Henry. Cousin Stewart, for instance, wrote that, "Mrs. Meredith died alone, and her only mourners were a Mr. Howse, and a Miss Bennet, and her former maid, Jane Wells. No tombstone has ever been placed over her grave, and the spot . . . is not marked even by a grass mound."

Because, of course, as every Victorian knew, if you have sinned you cannot, cannot possibly, expect to die surrounded by your family and friends. Victorians knew these things; they rearranged facts to fit with what they knew. Cousin Stewart tries to be handsome for George's sake: "Thus ended the sad life of Mary Ellen Meredith. There is no condemnation for her, for, whatever her errors, they were blotted out by her tears. Meredith himself never blamed her, for he realized his own share in the mistakes and misunderstandings that finally led to ruin."

The Halliford Biographer says: "Early in 1858 Mary Meredith was alone at Seaford; she was in debt, and unhappy; Henry Wallis helped her, and before the year was far advanced, she fled with him to Capri. Her father apparently never saw her again. She returned to England without Wallis, in 1859, and died at Weybridge, after many wanderings, in 1861. . . . Peacock did not attend her funeral. . . . No monument was set up to mark her grave. . . .''

This sad story sounds a bit like poor Lady Lowborough's, who ''eloped with another gallant to the Continent, where, having lived awhile in reckless gaiety and dissipation, they quarrelled and parted. She went dashing on for a season, but years came and money went; she sunk, at length, in difficulty and debt, disgrace and misery; and died at last, as I have heard, in penury, neglect, and utter wretchedness.'' But Lady Lowborough is an imaginary lady in Anne Brontë's *The Tenant of Wildfell Hall*, from which we can see how much biography owes to fiction.

For Mary Ellen, this was not a fictional event but a real one; her own death, to come to terms with in her own way.

''Yet have I seen that the race is not to the swift, nor the battle to the strong: but time and chance happeneth to all men,'' Mary Ellen had written in her Commonplace Book. And,

''There is a dreary satisfaction in knowing one can lose no more. I bowed down my face on my hands and rested satisfied in that knowledge.''

''He thought it might be better to flow away monotonously, like the river and to compound for its insensibility to happiness with its insensibility to pain,'' she had written.

That is how one dies from the disease that Mary Ellen had. One slips into a coma, like slipping into a river with the voices of the tired watchers growing fainter, blurring together like waves; and the light from the window strikes across the bed a dimmer beam, and darkness closes over, as the dark waters of the Shannon had closed around Eddy, or as the darkness of night closes around the bed of a small sleeper, and one flows away monotonously, insensible to pain, insensible to happiness.

⌐⌐.

Victorians knew death better than we. Many, like many who had lived before in other centuries, believed death was part of God's plan. He took unto Him each soul when it was time. People sorrowed but they had that solace. Some Victorians did not have that solace because they did not believe in God, and these had to come to terms with death as best they could and in a way that we do not, because death entered their lives more often, and more capriciously. Today we do not often believe that God comes down for every soul when it is time, but we have explanations that seem, though painful, sufficient. The deranged cell strays through the bloodstream, the walls of the artery burst, or a bubble of oxygen bursts in the brain. We are sad but scientific.

The Victorian father, watching his child sink into a fever, had no science. Capricious death could sometimes be routed by cool wet cloths or tea, you never knew. You hung on a pulse, on every shudder. The Dying himself was not protected from knowing his condition the way people often are today, if he was old enough to say his prayers and bid his family goodbye. Anne Brontë, dying, had been taken on a journey to behold a last beloved vista, and, feeling weaker, calmly asked the doctor if he thought she would live long enough to get home again, if they started right away. He did not think so, so she composed herself to die in lodgings; death had capriciously come a day or so early. Her brother, it is said, resolved to die standing up, and was indulged in this request by his family, who held the thin body up-

right until the light had gone out of its eyes. Death was a household event, since, of course, you died at home: pretty little
neighbor children died, with their fat braids and sailor suits;
young women at the height of their consumptive beauty; plump
mothers left their big broods; promising, fine, manly young men
were swept off suddenly by fevers; nice people you knew were
every day taken off, unaccountably; capricious death might any
day take you.

This is still true, of course. But Victorians thought about
death much more than we like to. Mary Ellen's acquaintance no
doubt concluded in their various ways that her death was:
God's will; tragic; regrettable; inevitable—a function of cosmic
malice *or* retributive justice; a release; a relief.

George was afraid that Arthur had "cried a little," when Mama
died. George could not bear tears in a boy. Perhaps little Arthur
cried in secret when his beautiful Mama died, or perhaps by
blinking and biting his lips he could keep himself from crying,
to please his Papa. Was he not eight years old now—a little man?

It is a funeral. George Meredith's wife is dead. Almost no one is
there. Papa is too stricken; his friend Henry Howes goes to the
funeral to see that it is done properly. Harold's nurse Mrs. Bennet
is there, and the maid Jane Wells. The people she loved are not

there. They are proud, intelligent people, mistrustful of easy, ritual comfort, resentful of death, and will not play death's games.

~~)·

But one day the lonely old man, Peacock, in his study sketched out an urn and a little epitaph, in Greek, and a Latin inscription:

IN MEMORIAM
MARIAE ELENAE
CONJUGIS GEORGII
MEREDITH   .

Marya Elena

Earthly love speedily becomes unmindful but love from heaven is mindful for ever more. . . .

A bitter irony.

)//

After Mary Ellen died, Papa fell into the deepest of depressions, broke off his correspondence, would not see people, could not bring himself to leave his home at Lower Halliford. When Mary Ellen had been dead a month, he brought himself to write to Lord Broughton: "I have struggled in vain against the double weight of mental depression and physical fatigue. A few quiet days with you and your daughters present, not merely the greatest, but the only attraction the external world can offer me: but I am totally unable to avail myself of your kindness. I have been too long, perhaps, in bringing my self to the conclusion, but you will pardon me in consideration of my extreme reluctance to admit it.''

By Christmas he is no better. On Christmas Eve he writes, ''I have not written a line since the last I wrote to you. I have striven from day to day to throw off the weight of physical and mental depression; but in vain: and I thought and felt that I must ac-quiesce under it for awhile, and await the natural reaction which comes in all cases soon or later. For I had always in my mind the words of Wallenstein:

> This anguish will be wearied down, I know:
> What pang is permanent with man? —
> From the highest,
> As from the meanest thing of every day
> He learns to wean himself: for the strong hours
> Conquer him.''

He clung to his family now — to May and Edith, and to Cousin Harriet, who is a kindly old spinster, living with her brother Henry, who, she worries, finds it dull living with an old-maid sister. ''You, are far better off with May, and 'the young lady who sings'! I am glad to hear she is still with you, for nothing is more delightful than the society of those who are cheerful, and light-hearted. If we are gloomy ourselves, we are unwilling that they should be so, and often imperceptibly recover our own lost spirits, by communion with theirs. I sincerely hope this will be your case, and that you will yet accomplish a visit to Lord Broughton.''

But he never did. He withdrew further and further into sor-row and solitude. Edith was scolded for admitting Thackeray, who called one day. Robert Buchanan was caught smoking and was turned away forever, for Peacock's dread of fire, always intense, grew pathological.

Towards the close of his life [*says little Edith*] *he grew much depressed in spirits; the loss of his two daughters was a terrible* grief to him, and a very short time before his death he was greatly shaken by a fire breaking out in the roof of his bedroom. He was taken to his library, which, being at the other end of the house, was away from the danger and the water. At one time it was feared the fire was gaining ground, and that it would be needful to move him into some one of the houses in the neighborhood, but he refused to move. The curate who came kindly to beg my grandfather to take shelter in his house, received rather a rough and startling reception, for in answer to the invitation, my grandfather exclaimed with great warmth and energy, "By the immortal gods, I will not move!"

He would not leave his books; and fortunately the danger passed. He never recovered that fire; he had been weak and ailing all the winter, and he took to his bedroom almost entirely after that; he died in a few weeks, in his eighty-first year.

That which you fear will always overtake you in the end; the fire raged through his safe and loved place. Those whom you love will be taken from you. The gods whom you serve are no better than the cruel Nazarene, whom you despise; and when Peacock began to die, Edith heard him calling upon these gods with reproaches, "because they persisted in tormenting one who had served them for a lifetime and never wavered in the service."

Cousin Harriet and Cousin Henry arranged for his tombstone:

SACRED

To The Dearly Loved
Memory of
THOMAS LOVE PEACOCK, Esq.

Late of the East India
Company's Home Service
Born at Weymouth
October 18, 1785
Died at Lower Halliford
January 23, 1866

Evidently, they did not take his writing too seriously.

Peacock brooded on death. The last thing he published was his solution to the famous enigma of Aelia Laelia Crispis:

TO THE GODS OF THE DEAD

Aelia Laelia Crispis

Not man, nor woman, nor hermaphrodite:
Not girl, nor youth, nor old woman:
Not chaste, nor unchaste, nor modest:
　　　　But all:
　　　　Carried off,
Not by hunger, nor by sword, nor by poison:
　　　　But by all:
　　　　　Lies,
Not in air, not in earth, not in the waters:
　　　But everywhere.
　　Lucius Agatho Priscus,
Not her husband, nor her lover, nor her friend:
　Not sorrowing, nor rejoicing, nor weeping:
　　　<u>Erecting</u>
　This, not a stone-pile, nor a pyramid,
　　　Nor a sepulchre:
　　　　But all:
　Knows, and knows not,
　To whom he erects it.

I believe this aenigma to consist entirely in the contrast, between the general and particular consideration of the human body, and its accidents of death and burial. Abstracting from it all but what is common to all human bodies, it has neither age nor sex; it has no morals, good or bad: it dies from no specific cause: lies in no specific place: is the subject of neither joy nor grief to the survivor. . . .

But considered in particular, that is, distinctively and in-dividually, we see, in succession, man and woman, young and old, good and bad; we see some buried in earth, some in sea,

some in polar ice, some in mountain snow. We see a funeral
superintended, here by one who rejoices, there by one who
mourns. . . .

~~)·

Mary Ellen's death came, of course, as a great relief to George.
He was momentarily afflicted, the way people are who find that
people have died before they have made themselves understood, or said they were sorry, or been forgiven, or somehow
straightened accounts so that no bad thoughts will creep in
some future sleepless night. George had an unfinished feeling
about Mary Ellen. He writes to his friend Hardman, "when I entered the world again," from a "dumpling state" of vacation,
"I found that one had quitted it who bore my name: and this
filled my mind with melancholy recollections which I rarely
give way to. My dear boy, fortunately, will not feel the blow as he
might have under different circumstances."

From this unfinished feeling his greatest books and poems
were to come. But even though he attained in them a kind of
perspective, this was never so in his life; he could never, his
whole life long, speak graciously of this experience, or refrain
from saying something defensive and rude.[34]

Mary Ellen was to cause him one bit more of worldly trouble.
When, in 1864, he fell in love with a pleasant girl named Marie
Vulliamy, her father insisted on a few explanations about his
"antecedents in the matrimonial way," as Sir William Hardman
put it in his memoirs. Meredith enlisted Hardman, whom he had
previously told nothing, to talk to Mr. Vulliamy. Meredith "is
and always has been very taciturn on all matters relating to his
personal history, and consequently he had now a great deal to
tell me. It is a curious and painful story. . . ." "To have been
separated from his wife, who afterwards had a child by another

man, is not a cheerful matter for contemplation by a prospective father-in-law."

So thought Marie's Papa, and enquired into the minutest details—the date and "mode" of the separation, where Mary Ellen lived after it, "at whose cost was she maintained?" "Whether after the separation she continued to be known and called by your name." Poor George answers all these questions as best he can by letter, and sends Hardman to answer the rest. The puzzled papa, Mr. Vulliamy, annotates George's letter:

1849–53: 4 years of affection.

53–57: Indifference increasing into mutual (I suppose) dislike and ending in separation from bed and board at the instigation of the wife. Up to this time [muses Mr. Vulliamy,] *he does not admit that he entertained any suspicion of conjugal infidelity on her part so the separation was not considered by him to be final until he became convinced of her adultery.*

1857–61. . . . After the Institution of Sir C. Creswell's Court in 1859, why did he not seek the Remedy which was now open to him? It seems very strange he should suffer this woman to bear his name and unaccountable that she lived partly with her father. Was her mother still living? What is her father? and where does he reside?

Here speaks the good Victorian. That such a woman might be accepted home into her family seems to him nothing less than completely "unaccountable."

The Biographer assures us that little Arthur had every advantage of exemplary training from George:

One day when his son had gone to play out of doors, Meredith heard a ring at the bell and went down to open the door. On the step stood a beautiful girl in riding-costume, holding her horse with one hand and a disheveled Arthur with the other.

"Your little boy fell in the road, just in front of my horse," she explained. *"But he didn't cry at all, because he told me that 'Papa says little men ought not to cry.'"*

Arthur was a good little man.

Another time, when Arthur was nine, George writes his friend Hardman "to chronicle the sudden and unexpected descent of a small man from a height of 17 feet to the ground. Poor Sons little intended the feat, and therefore performed it satisfactorily. In the crypt here [at Arthur's school], there is a gymnasium, fitted up under a regular professor, who is 5th master, one Reinecke. He did this and that, he went in and out and around and over, and his pupils did the like. Apparently Sons had their emulation violently excited, for while we were all engaged in other wonders, Sons must mount a ladder by himself, and from the top of it make a catch at a pole from whence to slip down naturally. Instead of which he came plump to the floor. I felt him tugging gently at my hand and couldn't make out what was the matter with him. He had come to tell me he felt queer, and 'what he had gone and done.' I took him up and his nerves gave way just a moment (not noisily). Then we rubbed him a bit and discovered him to be sound. He was jolly and ready for fresh adventures in a quarter of an hour: wiser Sons, as we trust. My parental heart beat fast under its mask.''

Arthur was Papa's little man, his brave little man who mustn't cry. How people admired Papa for being so good to Arthur. So brave a man to raise a little boy alone, with only a housekeeper to help, and all the wives of all his friends. Rossetti painted a picture of the sweet little fellow. The beautiful Janet rescued him when he fell from his pony. How brave George Meredith is, they must have said (and have you heard about the mother?). George nobly raised his ''darling little man'' and worked at his writing and at his rising in the world.

Arthur was a little in the way, though. About a year after Mary Ellen's death, Arthur then being nine, George decided it was high time to send him off to school. It is not uncommon for English boys, of course, to be sent away so young. Papa understands that Arthur will not entirely like it; had not he too been put in a school — an awful school at that — when he was a little boy?

Papa understands Arthur. Had not Papa's mother died too when he was a little boy?

George writes to the Reverend Mr. Jessop, headmaster of the school where Arthur will go, in September 1862: ''This is Arthur's character. It is based upon sensitiveness, I am sorry to say. He is healthy, and *therefore* not moody. His nature is chaste: his disposition at *present* passively good. He reflects: and he has real and just ideas. He will not learn readily. He is obedient: brave: sensible. His brain is fine and subtle, not capacious. His blood must move quickly to spur it, and also his heart."

So Arthur was sent to school and doubtless did not cry.

Doubtless, also, Arthur did not cry when he was sent away to the Continent to a cheaper school four years later. Anyway he was now a big "little man" of thirteen. Papa understood his feelings, though, no doubt. Had not Papa too been sent away to Germany to school at the same age? Arthur did not know he was being sent away for life. But Arthur rarely came home any more after this. Papa's new wife Marie didn't much like him, anyway, and there were a new brother and sister, whom he didn't know very well. He felt strange coming home.

George went to visit him in Switzerland in 1871, when Arthur was eighteen. George wrote home that Arthur was "a short man, slightly moustached, having a tuft of whisker; a good walker, a middling clear thinker, sensible, brilliant in nothing, tending in no direction, very near to what I predicted of him as a combatant in life, but with certain reserve qualities of mental vigour which may develop; and though he seems never likely to be intellectually an athlete, one may hope he will be manful. . . . In a competitive examination of fifty he would be about the twenty-fifth." George was always doing this, analyzing poor Arthur's character disapprovingly.

Shortly after this, Arthur's first notable manly act, exhibiting "certain reserve qualities of mental vigour," was to have nothing more to do with George.

How it came about was this: Arthur was feverishly clung to and caressed by the frantic, angry Meredith for two or three years and then, as a child of nine, sent away to school, first nearby, then farther and farther away, to Switzerland, to Germany, and had learned to live there by himself, without father or family. Without complaint. When he was a little boy he had many thoughts about Mama, about a beautiful mother whom he must not mention. Could not talk to Papa about. And when Papa finally allowed him to see Mama it was because she was going to die and then he would not ever see her any more. And he still could not talk of it to Papa, and so he got in the habit of not talking to Papa at all, and he somehow got the notion that Papa did not think too much of him anyway: Papa did not like people who sometimes wanted to cry; Papa seemed to think him very stupid and slow, but he was only silent. He made friends at his schools. He had no home, anyway. He wrote dutiful letters to George, fewer and fewer of them, and received boring, tendentious replies. In one exchange, Arthur has mentioned that he is not a practicing Christian. Of this George intones:

—What you say of our religion is what thoughtful men feel: and that you at the same time can recognize its moral value, is matter of rejoicing to me. The Christian teaching is sound and good: the ecclesiastical dogma is an instance of the poverty of humanity's mind hitherto, and has often in its hideous fangs and claws shown whence we draw our descent. . . . Belief in the religion has done and does this good to the young; it floats them through the perilous sensual period when the animal appetites most need control and transmutation. If you have not the belief, set yourself to love virtue by understanding that it is your best guide both as to what is due to others and what is for your positive personal good. If your mind honestly rejects it, you must call on your mind to supply its place from your own resources. Otherwise you will have only half done your work, and that is always mischievous. Pray attend to my words on this subject. You know

how Socrates loved Truth. Virtue and Truth are one. Look for the truth in everything, and follow it, and you will then be living justly before God. Let nothing flout your sense of a Supreme Being, and be certain that your understanding wavers whenever you chance to doubt that he leads to good. We grow to good as surely as the plant grows to the light. The school has only to look through history for a scientific assurance of it. And do not lose the habit of praying to the unseen Divinity. Prayer for worldly goods is worse than fruitless, but prayer for strength of soul is that passion of the soul which catches the gift it seeks.

Your loving father,
George Meredith

So much for the climate of emotional richness that surrounded little Arthur's formative years. He was nineteen now, and must have wondered what, if any, was the use. He and George do not correspond much, if at all, after this, or see each other for a long time.

"Arthur is coming here today," writes Edith to Henry Wallis. "This is his birthday. He is 21. He has been for some months with Tom Taylor, as tutor to his son but he goes next month into a merchant's house in Havre. He is a queer lad, very small, quiet and very studious. He found it quite impossible to live with the Merediths. I am sorry for the lad. He has been kept so long abroad that he seems to have no idea of home-life, and his affections seem to me never to have been awakened, and there is, I grieve to say, little sympathy between our natures somehow or other. I do not know why I should trouble you with all this. It has run from my pen without the least premeditation."

Arthur was no longer like an Englishman and so he did not come back to England when he left school in Stuttgart. First he went to Le Havre and worked, and then to Lille, where he worked in a linseed warehouse. Arthur had a little money from Mama, or perhaps from the Peacocks or Nicolls, and he took no money from George but made his own way. We do not know what he did with himself when he came home from the linseed warehouse each night. Studied Cicero, perhaps, earnestly as Papa had said to; or maybe he was witty in the French language and went to cafés. Maybe he had a little French girl for a mistress, with whom he lived a *vie de bohème;* or maybe he was always silent, applying himself in the hope that the brain Papa had convinced him was not capacious would expand itself with study. He was a man of twenty-eight now. One day when he coughed a great spurt of blood came out upon his handkerchief and over his shirt front.

He went to London to the doctor — perhaps he was an Englishman at that, heading for English shores at a time of trouble. He did not communicate with George, but a family friend did, and told George that Arthur was ill. George writes to him. He has not seen Arthur for eight years:

Let me know of your present condition immediately, and of how you feel affected, and what you think to be the cause of it. The account of the nature of your work makes me fully commend the wisdom of your decision to quit it and Lille. It would severely tax the strongest. You should have rest for a year. The first thing to consider is the restoration of your physical soundness, and rest in the right sort of atmosphere for you might do much in a few months: — either on our South Coast, or Devon; or if advisable at Davos-platz in the Grisons, where friends of mine of weak lungs have been with profit. Your pride, I hope, will not be offended if I offer to eke out your income during the term of your necessary relapse. You have laboured valiantly and won our respect, and you may well consent to rest for awhile, when that is the best guarantee for your taking up the fight again.

Arthur apparently has formed a life plan which the family friend tells George of. George tells Arthur:

When I was informed of your wishing to throw up your situation at Lille that you might embrace the profession of Literature, I was alarmed. My own mischance in that walk I thought a sufficient warning. But if you come to me I will work with you in my chalet (you will find it a very quiet and pretty study), and we will occupy your leisure to some good purpose. I am allowed the reputation of a tolerable guide in writing and style, and I can certainly help you to produce clear English. You shall share the chalet with me. Here you will be saving instead of wasting money at all events. It will in no way be time lost. After all, with some ability, and a small independence just to keep away the wolf, and a not devouring ambition, Literature is the craft one may most honourably love. I do not say to you, try it. I should say the reverse to anyone. But assuming you to be under the obligation to rest, you might place yourself in my hands here with advantage; and leading a quiet life in good air, you would soon, I trust, feel strength return and discern the bent of your powers. Anything is preferable to that perilous alternation of cold market and hot café at Lille. I had no idea of what you were undergoing, or I would have written to you before. No one better than I from hard privation knows the value of money. But health should not be sacrificed to it. I long greatly to see you. I would at once run over to Lille, if I could spare the time. . . .

In four days time he had Arthur's reply, that the lung hemorrhage had ceased, that he was better, that he was going to the mountains, that he had no need of financial help. George writes him, mostly about George:

. . . the thought of a child of mine having the prospect of life extinguished in his youth, is a cruel anguish. Hitherto my lungs

have worked soundly. — Nothing but the stomach has ever been weak. Unhappily this is a form of weakness that incessant literary composition does not agree with.

And:

We have been long estranged, my dear boy, and I awake from it with a shock that wrings me. The elder should be the first to break through such divisions, for he knows best the tenure and the nature of life. But our last parting gave me the idea that you did not care for me; and further, I am so driven by work that I do not contend with misapprehension of me, or with disregard, but have the habit of taking it from all alike, as a cab-horse takes the whip.

George was right, apparently, that Arthur did not care for him much.

More years passed. Arthur saw Papa occasionally, only occasionally. He lived mostly in Italy, and wrote a few articles for magazines, and worked at a book on English prose style, for which George sent a suggestion now and then. He was ill again in 1886, and had to come to London, and George visited him in the hospital. In 1889 it was clear that his tuberculosis — for of course he had that most typical of nineteenth-century diseases — was far advanced, and he decided to take a voyage to Australia to see if the climate there would help him. For that is what tubercular people did then, they sailed, and sought, and hoped; they were curiously innocent about their fatal maladies. George writes in February 1889 to Edith:

Please read and meditate on this before you speak of it to Arthur. I want you to use your influence in getting him to accept this little sum in part payment of his voyage. Tell him it will be the one pleasure left to me when I think of his going. It may not help much—and yet there is the chance. As I sat chattering yesterday afternoon and noticed how frail he looked, I was pained with apprehension. He may find on the voyage to and fro, that a rather broader margin for expenses will spare some financial reckoning and add to necessary comforts. Tell him that I now receive money from America—and there is promise of increase. And I live so simply that without additions to income I could well afford myself this one pleasure. He will not deny it if he thinks. I apply to you for an aid that must needs be powerful with him; I am sure you are rational; you have been sister and mother to him, you will induce him not to reject from his father what may prove serviceable. As for money—how poor a thing it is! I never put a value on it even in extreme poverty. He has an honourable pride relating to it; touch his heart, that he may not let his pride oppose my happiness—as far as I may have it from such a source as money.

It is not known whether Arthur took the money or not, but he took the voyage, and, it would seem, without George's help, for he went "saloon" class instead of first, and found himself with a "mad inebriate" in his cabin, whom he wrote Edith about.

"When I think of that poor boy with the mad inebriate in his cabin I am taken with rage. It shall be spoken of to the P. & O. But their management depends in part for dividends on the sale of liquor—just as the National Revenue does. Great Britain is on a beer-cask," fumes George.

⁓.

They say a sea voyage sometimes helps. Arthur hoped it would. Rest and a sea voyage and getting away from the English climate.

He hoped it would help. He didn't mind a lonely voyage—he was used to strange places and strange faces. Didn't mind long silences; days without speaking to anyone out loud; he had sometimes spent entire weeks with his thoughts anyway, with no one to talk out loud to.

Anyway, on a ship people would talk to a thin, dying young man wrapped in a robe in his deck chair with the sea air maybe good for him. Kindhearted ladies would remark among themselves that he looked a little improved, perhaps. Someone had a relative who had gone to the Antipodes a dying man and come back quite cured. You never knew. Arthur would be aware of faint solicitude beneath the well-bred reticence of his fellow passengers. They did not know, no doubt, that he was the son of a famous writer in England; perhaps it would surprise them. Perhaps it would interest them. Probably Arthur did not tell them.

Arthur was unlucky in his cabinmate, a violent alcoholic, who frightened Arthur a little, although Arthur understood a little, too, since there are forms and forms of desperation, which the frightened eyes of the quiet, dying young man and the glaring red ones of the "mad inebriate" might, for a second, communicate.

Arthur came back to England in the spring of 1890. He went to Edith's house, where she cared for him; she was very kind; but in September he died. George did not go to his funeral:

My dear Edith,

Will[35] is urgent to keep me away, as the long standing injures me, and I am at the moment oppressed. But I shall come if I feel better tomorrow. Woking is a place where I could wish to lie. Lady Caroline Maxse is there and Fitzhardinge her son, and perhaps

the admiral will choose it. The where is, however, a small matter.
Spirit lives. I am relieved by your report of Arthur's end. To him
it was, one has to say in the grief of things, a release. He has
been, at least, rich above most in the two most devoted of friends,
his sister and her husband. Until my breath goes I shall bless
you both. — As to the terms of the Will, they are fully in accord
with what I should have proposed. Will and Riette have seen
your letter and warmly think the same. They will each have as
much money as young ones need to have — under our present
barbaric system. Know that if you do not see me tomorrow, there
is physical obstacle. Believe me, that my heart is always with
you both and with your little ones.

Arthur left his "estate" of £2,007.18s5d to Edith. We do
not know if, in his last hours, he was comforted by the prospect
of being laid in his grave near such eminent personages as Lady
Caroline Maxse and Fitzhardinge her son.

Poor Peacock had died, calling on the immortal gods to let him
die, so it was clearly enough a merciful release, but now Miss
May was all alone at Lower Halliford. Or maybe Edith stayed
with her there sometimes. May stayed at Lower Halliford always. It was too late for her to marry; she was over forty now.
Papa left her all his money, and the cottages and everything
that he had; the real Peacocks didn't get any of it. Well, she deserved it, taking care of him until the last, all those years, and
never marrying.

And when May died, when she was just sixty, she gave it all
to her real family — her nephew Edward, the innkeeper, and her
brother William, the fisherman, and her other nephews Arthur
and Edgar Upsdill. Perhaps she might have been better off to

have stayed with her family, and might have become the wife of some sturdy fisherman, and, like her real sister, might have had a pair of such sturdy, sweet boys as Arthur and Edgar. Upsdill is a fine name for such rising young men; they will perhaps rise out of their social class into a finer one with Aunt May's money.

It is not known whether May regretted her fine chance in life at the Peacocks' house. It is certain that Edward the innkeeper, and William, and the Upsdill boys thought it swell of Aunt May, who had been so lucky in the world, to do so well by them.

~⁊.

When Mama died, little Edith Nicolls was a nearly grownup girl of almost seventeen and was living at Lower Halliford. After Mama's death, Grandpapa seemed to need her very much. He could scarcely be made to move, he was so sunk in depression. His words and thoughts were bitter and sad, but he was glad Edith was there. He confided in her and allowed her in his library, and she understood that some day her task would be to deal with Grandpapa's papers and writings. Edith did.

We do not hear of her until eight years after Grandpapa's death, when she is engaged on a biography of Grandpapa to preface an edition of his works which she was preparing under the aegis of an old Peacock admirer, Henry Cole. That she should do this, we feel, is only fitting; it is the duty of lesser lives, finding themselves appended to great ones, to set aside personal considerations and write memoirs so that posterity may know in greater detail the immortal words, the cherished anecdotes of its heroes.

Perhaps, at first, Edith stayed at Lower Halliford with May, as maiden ladies did in those days if they had property and were bereaved. But it is probable that the Nicolls stepped in and saw to it that Edith got some experience of London society—she would never meet an eligible husband in Lower Halliford, that was certain, and the time was 1866, when young girls still had above all things to find husbands, and Edith was nearly twenty-two.

Edith ought to have been a most eligible girl. We hope she was pretty, and it is possible that General Sir Edward and Lady Nicolls were able to "do a little something for her" in the financial way, and she had important relatives: the steamship-manufacturing Lairds, for example. Even if she was poor, Edith was genteel, with two famous Grandpas as a dowry, and—we hope—a pretty face.

But we do not hear of her, and she does not marry, and then it is suddenly 1874 and we come upon Edith again, and she is now over thirty, and has not married; she is still Miss Nicolls, so it is nearly up with her. She is writing a life of Grandpapa, as she ought, and the record of this survives in her correspondence with a man by the wonderful name of L'Estrange.

Mr. L'Estrange was an Irish gentleman and a self-appointed inquirer into the affairs of Thomas Love Peacock, whose writing he admired above anybody's. A good thing, too, because he wrote very intrusive letters to ask Peacock biographical questions which Peacock answered, and to which, if he had not, the answers would not be known.

Now of course such a gentleman must be of service to a young lady writer, or even a not-so-young one, and Edith appears to have been grateful for his help—not only because he could tell her things about Grandpapa that she herself had never thought to ask, but because he was a stern critic of her writing, constantly admonishing her to be more interesting, to include anecdotes, to make old Peacock come "alive": "If you suppress or exclude all matters of human interest what value do you attach to your notes?" Edith confided matters to Mr. L'Estrange that were not known before, and he admonished her to include them: "The Disappointment you speak of might explain the querulous tone of the greater part of his prose. Does it do so? From your notes and from your letter I infer Newark Abbey refused him and that then he proposed for the Philosophy of Melancholy. Is this so? If it be so, it is a cardinal point in a life . . . ,'' which Edith ought not to omit. Every Biographer since has been grateful to Mr. L'Estrange, because Edith's memoir, and the notes Cousin Harriet made for Edith to use, have been the foundation for all Peacock biography since, and little has been added.

Certain things troubled Edith — Grandpapa's amours, for example. It was not that she minded his having them, but what was proper to print? Mr. L'Estrange was very judicious: "I do not think we need touch on the second lady unless you see unmistakeable traces of her, which I do not." (Marianne de St. Croix, of whom unmistakable traces would appear in Mrs. Shelley's diary.) Or, "you are quite right to omit that 'thousand and one loves.' Surely of how many millions of young men ought not the same story be told."

In some things Miss Nicolls betrayed a knowledge she should not have had — of the scandalous Shelley circle, for instance. Mr. L'Estrange is shocked: "I am very much obliged to you for making the Shelley mystery clear. . . . That school of philosophy considered — and acted on the consideration — that the appetite which nearly fills our jails with convicts, crowds our cities with beggars, and spreads woe and desolation [dissolution?] into families is the only appetite which is not to be restrained." (The question is whether he is objecting to greed, drink, or sex.) Edith, in any case, had seen a little of the wages of all three.

With Mr. L'Estrange she began a debate that still continues, about Mama's cookery article. Edith remembers that Mama wrote the article at Lower Halliford, in Grandpapa's study, with Grandpapa's suggestions and advice. Mr. L'Estrange refuses to believe it: "If anyone except your Grandfather wrote it your Grandfather must have transferred all his wit and peculiar views to that writer, or your Grandfather must have *rewritten* the article . . . completely" (as the *Odyssey* poet rewrote the *Iliad*). Not too long afterward, Meredith biographers will contend (Meredith having been around at the time it was composed), that *he* must have written most of it. The implication is always that Mama, a woman, could not have done such a clever thing. One wonders if little Edith, at her writing, minded these assertions by Mr. L'Estrange.

So far, what we see of Edith is not what we could have wished for her — she is over thirty, unmarried, portionless, immersed in dead papers and books — but it is more or less what we might have expected. We can imagine her living in New Grub Street and spending time at the British Museum, like someone in a Gissing novel, and occasionally visiting her more prosperous Nicolls relatives in the country. She will wear dark-green bombazine and old bonnets.

But then something turns up in 1875 that must dramatically alter our view of Edith. In that year, we learn, she assumes the principalship of — has perhaps herself established — the National Training School of Cookery. After a moment's consideration this should not surprise us. Or, it surprises us but we see it follows. This forlorn Orphan, Edith, has not escaped drawing conclusions from the many strange and sobering sights she had seen around Lower Halliford, at Seaford, in odd and dingy lodgings with Mama and George Meredith; at the Nicolls's at Blackheath. Edith had kept her eyes open. There, on the one hand, was adopted Aunt May, rocking idly and thinking her not-very-complicated thoughts alone in Lower Halliford. So much for a life of devotion. And, on the other hand, there was Mama, with her writing and her passion and restlessness, her strong desire for freedom, and her tears. Mama: such a pariah that you could not convince a respectable man like Mr. Vulliamy that she could possibly have been received into her home again, or that she could possibly have written anything by herself. And men like Mr. L'Estrange, kind but patronizing, who did not take you seriously if you were female, and to whom you had to send things to be translated if they were in Greek or Latin, since no one thought you needed to learn such things.

And what would a sensible girl with her eyes open conclude from all this? That a woman had better get herself secure in something, some work to assure her independence, and she had better not get mixed up with men, either, until she had. And that the world was a very hard place full of hard people, and you had to defend, to defend, and to be clever, and to see your chance, and to get ahead, like a man.

Fortunately, little Edith had learned a lot about cookery from Mama and Grandpapa, who were forever discussing it and observing that they were living in a nation where no one could cook so much as a mutton chop decently, and where people were starving — literally starving — because of their insular food prejudices, and ignorance of proper cookery, and their notion that they would rather die than eat like a Frenchman or a Turk.

But Edith had learned better, and had a book of recipes besides, and a reverence inherited from Grandpapa and Mama for fine cookery,[36] scientific cookery, and a knowledge of these, and a missionary zeal for imparting what she knew to others — and she had ambition and a strong need to save little Edith.

So she became an Expert and a Principal, and then, in 1876, when she was secure, she married a Charles Clarke from the India Office — perhaps someone she had known a long time. And they had three daughters. But Edith went on being remarkable and peculiar for a Victorian woman; she continued her career. She was head of her cooking school until she was seventy-five, "the pioneer of Domestic Subjects Training" for girls in school — this being rather like home economics in America. And she wrote cookbooks: *Plain Cookery, Fancy Cookery, High-Class Cookery, Work-house Cookery;* these went into many editions, so she did all right by them, and a lot of good by them too. And she was given a gold medal from the Royal Society of the Arts — conferring upon cookery a status it had theretofore lacked in England, and was given (for some reason) a tea set by the Committee of the Fisheries. And she was made a Member of the British Empire, so that she could always put initials after her name, Edith Nicolls Clarke, M.B.E. And all her life Edith often thought of Mama, and what could happen to a woman, no matter how brilliant and energetic, if she was just a little unlucky.

The Baby Harold—Felix—was too young to remember, only three when Mama died, but when he was bigger he would look at the little clothes she had sewed him and that Papa had laid away in a trunk, and at the tiny envelope addressed to him in her own hand, with a lock of her hair in it. Harold loved his nurse Mrs. Bennet almost as well as he might have loved a mama, and he loved Dottie Bennet and Auntie and Joy Farm near Birkenhead, where they lived, and there were roosters and two pug dogs and ever so many other things. It was a great comfort to Henry that Harold was so well taken care of; Mrs. Bennet was a sensible woman who let Henry know what Baby needed: "I am going to ask you if you would be so kind as to see if you can get for me a good collection of the old fashioned English nursery stories, not put into modern dress. I do not wish to have any German mixture, but simply such tales as Jack the Giant Killer, Tom Thumb . . . Jack and The Beanstalk which is Harold's favorite—so far as I can tell it to him, but unfortunately I always stick fast in the middle for want of memory. I do not want expensive binding or illustrations."

How Harold got on was a matter of some anxiety, for he was a delicate little boy, very blond and fragile-looking. Henry was afraid he might take after the delicate Peacocks, though he rather resembled his grandfather Thomas Love, who was a robust old man still. To be safe, Henry took Harold out of England each winter—in 1861 and 1862 to Capri, where he had taken Mary Ellen; Henry was still convinced that Capri was good for you. In 1863, they went to Rome instead, and it was cold; Henry writes his own Mama that "some of the fountains with figures of Tritons and Neptunes etc. presented rather a curious appearance, being quite draped in ice with icicles hanging from their arms and legs, which amused Harold immensely. I put him in extra flannels and he seems to have got on very well." In another letter Harold is "Pretty well"; but not quite equal to the previous winter in milder Capri. They plan to be back for the English spring.

Harold seems, like his half-brother Arthur, to have been interested in philology; when he was but five, Henry reports of him that "he is very fond of acquiring languages. I think I shall let him begin German. He has been trying his hand on Greek lately—the joke against him is that he begins a fresh language every day."

Harold and Arthur had other boyhood similarities; like most boys, for instance, they were both afflicted with measles. Mary Ellen, being dead, was spared the nursing of her two little boys through that disease, but the two fathers had to cope. Arthur was with George. George writes to a friend for advice:

Dear Tuck,

Little man has got measles coming out.

Now, may I trouble you to send me globule bottles of Puls: and any other medicine necessary; stating what to be given during the dort of fever etc.

And later:

Dearest Tuck,

Your medicines and directions came opportunely, deciding me not to send for Izod. Sons are as a mulberry in the shade. They are spotted like the pard. They are hot as boiled cod in a napkin. They care for nothing but barley-water, which I find myself administering at all hours of the night, and think it tolerable bliss, and just worth living for, to suck an orange. I am sorry to say they have a rather troublesome cough. Otherwise all goes well.

Harold, now always called Felix, was staying with his grandmama Wallis. Henry writes from London:

My dear Mother,

I was sorry to hear Felix is no better. If it is measels I suppose you had better let the doctor see him. I do not think it is necessary to give medicine for measels or only something very simple.

Write and let me know how he comes on. Give him my love &
kisses & tell him I hope to hear that he is patient I shall come &
see him the first opportunity.

George is cleverer but Henry is more truly kind, which may have
been the way Mary Ellen saw it too.

SANGER'S GREAT HIPPODROME

AUG. 16

THE PROPRIETERS HAVE, AT AN UNHEARD-OF OUTLAY,
PURCHASED ONE OF THE MOST GIGANTIC

TRAINED ELEPHANTS

EVER SEEN IN EUROPE. THE NOBLE ANIMAL IS
THE MOST DOCILE OF ITS SPECIES, AND WILL APPEAR
AT EACH REPRESENTATION IN ITS WONDERFUL
AND (FOR ITS HUGE SIZE)

ELEPHANTINE PERFORMANCE,

WHICH MUST BE SEEN TO BE CREDITED.

Sometimes Henry takes Felix to the circus.

Felix was somewhat more fortunate than Arthur in the matter of
schools. When it was time for him to begin instruction, Henry
put him in the care of a Reverend Mr. Wicksteed and his wife, a
concerned and kindly couple who kept a small school for six
children. Henry seems at one time to have contemplated a

French school for him, and immediately incurred a torrent of pedagogical advice, first from Mrs. Wicksteed:

June 29, 1867

My dear Sir,

We have had a nice note from Felix this morning telling us of his safe arrival in Chester. I enclose it for your edification. He left us well and happy yesterday. Indeed contrasting his delicacy, and your anxiety about him when he first came to us with the present, we have all great reason to be thankful for his increased robustness, and soundness of constitution. The last half-year he has particularly developed in physical power and bearing, and in those moral qualities which are the most sympathetic with these. I used to observe with some pain and more puzzlement a certain shrinking, frightened look about him — as if he were expecting a blow — and a suspicious and guarded out-look of the eyes, of a self-protecting and untrusting character. I never could account for it, as he had never been exposed to anything anywhere that I could make out to cause or explain. But as the older boys have gone, and younger ones succeeded (altogether of our present six, he is still the youngest but one) he has blossomed out into an increased confidence and courage — speaking in a more assured and manly manner — holding his own better and altogether taking a more individual and independent position. This has been accompanied also by more kindness in his behavior to his schoolfellows, and more confidence and affection in his bearing towards our school. I think possibly that having beat about a good deal, and having been mostly with older people, he has naturally fallen into some want of that hearty unreserve and unshrinking sense of equality and security, which now that he is thrown among boys not sensibly much older than himself, he seems to be acquiring, to the great gain of his [?] and happiness. I think the present is rather a turning point with him, and I should be sorry to see this process, which I consider particularly salutary for him, interrupted too suddenly. It may be indeed and I should not much wonder at making the discovery any month, that the work is done, and that he may be becoming a little too cocky for a young set — or for ladies' management — inclined to rebelliousness. In such case a change would be unquestionably desirable for him. But are you quite sure of the effect of a French School at his very early age? The result of a rather lengthened observation and experience in reference to my own and my friends' children is to incline me to defer a superinduced foreign education, whether in France or in Germany — to a later age, say 16 or 17. If a great deal earlier before a thoroughly English schooling and training are completed, I have sometimes noticed a kind of mongrel result — confusion of knowledge, and even a confusion of tongues. Each nation has its own character and characteristics, and I think such a question always involves the question of a boy's nationality. His history, his geography, his very arithmetic, his politics, his manners, his religion, his sympathies, his form and scheme of life, his Latin and Greek — all take a mixed, individual and confused form — which sometimes even reflects itself in his mind and pursuits. When on the basis of a clear, firm, national foundation the larger superstructure and wider sympathies of study and intercourse in other countries is added — the effect is purely accretive — enlarging and enriching, like a handsome house on a grand foundation. But before that foundation has been much laid, I think weakness, vacillating, uncertainty, confusion and want of strong leanings and preferences (of a kind in harmony with original natural inherited and national antecedent instincts and tendencies) are apt to manifest themselves.

I am afraid you will think I am losing any ideas I may have in a multitude of words. But I feel very anxious my dear Mr. Wallis, as you have confided your dear and beautiful little boy to my care, to be as frank with you and as helpful to you in forming a judgement of what is best for him as I can be. . . .

⌒⌒.

Felix had left school for the holiday and was visiting a Mrs. Smith, to whom the confused parent sent Mrs. Wicksteed's letter. Mrs. Smith feels that although she

cannot judge on some of the points she speaks of I cannot but feel inclined to fear that Felix is not strong enough, or independent enough yet, to enable him to bear roughing it, at a foreign school—the School Mrs. Bennet mentioned to you, I know more particulars of than she did when she spoke to you; two of Dottie's young Uncles went there—the eldest who from a little fellow was very forward, manly and independent got through all well, suffering but little—he was there 2 or 3 years. But when he came back tho' a good French scholar and trained somewhat like a soldier—he was obliged to go to school to rub up his English and fit himself for his uncle's office. The younger, Lyell, was of a very different disposition and suffered very much bodily and mentally—he was so ill that he would scarcely have recovered had there not been a lady at the place to whom he was known and she had him at her house and he gradually recovered—he was there only one year—There are 300 boys at this school—and the arrangements and discipline are good— but not such as such boys of at all delicate constitutions—or such as cannot make their own way in the world—no home comforts.

Poor little Arthur Meredith was already placed at such a school. Henry continued to investigate the problem of schools, and sends a copy of Matthew Arnold's report on schools to the Wicksteeds. Now Henry rather inclines, through his reading, that Felix should go to a German school. A Matilda Lufton, one of the teachers, enters the fray:

I feel very glad that you should have decided on Germany in preference to France, but do you really think that English boys or indeed any boys are benefited by a foreign education commenced so early. I mean before 16 or 17? My impression was the contrary. I know I have heard that the greatest scapegraces in the German schools are the English boys, and I, perhaps somewhat luckily [?] took it for an axiom that boys were better for the control that the public opinion of their own country exercises on them. I have fancied that I perceived in children brought up abroad a sort of homeless feeling. They do not regard the feelings or opinions of those among whom they live, and they are too far from their own country to feel it home, and when they return, often seem more aliens than many foreigners.

This is rather Edith's comment on Arthur, when he returned to her in 1874, after eight years in a foreign school.

Eventually, Felix went to London University School in England, and was not exposed to the rigors of a foreign education at all, but he accompanied Henry on his many travels, and so it must be supposed that he had the advantages of foreign "culture" nonetheless. He received the third certificate in his class in French, and the eighth in his class in English. But only the fourteenth, we are sorry to see, in mathematics, which suggests that he may have inherited more from the artists in his lineage than from the businessmen, though a businessman he would be.

Whether Felix grew up to be like his Mama, or his Grandpapa, or his Papa, it is impossible to say. An old solicitor at the firm that always took care of Henry's business remembers that he was a "tall thin man who always appeared to wear a long black cloak." Just before his twentieth birthday he entered the Bank of England and there worked with distinction, whatever working with distinction in a bank may involve, as Manager of the Dividend Department, for more than forty years, and received a table service when he retired. He was happier than Papa, or Arthur, or so it may be hoped, in that he married a pretty girl named Alice and had two children. Now they are all dead.

Henry Wallis was a good fellow. He had a lot of friends. Henry had wanted to become a great painter. He had studied hard at the Royal Academy and at Cary's Academy of Art, and in Paris at Gleyre's Atelier and at the Académie des Beaux-Arts. He had done patient, beautiful drawings of all the statues in the Louvre, to perfect his knowledge of anatomy, and drawn from models, and learned to use charcoal, the pencil, watercolor, oil. He had learned to paint in the Pre-Raphaelite manner, so beautifully clear, fine as a photograph, radiant with feeling, with the sort of patient passion it took in those days to paint in that manner. It was Henry who painted *The Death of Chatterton* and *The Dead Stonebreaker,* famous paintings, and everyone thought he would become the equal of Hunt or Millais. But somehow he did not.

After Mary Ellen's death, Henry took to wandering, ostensibly to paint. Did paint; sent his fine little canvases back to England for the Royal Academy shows each year for another twenty years, nearly. But fewer and fewer of them. Partly it was that he had never repeated his *Chatterton* and *Stonebreaker* successes. Needed England perhaps, and fellowship, and the encouragement of a pretty and devoted woman. And he was never elected to the Royal Academy, a disappointment; one of those uncomfortable ambivalences lurking deep at heart. Henry did not believe in the R. A.—exclusive, conservative, a silly club that kept talented unconventional painters out; foolish snobs; a legion of untalented painters whose works do not hang in the Tate today. Holman Hunt and Dante Rossetti were never R. A. But Henry would have liked to belong. Anyone would.

Partly, Henry was not successful because he got absorbed in his wanderings. Things caught his eye, all sorts of things: a fragment of Titian's canvas, leaves of a fine old Koran; "I bought a few days ago some old lace that you would enjoy immensely. It has been part of altar clothes. I think the pattern is wonderfully rich. It was at an old shop in the Jews quarter. I saw at the same time some net would do for collars but was not sure it was genuine. I will ask some lady about it and if good will buy you some. I picked up some bits of old silk brocade with silver worked in it, and a large piece of tapestry enough to cover the side of a room for 12," he writes to his mother from Rome in 1863.

He liked beautiful bits of things and he liked to observe foreign customs in strange places: "On Christmas Eve I went to the Sistine Chapel in the evening. Men are obliged to go in evening dress and the ladies in black with veils of the same color. There was a grand mass at which a lot of cardinals attended, who looked very picturesque in their red silk dresses. They evidently found the ceremony wearisome as they yawned a good deal. It was curious that the congregation were Protestants, being nearly all English."

He began more and more to spend his time making watercolor sketches of old buildings, like the perfect English traveler: "Your drawing in the last Old Water Colour [exhibition] was of a favorite facade of mine," Holman Hunt writes him, "but I don't know how you escaped the bad odour in the opposite mosque. Edith nearly got her death there."

Henry continued to exhibit at the Royal Society of Painters in Water Colours, of which he was a member, and he began to draw pictures of the beautiful ceramic vases and tiles he saw in foreign museums, and to collect pots and fragments of pots for himself. As he did so he became increasingly interested in the romance of these pots; old glazes, traditional designs; the meaning of the forms. His taste was perfect; he had money and could travel; he began to learn more about pottery, and to think more about pottery. His was the good Victorian's fascination with the archaeological and the artist's fascination with exquisite craft.

Pottery finally preoccupied him altogether, and, as his old friend Albert Van de Put of the Victoria and Albert Museum wrote of him in a memorial pamphlet, he ultimately became "a prominent personality, whose memory will be cherished for its embodiment of sterling qualities with a rare knowledge and experience of the ceramics of Southern Europe." About these he wrote some seventeen books and articles, and "none more enlightening or beguilingly suggestive are likely to be written than the series of volumes, mostly in themselves artistic productions, which are Mr. Wallis's tribute to the potter's art. Everywhere peeps out the wisdom begotten of pilgrimages to little known museums, in quiet old cities: of the quest-ceramic pursued between Berlin and Bitonto, and from Sèvres to Fostât, sketch-book in hand; of discussions with *conservatori;* and of arguments with all and sundry: *canonici, sacristani, ciceroni, Fellâhîn.* Mr. Wallis's real knowledge of ceramics in certain departments would have equipped two or three professed archaeologists to treat thereof with greater appearance of learning, but with the dryness still supposed, in certain quarters, proper to the exposition of all manifestations whatsoever of art or science."

And so on. Henry: traveling alone, sketchbook in hand, until he was over eighty. Little letters from Mary Meredith tucked away in a trunk at home, with her parasols, where he could always look at them.

And though he had his little sketch of her, and he had Felix, who resembled her, no doubt as the years—fifty, sixty years— went by, it became harder and harder to remember what she had looked like. For company in those foreign places, Egypt, Italy, he had *canonici, conservatori, ciceroni, sacristani, Fellâhîn;* but whether, ever, of another pretty woman, we cannot say.

⌐⌐.

His friendship with the Pre-Raphaelites and other painters of his day continued undiminished throughout his and their lives, and is recorded by scraps of correspondence here and there. They are all busy with painting. In 1867 Henry wants to borrow a suit of armor from William Morris—Morris can't remember but he thinks Hughes has it, and Henry can get it from him— "only fisticuffs to be avoided, it is not respectable; and you can't expect that any body who has had my armour for say 8 years can think it belongs to any body except himself."

In 1871 Henry is planning a picture of Shelley, in whom he has always been interested; he had been given some of the hair from Shelley's head by Peacock, and has given two hairs of this to William Michael Rossetti, who has lost them. Dante Gabriel Rossetti thinks that Robert Browning has a bust of Shelley that Henry could use as a model, and writes to Browning, who says that Henry may come and see it any time. "I remember I made some rough sketches myself for a picture of it, which I projected calling 'Percy Bysshe Shelley. Cor Cordium,' followed by the quoted incident," Rossetti says. This, or another time, Rossetti writes that he is in "consternation at the state in which I hear the bust has reached you. I am quite confident that . . . I gave full directions for the thing to be sent on to you and at any other time should have remembered to inquire again if it had been done but was in a confused state of mind just then." Henry must have known about Gabriel's confused states of mind.

For another painting, subject unknown, Algernon Swinburne suggests Henry ask Burne-Jones for his memories. Burne-Jones replies, "I should be very glad to be of any help, but Swinburne has surely much overestimated my knowledge, though not my interest in the subject—I greatly question if I can be of any good to you, but if you will tell me when you shall be in I will come and talk it over and see more exactly what you mean. If one had a perfect memory of what struck one's imagination most as a child, doubtless that would [be] a good direction to work in, but unfortunately for any help in this way I had the stupidest of infancies and childhood, and don't think I was taught or told anything but Hymns — how the word makes one creep." Henry missed finding Burne-Jones at home and Burne-Jones was "aggravated to find your card the other night and to think that the only night you had come to see me for a year I should be dissipating at Rouge et Noir — it was at the Lyceum and very harmless, and I must say you had your revenge for any annoyance the journey out here cost you."

William Michael Rossetti introduces Henry to Baron Kirk [?]. Henry introduces someone named Hotchkiss to Holman Hunt, who has promised to look at Hotchkiss's sketches and help him. A physician in Moorgate Street writes to Henry agreeing to see without charge another of Henry's friends, an American painter, and adds that "at any time I shall be very happy to see without Fee, any poor artists whom you may send to me." They are all very kind to one another.

Holman Hunt wonders if Henry may have an Egyptian scarf like one he had begun to use in a portrait and which had been stolen:[37] "It was of substantial silk — which the silk in Oriental shops are not now — it was about 7 feet long and 2 feet broad at either end was an extent of about 20 inches with stripes of hyacinth color 1–1/2 inch wide 3 or 4 inches apart and between these were bars of gold color half an inch wide (not gold fibre) the body of the scarf was of a delicate pink tint, formed by a shot of whiter woof upon a sort of strawberry cream warp: in the middle space there was no pattern." Another friend supplies it in time.

How very 1890's these men are now, with their exquisitely developed aesthetic sensibilities. They had grown with the times. Or, perhaps, the times had grown with them, for had they not begun all this fifty years before?

Henry, the father of one of Peacock's grandchildren, seems to have kept up with Peacock family affairs; and they seem to have regarded him most cordially. There are a few records of the acquaintance. It is to Wallis that James Hanway writes in 1866, after his article on Peacock in the *North British Review,* that he hopes "Peacock's people and his friend Howes were satisfied with the line I took about him. . . ." In 1874 Edith writes "to ask you a favour, which is this, have you any Photo, or likeness of my Mother which you will give to me? I have no likeness of any kind of her and I much desire to get one. I understand that the miniature of her taken as a girl with long curls, was given either to you or Harold by Mary Anne Rosewell; this should surely have come to me as it was painted for my Father at the same time that one was painted of him for Mamma, this latter I have. If you or Harold object to give me that miniature, then will you please lend it to me that I may have a copy made of it? when I will faithfully return it to you again." And she asks also for a photo of her brother Harold. In 1906 Henry writes to Felix that he has given some advice to Edith in the matter of a Peacock manuscript which was being auctioned and which Edith felt to be hers: "As to the MS of *The Last Day of Windsor Forest* I have suggested to her that if she thinks she can claim a lien on it she might ask the auctioneer to withdraw it, but I don't suppose she will. I have asked Quaritch if he can buy it for me for a low sum to do so."

Edith's daughter, Mrs. Hall Thorpe, remembered old Henry Wallis coming to call on her mother as late as 1911.

One of Henry's worthy projects was to be honorary secretary of a committee for the preservation of St. Marks in Venice in

1880. In this he seems to have been joined by another en-
thusiast, William Morris, who writes rather crossly, "I understood when I saw you last that we were to meet here at 1/2 past
4 today; so I came; but after waiting til 1/4 past 5 concluded
thare [sic] must be some mistake." But Morris has good news
about the committee: "Ruskin written to by Jones has tele-
graphed to say that he joins; Burne-Jones joins . . . Civil note
from the American legation on Lowell's part accepting. Also
from Mark Pattison, Rector of Lincoln College in Oxford accepting."

Beside Morris, Henry has letters from such various figures
as Turgenev, and Charles Eliot Norton, who adds a postscript:
"May I ask you to see that, in future issues of the statement, my
initials are given correctly?" Norton suggests Henry ask William
Wadsworth Longfellow, but Longfellow declines on the grounds
that "anything that looks like foreign interference will do more
harm than good with the sensitive Italians." They, or something,
seem to have succeeded in preserving St. Marks anyhow.

~~?.

Throughout their lives these men assist one another's little
projects. Henry has for a long time been interested in ceramics.
Eyre Crowe writes that he has done as Henry asked in looking
at some pottery at Alwick Castle near Aberdeen. He sends some
sketches and asks about Felix. Henry sends a scrap of Titian's
canvas to Sir John Gilbert, in case the paint and the ground and
grain of the canvas would interest him. The great archaeologist
W. M. Flinders Petrie writes from Cairo that a dealer there is
selling a "fine Rameses II green brick" and some other things
he thinks Henry would be interested in, and offers to have them
shipped back with his own things. Poor old William Bell Scott
writes "to my old friend Henry Wallis" that he is at last giving

up the lease of his Chelsea house and selling off some things, "and if you want the little early Italian pots you once called to see or anything else I advise you to go" to the sale. "There are a number of Hispano: Moros if you still collect such, and a remarkable Majolica platter with the subject of Jupiter and Juno in an interesting position (not improper) on it." "The Hispano Mooresque Water vessel I have presented to the SK Museum. I expect things will go dirt cheap. All my Nankin [?] ware will go with the rest and the wine in the cellar, among wch is 3 or 4 dozen very old Port, really regretted by me, but impossible to send down here."

William Bell Scott is old. They are all old now. The nineteenth century draws to a close.[38] George Meredith has become the most famous author of his day.

George Meredith as he grew old got deaf. As Henry got old, it is said, he got "difficult." But to him it seemed that the world had gotten difficult. War threatened. Automobiles were everywhere, and more soot than ever, crowds and violence. Once an ardent democrat, Henry now wonders about Democracy. He writes to Felix, when he is over eighty: "It appears we are returning to a state of barbarism, and encouraged thereto by the present government. I am inclined to agree with those who say that constitutional govt. has become such a squalid farce that the only remedy is the government of the strong man—cld. he only be found! But he must be something different than the cackling Kaiser, who is what Carlyle wld have called a *simulacrum*."

On Christmas day, 1914, the world was well embarked on the most grotesque madness of its history (until then). Henry is eighty-four now and doesn't much leave home:

My dear Felix,

Thanks for your good wishes, and the same to Alice and Violet.
But with all this savagery going on it seems rather a mockery to talk of the Christmastide as it was understood in the days of Charles Dickens?

Now only a few can remember the days of Charles Dickens. Henry and one or two of his friends are left, that is all. They are all old. Peter Daniel is nearly ninety, poor fellow, and cannot move, he is so weak and crippled. George Meredith has been dead for a decade; Mary Ellen for half a century.

Henry had been a disciple of the Pre-Raphaelites and their friends, Arthur Hughes and Brett and Seddon. In the 1850's there had been the Hogarth Club—Henry and Swinburne, Burne-Jones, Morris, and F. G. Stephens as secretary.

But now, half a century later, Arthur Hughes writes Henry:

My Dear Wallis

I am laid up on my last illness—and so despairing at leaving my dear people in dire want and trouble (all from my want of care and dutifulness) that I try to think among the old pictures I have—there might be one that you remember with favour, such as Botticelli "Calumny" old copy—or the St. Jerome I lent the Burlington Club—reproduced in Burlington Magazine—Do you think at a modest price you could add such to your collection?

Affectionately yours
Arthur Hughes

And, when Henry replied a few days later,

Alas and Yes it was this Hughes who wrote the dismal letter.
How to thank you I hardly know, for the kind thought.
I am awfully sorrowful and I am very sorrowful too by the
evidently diminished sight as shown by your writing. but you
have done supreme work with those eyes — and I hope there are
loving other eyes to read to you about you at hand.
This is only to thank and acknowledge this mornings letter

Affectionately yours,
Arthur Hughes

Hughes's letters are dated November 1915, to an eighty-five-year-old Wallis, who takes a fall shortly thereafter, and cannot answer a letter from another old friend, Peter Austin Daniel, who is eighty-eight. Hughes was right about Henry's sight, which had failed so that his writing was a mere scrawl, and this apparently embarrassed him. In his last letters he always apologized for being illegible and would add "in haste," as if to explain it.

In the year of his death, Sir Laurence Alma-Tadema writes to Henry: "It was truly nice to receive your wishes on my birthday; I felt much gratified. One loses so many friends who depart for ever that those who remain are somehow doubly precious especially when life feeds principally on recollections."

F. G. Stephens is dead, even his son Holly is old now, who writes that Henry and Felix are his oldest friends alive.

1916. The world is still full of the sound of gunfire and bombs, and women wear drab dresses, and it is Christmas eve of 1916. But Henry hears neither gunfire nor bells.

Old Peter Daniel is writing to Felix:

The death of your dear Father on the 20th instant ends for me a long life of intimacy and friendship; I first made his acquaintance on the benches of the Classical school of the Royal Academy, and on Saturday, 23rd Dec. I reached my 90th year. He was a few years my junior, tho' as a distinguished man he was always my senior and I always looked on him as such. In fact I felt distinguished by his recognition of me.

I regret therefore that I cannot be present at the last sad scene to do honour to his memory. For years now bodily weakness will not permit me to venture into the streets or even into our little garden.

They put Henry in Highgate Cemetery, grave number 19216, SQ 109, which grave to be maintained for the cost of 10/6 yearly payable to the London Cemetery Company; but costs have gone up since then, and the London Cemetery perhaps does not even know, any more, where to send the bill.

After his death, museum officials fell into squabbles about his possessions. Sir C. Hercules Read, Keeper of the British Museum, writes to Felix:

Dear Mr. Wallis,

. . . I was a little surprised, though I had no cause to complain, that I had heard nothing of his death. As I dare say you are aware, I was a very old friend, of something near to forty years' standing, and I think he confided in me as much as he did in any-

one. I knew, moreover, that at the time of his death he had a good number of things in his possession that he would have liked to remain in this country, if possible. This made me anxious to know what was likely to become of this branch of his estate. . . .

And Bernard Rackham of the South Kensington (or Victoria and Albert) Museum by the following September, is writing crossly to Sir Hercules:

27th September, 1918.

Dear Sir Hercules,

. . . I understood from Hobson that the fine turquoise vase with black inscriptions from Rakka (fig. 8. in "the Oriental Influence") is one that you would be glad to have for the British Museum. It is also a thing I should like to see kept here, but it is not essential to us, as we have already fairly good pieces of that type. The blue and white hexagonal vase, on the other hand, I feel to be highly desirable for us to exhibit side by side with our panels of hexagonal tile from the Great Mosque in Damascus, many of which came to us through Henry Wallis several years ago. It also has a great value, as a splendid type of industrial art, from the special point of view of this Museum. There are further reasons I should like to put before you which, may I say candidly, in my opinion strengthen our claim to this vase. . . .

I hope therefore you will not mind if he sells us the blue and white vase. We should in return be willing (the Director agrees to this) to waive our claim to the turquoise vase from Rakka.

Yours sincerely
Bernard Rackham

They are all dead now—all the Peacocks, all the Merediths. Mary Ellen's little boys, Arthur and Harold, and their sister Edith, and George Meredith, and Henry Wallis and Edward Nicolls, and all their children, and all the people they knew. And Sir C. Hercules Read, and Bernard Rackham, too. Hands that held needles, paintbrushes, pens. The potter who drew, with a fine brush, across the face of the handsome majolica platter he has made, the smiling gods at their earthly pleasures.

The books by George Meredith in fine bindings line shelves. In the cupboard in a velvet case lies a drawing from the hand of another young lover, of a beautiful, large-eyed woman smiling a little, demure in her bonnet. Perhaps the artist is saying something that causes her to forget, for a moment, some bitter things she has learned. His enamored pencil does not catch, perhaps, a certain fated expression in her eyes. Kisses, from whomever, have left no imprint on the pretty lips. The young lover sees only his own kisses there. She will die soon. He will grow old. All this is more than a hundred years ago now. "Earthly love speedily becomes unmindful but love from heaven is mindful for ever more," it was to have said on her tombstone. No one knows where her grave is now.

Painters, writers, potters—all are dead. The greater lives along with the lesser. Things remain. Mary Ellen's pink parasol lies in a trunk in a parlor in Purley. Henry's drawings lie in the boxroom upstairs. Henry's little painting of George as Chatterton hangs in the Tate Gallery, properly humidified. The hair from Shelley's head that Peacock gave to Henry, hair from the sacred head of Shelley, Henry had put into a little ring, and people always kept it safe, but thieves broke into the house in Purley a year or two ago and stole it, and who can say where it is now? The turquoise vase from Rakka is safe in the museum; but I don't know what happened to the majolica platter.

NOTES

BRIEF LIVES

A LIST OF MANUSCRIPTS USED

SELECTED BIBLIOGRAPHY

NOTES

1. Holman Hunt remembers her as a "dashing horsewoman" in his memoirs. Sir Edmund Hornby says, in his *Autobiography*, "there are only three poets whose poetry I can appreciate, and they are Pope, Dryden, and Oliver Goldsmith. Tennyson, Swinburne, Morris & Co. I simply do not understand. Perhaps Mrs. Meredith, the wife of George Meredith, was right when she declared I had a 'Manchester mind.'" Clodd says in his *Memories* that those "who knew her say she was charming, with intellectual gifts far above the average."

2. The belongings described here were carefully kept by Henry Wallis after Mary Ellen's death. *Fireside Reverie*, like many of Wallis's important paintings, seems to have disappeared.

3. We are so used to the paradigm of family conflict in the modern family—conservative parents and radical children—that it is hard for us to remember that in the mid-nineteenth century the situation was almost exactly reversed. That is, the hard-working, serious, earnest, increasingly proper young people must have sometimes been scandalized by the wicked and irreverent older generation, with its eighteenth-century heritage of individualism, atheism, freedom, and defiance. The Victorian Mr. L'Estrange, for example, wrote to Peacock's granddaughter in 1875 that Peacock's dear old friends, "the Shelley group were 'a rum lot,'" and that old T. J. Hogg was one of the "monsters of the male sex." "But let these riff-raff rest." What the granddaughter, Edith Nicolls, thought, who had been bounced on the knees of this kindly riff-raff, is not recorded. It is easy to see Mary Ellen having more in common with them than with her own generation—being born too late, perhaps, rather than having been born too early, though in many ways she was a modern woman. Her conflict with George Meredith,

then, can be seen as a conflict between eighteenth- and nineteenth-century modes of life, whose tragic outcome ironically had the effect, via Meredith's novels, of in some degree influencing social theory to return to values that she would have found more comprehensible.

4. This obituary of Mrs. Love is printed in K. N. Cameron's *Shelley and His Circle* (Cambridge, Massachusetts, 1961), vol. 1, pp. 284–5. The same volume also contains Dr. Eleanor Nicholes's useful short biography of Peacock, to which, together with Edith Nicolls's "Biographical Notice" in the Cole edition (1875), and the "Biographical Introduction" in the Halliford edition (1924–34) of Peacock's works, I am chiefly indebted for details of Peacock's life. The principal biography of Meredith is Lionel Stevenson's *The Ordeal of George Meredith*. Because all of these biographies are standard and easily available, I have not burdened the text with specific sources.

I do refer in the text, however, to a hypothetical composite figure, the Biographer, who is responsible for handing down traditional biographical information. Without meaning to impugn individual real biographers, I am sometimes severe upon the Biographer, for he is the purveyor of received attitudes and accepted traditions that often turn out to be misinformed or even willfully benighted. This is usually a function of his imprisonment in a curious set of Victorian attitudes, which seems to plague modern biographers as well as Victorian ones.

5. Here, for instance, the Biographer is actually Mr. L'Estrange, mentioned above, and to whom we will return later.

6. We might ask here what, if any, are the special problems and responsibilities of the Biographer? Biographies of literary figures seem fraught with special perils because they do have an obligation to literary criticism. Some literary critics would deny this; in an effort to avoid the obvious pitfalls of the "biographical fallacy" and its tendency to make facile connections, especially reductivist, Freudian ones, criticism has exerted a great deal of effort to develop ways of looking at literature and leaving the writer out of it. Biographers of literary figures have often erred in the opposite direction, revealing that at such-and-such a time the writer was engaged in such-and-such a work, without imagining that there was much connection between that work and the writer's ongoing life experiences, except when the subject matter of the work is too autobiographical to be ignored – as in Meredith's *Modern Love*. But this is wrong, and Mr. L'Estrange (see pages 166–8 above) was on the

right track when he inquired of Edith Nicolls whether "the Disappointment you speak of might explain the querulous tone of the greater part of his [Peacock's] prose. Does it do so?" Very likely. Disappointments affect tone. The people the writer knows may affect or alter the controlling themes and metaphors of his works. That they do so is really the ultimate reason for concerning ourselves with the lives of writers at all, and would be the ultimate justification for books such as this one.

Admittedly, the present work carries the assumption about the relation of the writer and his work to its logical extreme by using literary works to comment upon lives with no qualifying commentary at all. This can be more easily justified on artistic grounds than as sound biographical methodology. Literary works are reality digested, not transcribed. But this work, really, has an axe to grind in the service of the Lesser Lives, and I have been more concerned to attend to its coherence as a work of art. I shall refer to biography considered as art, specifically fictional art, presently.

This is partly just an argument for attention by literary critics to what Frederick Crews has aptly called "a sense of historical dynamics," or, more simply, plain sense about the realities of human nature and human experience, which must shape literary works. Literary critics are often colossally insensitive to even the most ordinary considerations — let us say chronological and spatial ones; a literary work must be composed somewhere, takes a certain amount of time to do, will turn out differently if written longhand or typed on a typewriter. This is not an argument for straightforward biographical criticism, whose problems are well known, but for requiring of literary critics that they be something of the psychologist, and more controversially, of the novelist.

Like the critic, the biographer should have in him something of the psychologist and the historian, and he should have something of the novelist in him too, which seems on the face of it to be a heretical remark, for everyone knows that the biographer cannot make anything up. A biography is not and should not be fiction, precisely because a balanced and accurate biography must be at the service of the literary critic who hopes correctly to discern the operative pattern of works, or groups of works. This view, of course, tends to see biography wholly as the tool of the critic and to ignore its artistic function, to which we will return.

The critic of literature, and especially of Victorian literature, is still largely at the mercy of the Victorian biographer whose prudery, reticence, and, from the twentieth-century point of view, lack of common sense are well known. This being the case, the extent to which biographical traditions established in the Victorian era are still upheld is truly astonishing. The Merediths are a case in point, but almost any Victorian figure is another. Peacock's relationship with his wife, for example, has been left undisturbed by the reticent Biographer, who does not stop to inquire, say, into the emotional and physical probabilities of the behavior of a man only forty, a "pagan," moreover, unconstrained by religion or Victorian mores—a worldly man whose wife became mad. Is it likely that he spent the next forty years in disappointed chastity? Is it important? Or, take the assertion of the biographical tradition, unchanged until the 1950's, that Peacock never saw Mary Ellen again after her sexual adventure with Wallis. Its importance is easier to see: it has had the effect of ascribing to Peacock a completely different set of moral values than he in fact held, making the sophisticated, eighteenth-century gentleman into a Victorian Heavy Father because rigid unforgivingness was the only sort of behavior a Victorian biographer could imagine. And thinking of Peacock as being full of moralistic vindictiveness cannot but affect a critical evaluation of his works. (Peacock himself, it should be noted, was a firm believer in reticence in biography and would take great issue with these remarks. It is said he was vigorously indignant when Trelawney wrote about Byron's deformity.)

The tradition of Peacock's reticence provides another case in point. Reticence, vaguely equated with modesty, seems to be a quality attributed to all famous people by their biographers. Peacock's, it is said, was so extreme that he would allow no one in his library. But a recent critic, Carl Dawson, in *His Fine Wit,* makes the sensible speculation, based on the poet Robert Buchanan's disapproving remark that Peacock's mind was a "terrible 'thesaurus eroticus,'" that the library was full of dirty books—ribald classics, anyway—which Peacock was fully aware were not compatible with bourgeois Victorian notions of decency. (Mary Ellen, and later her daughter, Edith, were given full run of the place, in any case.)

Biographers, especially Victorian but modern ones too, favor reticence and inattention to emotional realities or probabilities—but they are also afflicted by the literary conventions operative when they are writing. This is the oddest part of all. We are familiar with the circular relation of life and art, and the difficulty sometimes in telling which is which. Although fictional characters ostensibly behave like real people the author has seen, people do sometimes behave like people in books they have read. It would be difficult to analyze the relationship among (1) Anne Brontë's description of the death of her heroine, the wicked Lady Lowborough (see page 145 above), who after an elopement like Mary Ellen's, "died at last . . . in penury, neglect, and utter wretchedness," and (2) S. M. Ellis's description of Mary Ellen's end: "But the poor woman never found happiness, and her short, tragic life was nearing the end. . . . Ever restless, she wandered from place to place, seeking to drown bitter memories and regrets. . . ." And "all those who remember Mrs. Meredith in the last years of her life state that she was always sad and constantly in tears. Her warm, vehement nature could not meet sorrow with resignation or be softened by it. She would pace up and down the room in uncontrollable emotion," and so on, straight down to the unmarked grave. Needless to say that Debt, that awful Victorian specter, was also present, and (3) Mr. Justin Vulliamy's notion that the adulterous wife going home to live with her father, was "unaccountable," inexplicable.

There is a relationship among these three attitudes. Fictional endings are dictated by a sense of retributive justice; the interpretation of a real life, by both Mr. Vulliamy and the Biographer, appears to be influenced by notions of decorum and retribution, but also by fictional convention.

Biography, being affected by the fictional conventions with which it is contemporary, thus can be seen to have the same function as fiction, especially for the reader. In a sense it is fiction. Fiction, conversely, presents itself as "real," as a version of reality. In either case the controlling vision or imaginative grasp of the writer in managing the materials of human experience will produce an effective (or ineffective) work of art, whose origins in the verifiable life of a historical figure, or in the same material controlled by the "imaginative" writer— put through his personal systems of defense and so on—are probably a matter of very little importance to the reader. As far as the reader's responses are concerned, there is finally very little difference. It is in this sense that the biographer is after all a novelist, as far as his responsibilities, if not his powers, go—and in this sense that the critic must also be one. Like the biographer, the critic, in commenting upon fiction, must perform an empathetic (fictional) act. This is especially demanded of a critic if he does not have at his service reliable biography: that is, undistorted by factual error or by a really unreliable sensibility on the part of the biographer. Good critics would no doubt be better off with mechanically compiled lists of "facts" from which to work, rather than with those persuasive, interpretive fictional biases that are often so hard to spy out.

But what, anyway, are the "facts" of a writer's life? That George Meredith had an erring wife is a "fact," but for him, the existence of those fictional heroines Mrs. Mount and Mrs. Lovell is also "fact." The one is an external, the other an interior fact. The danger for the biographer, or critic, lies in mismatching external and interior equivalents. I suppose there is no safeguard against doing this except, one hopes, common sense and a (no doubt) suspect degree of empathy, especially with the "seamy" side of human nature; it is this side of himself the writer is likely to be in conflict about, and to find himself impelled to deal with—or to sedulously avoid dealing with—in his works. The writer is more likely to treat, directly or between the lines, his relationship with his wife than the one with his grocer. Which returns me to my point: the biographer must be a historian, but also a novelist and a snoop.

7. It seems, in fact, to have been Dr. Gryffydh's neck which was almost broken. Here is Peacock's story of his adventure in a letter to a friend.

The other day I prevailed on my new acquaintance, Dr. Griffith [sic], to accompany me at midnight to the black cataract, a favorite haunt of mine, about 2¼ miles from hence. Mr. Lloyd, whom I believe I have mentioned to you more than once, volunteered to be of the party; and at twenty minutes past eleven, lighted by the full-orbed moon, we sallied forth, to the no small astonishment of mine host, who protested he never expected to see us all again. —The effect was truly magnificent. —The water descends from a mountainous glen down a winding rock, and then precipitates itself, in one sheet of foam, over its black base, into a capacious bason [sic], the sides of which are all but perpendicular, and covered with hanging oak and hazel. —Evans, in the Cambrian Itinerary, *describes it as an abode of damp and horror, and adds, that the whole cataract cannot be seen in one view, as the sides are too steep and slippery to admit of clambering up, and the top of the upper fall is invisible from below. —Mr. Evans seems to have labored under a small degree of alarm, which prevented accurate investigation, for I have repeatedly climbed this* unattemptable *rock and obtained this* impossible *view; as he or any one else might do with very little difficulty; though Dr. Gryffydh, the other night, trusting to a rotten*

branch, had a fall of fifteen feet perpendicular, and but for an interven-
ing hazel, would infallibly have been hurled to the bottom.

8. *Maid Marian,* a Robin Hood story, contains another of the sprightly, independent, and intellectual heroines Peacock so admired. When she grew old enough to read, Peacock gave a copy of this work to his own Mary Ellen:

> To Miss Mary Ellen Peacock
> From the Author, her dear Papa.

Later, George Meredith writes a poem entitled "Marian," which describes Mary Ellen. It has been suggested that he meant to associate the heroine of the poem with Peacock's heroine. Still later, after Mary Ellen has left him, Meredith calls a succession of mad or degenerate women in his books "Marian."

9. Hogg never seemed to follow his minister's advice and associated all his life with "advanced" women. So did Peacock, feeling, in the words of his own fictional character, "I can answer for men, Miss Melincourt, that there are some, many I hope, who can appreciate justly that most heavenly of earthly things, an enlightened female mind; whatever may be thought by the pedantry that envies, the foppery that fears, the folly that ridicules, or the wilful blindness that will not see its loveliness." (*Melincourt:* Works, 2, p. 167.)

10. It is hard for us not to wonder at the conventions of Victorian domestic address. Here is a fictional episode from Charlotte Yonge's *Heartsease,* which Mary Ellen read. A young couple has been married for a few weeks and is just coming home to meet his relatives for the first time. The husband is the younger son, not technically entitled, according to Victorian usage, to be called "Mr. Martindale"; he would be called "Mr. Arthur."

> *"I am glad I have seen Mr. John Martindale," sighed she.*
> *"Don't call him so here. Ah! I meant to tell you you must not Mr. Martindale me here. John is Mr. Martindale."*
> *"And what am I to call you?"*
> *"By my name, of course."*
> *"Arthur! Oh! I don't know how."*
> *"You will soon. And if you can help shrinking when my aunt kisses you, it will be the better for us. . . ."*

11. As an index of Peacock's own views on female dress and nudity, we may perhaps consult Mr. Crotchet, in *Crotchet Castle:*

Mr. Crotchet: Sir, ancient Sculpture is the true school of modesty. But where the Greeks had modesty, we have cant; . . . And, sir, to show my contempt for cant in all its shapes, I have adorned my house with the Greek Venus, in all her shapes, and am ready to fight her battle against all the societies that ever were instituted for the suppression of truth and beauty.

The Rev. Dr. Folliott: My dear sir, I am afraid you are growing warm. Pray be cool. Nothing contributes so much to good digestion as to be perfectly cool after dinner.

Mr. Crotchet: Sir, the Lacedaemonian virgins wrestled naked with young men: and they grew up, as the wise Lycurgus had foreseen, into the most modest of women, and the most exemplary of wives and mothers.

The Rev. Dr. Folliott: Very likely sir; but the Athenian virgins did no such things, and they grew up into wives who stayed at home, — stayed at home sir; and looked after the husband's dinner, — his dinner, sir, you will please to observe.

Mr. Crotchet: And what was the consequence of that, sir? that they were such very insipid persons that the husband would not go home to eat his dinner, but preferred the company of some Aspasia, or Lais.

The Rev. Dr. Folliott: Two very different persons, sir, give me leave to remark.

Mr. Crotchet: Very likely, sir; but both too good to be married in Athens.

The Rev. Dr. Folliott: Sir, Lais was a Corinthian.

Mr. Crotchet: 'Od's vengeance, sir, some Aspasia and any other Athenian name of the same sort of person you like —

The Rev. Dr. Folliott: I do not like the sort of person at all: the sort of person I like, as I have already implied, is a modest woman, who stays at home and looks after her husband's dinner.

Mr. Crotchet: Well, sir, that was not the taste of the Athenians. They preferred the society of women who would not have made any scruple about sitting as models to Praxiteles; as you know, sir, very modest women in Italy did to Canova: one of whom, an Italian countess, being asked by an English lady, "how she could bear it?" answered, "Very well; there was a good fire in the room."

The Rev. Dr. Folliott: Sir, the English lady should have asked how the Italian lady's husband could bear it. The phials of my wrath would overflow if poor dear Mrs. Folliott — : sir, in return for your story, I will tell you a story of my ancestor, Gilbert Folliott. The devil haunted him, as he did Saint Francis, in the likeness of a beautiful damsel; but all he could get from the exemplary Gilbert was an admonition to wear a stomacher and longer-petticoats.

Mr. Crotchet: Sir, your story makes for my side of the question. It proves that the devil, in the likeness of a fair damsel, with short petticoats and no stomacher, was almost too much for Gilbert Folliott. The force of the spell was in the drapery.

The Rev. Dr. Folliott: Bless my soul, sir!

Mr. Crotchet: Give me leave, sir, Diderot — . . . .

The Rev. Dr. Folliott: . . . Sir, Diderot is not a man after my heart. Keep to the Greeks, if you please; albeit this Sleeping Venus is not an antique.

Mr. Crotchet: Well, sir, the Greeks: why do we call the Elgin marbles inestimable? Simply because they are true to nature. And why are they so superior in that point to all modern works, with all our greater knowledge of anatomy? Why sir, but because the Greeks, having no cant, had better opportunities of studying models?

The Rev. Dr. Folliott: Sir, I deny our greater knowledge of anatomy. But I shall take the liberty to employ, on this occasion, the argumentum ad hominem. Would you have allowed Miss Crotchet to sit for a model to Canova?

Mr. Crotchet: Yes, sir.

"God bless my soul, sir!" exclaimed the Reverend Doctor Folliott, throwing himself back into a chair, and flinging up his heels. . . .

12. The first of the two letters that follow (addressed to "My kind dear father") is not, in fact, in Mary Ellen's hand, and seems to have been copied by someone else (perhaps Peacock), perhaps with a view to suppressing some passage in it. Victorian families were most unscrupulous in this respect. It is just possible that the second letter (to "My own darling Eddy") is written to her brother Edward rather than to her fiancé, for Victorian siblings were effusively affectionate and loverlike in their addresses. Both letters are unpublished and are quoted here by permission of the Carl H. Pforzheimer Library.

13. Victoms. "I fear," remarks his descendant, Lady de Montmorency, "that his early entrance into Service did not improve his spelling." That Fighting Nicolls was a man of action is demonstrated by this account, from Colonel C. Field's Britain's Sea-Soldiers, pp. 237–9.

It was the year 1803, and the <u>Blanche</u> frigate, Captain Zachery Mudge, was cruising off the Island of San Domingo. Intelligence had been received that the French armed cutter <u>Albion</u> was at moorings in the roadstead of Monte Christi on the North coast of the Island, and an attempt was made to cut her out by daylight, three boats being sent in under Lieut. Braithwaite, R.N., but the boats were driven off by the fire of a battery which covered her. It was in the early part of November, the nights were long, and it was determined to take advantage of them, and make another attempt to cut her out under cover of the darkness. Lieutenant Nicolls of the Royal Marines volunteered to carry out the job if he could have one of the cutters and twelve men. His offer was accepted, and late on the evening of the 4th of the month, he shoved off from alongside the <u>Blanche</u> on his little expedition. He had not long left the ship when Captain Mudge, fully aware of Nicolls' daredevil disposition, conceived the idea that he might attempt more than his diminutive force would possibly be able to do, for the object of their attack was lying within a hundred yards of a shore battery, mounting four 24-pounders and three field guns. He therefore called away the barge with her crew of twenty-two men, and putting Lieutenant the Hon. Warwick Lake, R.N., in charge of her, ordered him to reinforce Nicolls and take personal charge of the attack. The bigger boat having come up with the Red cutter — Nicolls' boat — the two pulled steadily in together until the Marine officer was able to point out the dim form of the <u>Albion</u> as she lay close under the land. He had probably located her before he volunteered to cut her out and had taken her bearings. Lake, however, would not have it that the craft they could see was the one of which they were in search. He maintained that the <u>Albion</u> was lying right away at the opposite side of the Bay. However, although he was in command, he did not insist on the red cutter accompanying him when he headed his boat in the new direction, but told Nicolls to keep an eye on the vessel they had already discovered. This was about half past two in the morning, and though the bay was overshadowed by high mountains there was not very much time to waste if the <u>Albion</u> was to be captured and taken out before there was a glimmer of light in the East. Besides, there was now a favourable breeze for bringing her out, and this might very likely drop or change its direction at daybreak. Anyway, Nicolls felt quite certain that the vessel he was watching <u>was</u> the <u>Albion</u> and headed his boat towards her. An attack was evidently looked for — the <u>Blanche</u> had probably been seen standing off and on in the offing at sundown, and as soon as the red cutter was within pistol shot she was hailed by the French look-outs. Three rousing cheers was the answer from the little boat, whose crew, bending to their oars, dashed alongside. One volley from the _Albion_ whistled overhead, a second badly wounded the coxswain, the bow oar and a Marine. Before the compliment could be repeated the red cutter had hooked on, and Nicolls had sprung on board. As he jumped on deck the French Captain's pistol cracked and the ball pierced the skin of the Marine's stomach, came out and lodged in his sword arm. Nicolls, or one of his men, instantly shot the French officer, and after a short scuffle with cutlass, bayonet and boarding pike, the crew were driven below with the loss of five men wounded, one mortally. So far, so good; the _Albion_ was taken and Nicolls now had to get her out. But the battery close by could easily blow her out of the water, once the gunners became aware of Nicolls' success. A stratagem was necessary to throw dust in their eyes, and Nicolls therefore ordered his Marines to continue to discharge their muskets in the air in order to produce the impression that the French crew was still holding its own, while the seamen of his little party cut the cables and got sail on the prize. All would have been well, had not the barge, attracted by the firing, now come bumping alongside. Lake, of course, at once assumed command. There was nothing for him to do, but he, by way of taking a hand in the proceedings, ordered the Marines to cease firing. Instantly followed the red flash and boom of the battery guns, round and grape shot came humming and whistling on board, and two of the _Blanche_'s seamen fell dead. But the wind was fair, and with both boats towing ahead the _Albion_ was soon out of gunshot, and lost in the darkness.

There is no doubt that Nicolls had done the whole thing "off his own bat," but Captain Mudge, in his report, put quite a different colour on the affair. He said that the _Albion_ was "gallantly attacked" by _two_ boats, Lieutenant Lake in the _cutter_, and Lieutenant Nicolls of the Marines, in the _barge_. Here are no less than three misstatements to begin with. Neither did he make any mention of Nicolls being wounded, although he had been pretty seriously hurt. The Admiralty, misled by Zachery Mudge's "terminological inexactitudes," naturally selected Lieutenant Lake, the senior of the two officers, for promotion, while the Committee of the Patriotic Fund, although they presented Nicolls with a sword of the value of £30 for "having commanded one of the boats," gave Lake one valued at £50 for "his gallantry." How the latter could have accepted it, without suggesting that it ought to have been given to Nicolls, is a question which can never be answered.

14. Of course, we all know that experiences described by novelists in their novels are not often verbatim accounts of things that have happened to them. Strictly speaking, it is not fair to infer Mary's life style from George's books. At the same time, it is true that a writer has nothing but his own experience to fuel his imagination; when certain scenes or characters recur in his work, and when they resemble the people he is known to have known in his life, it is fairly safe to say that the latter inspired the former. We may say that the scenes in a novel are fundamentally true to the life experience of the author and superficially distorted. Meredith's witty *femmes du monde* have different coloring, various personal histories. But consider how their names — Bella, Mary, Marian — play variations on "Mary Ellen."

15. And Mary Ellen must have been like Bella and Mrs. Lovell; "She was a brilliant, witty, beautiful woman, thirty years of age, and a widow. . . . Meredith was immediately attracted by Mrs. Nicolls and she to him, but the mutual attraction was probably only of a physical nature," explains Cousin Stewart Ellis disapprovingly (George's second cousin and first biographer).

16. I have provided the translation for Mary Ellen's essay that appears in the text, with thanks to Toni Roby:

LA MORT

Qu'est-ce que la mort? Ce voyage, cette peine inconnue au milieu de laquelle nous vivons, mais que nous craignons tous; et cette crainte d'où vient-elle? car nous la trouverons dans le coeur de tous les hommes, même dans ceux qui désirent le plus d'être morts; ils désirent être morts, mais ils craignent de mourir. Cette crainte n'est-elle pas une sentinelle que Dieu a placee à la porte de la seconde vie, ou comme nous la nommons l'autre monde, elle est là pour nous en défendre l'entrée jusqu'à ce que notre heure nous appelle et quand elle arrivera peut-être cette crainte abandonnera-t-elle la porte qu'elle ne devait plus garder quand on présente le billet d'admission signé du doigt de l'Éternel.

Ordinairement on regarde la mort comme un arrêt final, comme la fin de la vie, la cessation de tout ce que nous avons connu et senti: arrêt suivi d'un état nouveau où nous n'avons rien de ce qui fait notre bonheur ou notre malheur ici-bas; mais il ne peut en être ainsi, nous voyons que dans la nature toute mort est naissance. La plus vilaine corruption qui pourri [sic] sur la terre a-t-on fini avec elle? Non, et on

voit au contraire que la terre bienfaisante la change en quelque nouvelle
vie. Les feuilles de la jolie fleur ne tombent-elles pas pour donner place
à la nouvelle vie du fruit? et le fuit ne jette [sic] il pas ses riches sucs
pour que la graine prende [sic] naissance? et elle, quand elle tombe,
n'est-ce pas pour créer une nouvelle vie? Or la nature qui par ses belles
analogies nous révèle si souvent le surnaturel, ne nous montre elle pas
l'infaillibilité de ce principe, que la mort est aussi la naissance. Quand
nos âmes sont mûres, quand elles ont gagné des chaleurs ou des froids
de ce monde tout ce [sic] peuvent ou les nourrir, ou les détruire, la
nouvelle naissance ne brise-t-elle pas les liens qui ne peuvent plus la
contenir; la mort n'est qu'un passage, un moment, mais elle est suivie
de l'éternité! Et dans cette éternité autant de joie pour celui qui vient
de naître, qui'ici-bas de douleur pour celui qui vient de mourir.

Mais, pourtant il y a beaucoup d'inconnu, de mystérieux pour nous
dans ce passage de la vie. Qui sait quel changement, quelle division elle
a pu mettre entre ceux que nous avons perdus de vue par cette action
étrange: nous sont-ils enlevés à jamais? nous poursuivent-ils avec les
mêmes regards d'affection qu'ils nous prodiguaient ici-bas? nous n'en
savons rien, mais pour donner ce qui manque à la connaissance avons
l'ange de la foi, et elle nous enseigne que Dieu n'a créé rien en vain,
et assure qu-il ne nous a pas donné les affections que pour un moment
ou pour un jeu.

---

17. The cookery book was probably *The Science of Cookery*, which is
mostly in Peacock's hand, but which Mary Ellen was apparently ready-
ing for print by adding a preface and more recipes. Among his wise
sayings in the Preface:

It is said that there are Seven *chances against even the most simple*
dish being presented to the mouth in absolute perfection; for instance a
Leg of Mutton

1st — The mutton must be good
2nd — Must have been kept a good time
3rd — Must be roasted at a good fire,
4th — By a Good Cook
5th — Who must be in good temper,
6th — With all this felicitous combination you must have good
luck, and
7th — Good appetite — the meat and the mouths which are to eat it
must be ready for each other.

Clement Shorter, in *The Sphere* (vol. 64, March 25, 1916, p. 328), remarks of a cookery article of Mary's, "Here Mrs. Meredith shows so amazing a knowledge of cookery that one half suspects that she inspired the book, although the fact that much of it is in Mr. Meredith's handwriting suggests a joint authorship." This remark, in turn, suggests a second cookery manuscript, with more evidence of participation by George; the one from which I have quoted above is largely Peacock's. But I have been unable to locate this second manuscript, which was sold at Maggs in 1916. The Maggs catalogue describes it as extracts from an unpublished manuscript in Meredith's hand, "extending to some 19 pages, and interspersed with occasional notes" by Mary Ellen.

18. Perhaps George is fibbing about Mary Ellen having written some of his early poems. Scholars since have preferred to think that he himself wrote all of them. His son and first editor, Will, who is not credited with having a reliable character, appears to believe his father in the matter; he at least believes in collaboration between his father and his father's first wife. So, too, does Cousin Stewart, who says, "It is possible that some of the intervening numbers [of *Household Words* poems] were the work, wholly, or in part, of Mrs. Meredith." It may well be, then, that some of the unpublished early poems were Mary Ellen's, or part hers, but the only poem she is known certainly to have written is *The Blackbird.*

One poem George disowned, *The Gentleness of Death,* in *Household Words* for October 4, 1851, is reminiscent of Mary Ellen's essay on the subject, and begins:

> Who that can feel the gentleness of Death
>   Sees not the loveliness of Life? and who,
> Breathing content his natural joyous breath,
>   Could fail to feel that Death is Nature, too?
> And not the alien foe his fears dictated,
> A viewless terror, heard but to be hated.

It is equally hard to discover her prose works. It would appear from Dickens's plain reference to her work and from the circumstance that only George's name shows up in the contributor's book, that George was paid for both of them. Articles in British periodicals at this time were, of course, usually unsigned.

19. Mary Ellen was by all accounts an exquisite cook, but I do not know that we would care to drink her coffee:

The proportion of one ounce of coffee must be allowed to make two breakfast cups. When it is ground, mix it thoroughly with beat-up egg, so that each grain is equally moistened; then pour boiling water on it, and suffer it to boil up three times; let it stand a minute or two after the last boiling up, and it will be fit to pour out, requiring neither filtering nor straining.

Here are two of Peacock's recipes for salmon:

2 T liquor [stock] boiled in 1 T of salad oil
a dessert-spoon of chili vinegar
1 dessert-spoon of Cucumber vinegar
a tsp of Capers, a tsp of anchovy sauce.
Mix, marinate salmon, mix sauce with breadcrumbs and cover fish. Warm.

or

mix oil, parsley, gherkin, shallot, and anchovy chopped fine, with $\frac{1}{2}$ tsp cayenne sauce. Mix, rub over fish, wrap in buttered paper and bake.

20. Retrospective diagnoses are of course highly conjectural, but it does sound as if Meredith had an ulcer, to go with his ambitions and anxieties. It is certain that doctors subsequently recognized the nervous basis of his stomach affliction, whatever it was.

21. The "Anapestic Ode to Christ" is not printed in the Halliford *Works*, but its story is told under a section devoted to "Lost" works (vol. 8, p. 46), and is cautionary for those who have learned to be wary of the Biographer. In 1862, Peacock, in the bitterness of his spirit after Mary Ellen's death, wanted to have this ode printed up, and mentioned it to Mr. L'Estrange, with whom he corresponded. After his death, L'Estrange asked Edith for a copy, which Edith sent him; she could not read it anyway because it was in Greek. "He translated the closing words," the Halliford Biographer continues, "to show the uncomplimentary nature of the ode," and evidently thought it too controversial for the projected edition of the *Works*. Edith was "rather shocked," and, the Biographer speculates, destroyed Peacock's Greek text. Mr. L'Estrange's translation is all that survives.

22. One of the functions of these notes and of this work is to suggest an interpretation of George's great poem, *Modern Love*, rather dif-

ferent from the one critics have usually given. It is most often seen as "modern" because of its psychological subtlety and daring theme—an adulterous marriage—in which Meredith, having achieved a remarkable detachment from his tragic experience, skillfully analyzes the mutual guilt of the pair in the face of Victorian moral attitudes—which would have unquestioningly blamed the woman. Rather handsome of Meredith, it is felt, to confess a measure of personal responsibility for the whole mess, and to express, for a Victorian, an impressive degree of charity. He seems to blame the inadequacy of the education of Victorian females ("More brain, O Lord, more brain") and his own over-idealistic attitude toward Love. A magnanimous poem.

But George, as we shall see, was vindictive not magnanimous, and he was bound to have written this poem in a mood of self-vindication, for it would be read by people who knew his personal history. It is not a modern but a Spasmodic poem, in a mode then current.

What Meredith meant by "Modern," in his title, is not that he was treating adultery—that is very old indeed. By "Modern Love" he meant sentimental love, the "morbid passion of our day," as he called it. The narrator of the poem has too exalted a notion of Love, as something holy and enduring in a real world where real women are faithless and over-sophisticated. "Madam," the heroine of the poem, like Mary Ellen reads French novels, emblematic of worldly cynicism.

Of course the Victorian reader had the same exalted notion of pure and holy wedded love that the narrator condemns in himself. Meredith is seeming to say, "Perhaps I was wrong to feel as I did, considering how it turned out," and his readers would be sympathetic. They would secretly approve his idealism. You are too hard on yourself, dear George, we can hear them saying. Your sentiments do you honor. The woman was unfaithful. Do not apologize.

At the same time that the poem makes a serious statement condemning notions of Romantic love, it assuages George's stung male vanity by making the narrator a bit of a rake with a mistress and a desk full of old "wanton-scented tresses,"—something George was apparently not. The ending of the poem, in which the wife magnanimously kills herself in order to make way for his pursuit of a new love, is sheer wish-fulfillment, but George may unconsciously have hoped it would suggest to his friends that Mary Ellen had left him for something like the same reason. It is sometimes more bearable to think of yourself as the sinner than the sinned against.

If notions of Meredith's farsighted modernity—which, after all, he never showed again — are dismissed, it is easy to see the relation of *Modern Love* with the Spasmodic poetry, for instance with Tennyson's contemporary "Maud" (1856), with which it shares the neurotic, over-wrought, self-dramatizing hero. It is easier to see Meredith in this tradi-tion than to explain why he was able to write a highly innovative and capable early poem and never come close to it again. Though he was to write some good poetry later, *Modern Love* is unique among his ac-complishments.

23. Mary Ellen's religiosity seems to have been an invention either of Cousin Stewart Ellis, Meredith's first biographer, or of Meredith. In one letter to her, T. J. Hogg remarks, "Duty to Our Future Laureate, and Love to the child of Wrath, about to become a Son of Adoption and Grace," which implies no more than that they were having Arthur baptized. Her letters and Commonplace Book are rather strikingly free of religious allusions, and her behavior was clearly not derived from any prevailing Christian ethic.

24. This is Rossetti's sonnet "Nuptial Sleep":

> At length their long kiss severed, with sweet smart:
>   And as the last slow sudden drops are shed
>   From sparkling eaves when all the storm has fled,
> So singly flagged the pulses of each heart.
> Their bosoms sundered, with the opening start
>   Of married flowers to either side outspread
>   From the knit stem; yet still their mouths, burnt red,
> Fawned on each other where they lay apart.
>
> Sleep sank them lower than the tide of dreams,
>   And their dreams watched them sink, and slid away.
> Slowly their souls swam up again, through gleams
>   Of watered light and dull drowned waifs of day;
> Till from some wonder of new woods and streams
>   He woke, and wondered more; for there she lay.

25. George was unlucky in this wife too. Marie Meredith, apparently a pleasant and docile woman, died of cancer when she was forty-five, after two painful operations and a long illness, during which she could not move or speak, and so met her end, with whatever emotions of re-sentment and despair, literally uncomplaining.

26. The affair probably did not begin until some time after February 1857. Meredith records in his notebook little remarks by Arthur, aged

three years, seven months, to his nurse. This suggests that they were all sharing the same household as late as February, and that the marriage was therefore officially intact.

27. *If* she removed them. Ladies often wore no drawers in those days, for drawers, though known, were new in 1856, and were thought to be "masculine," in that they imitated trousers. So the whole thing may have been simpler than we think. Not much is known about Victorian notions of propriety in dress for erotic occasions. Did they remove their clothing? Or only the better classes? Or only prostitutes? Much would depend too, no doubt, upon the season of the year.

28. This friend is a Mr. Evans, perhaps F. M. Evans, publisher of *Once a Week*. This, as well as later, friendly letters to the Chapmans, suggest that Mary Ellen remained on friendly terms with many of the Merediths' acquaintance, even those who were in contact with George too, and this despite Victorian conventions of social ostracism.

29. "We are marrying Mademoiselle Corneille to a neighborhood gentleman, a dragoon officer, wise, gentle, courageous, a fine figure, loving the service of the king and of his lady, having about ten thousand pounds of yearly income, near Ferney. I am putting both of them up. We are all happy. I am ending up a patriarch.

"Our intended's name is Dapuits. Brother Thériot must be happy about Mademoiselle Corneille's good fortune. She deserves it. Are you aware that that child supported her father and mother for a long time by work done with her own little hands? And now she is rewarded. Her life is a novel." Translated by Toni Roby.

30. The name Felix was perhaps appended to Harold after Mary Ellen's death, for she never refers to him as Felix. But one hopes the name was prompted by the felicity he brought to her as well as to Henry.

31. "Has she been paid for her paper or papers? This passage in her note looks to me as if she had not been paid." This passage in Dickens's note looks to me as if Mary Ellen had written some things for *Household Words,* but what they were is not known.

32. Her affiliation to what we can call, for convenience, the eighteenth-century tradition, and the inability of either Meredith or his Victorian biographers to understand this, has led to the subtle but interesting distortions in the biographical account of Mary Ellen's "elopement." The actual circumstances of female life in the nineteenth century were such that an elopement was a frequent and almost the only way out of a mar-

riage. Women, at least in the middle class, who were not protected legally and who had no financial recourse in case of marital difficulties —unable to own property and unable to get jobs—had almost no other way out of an unhappy marriage except to throw themselves on the "protection" of another man. (Neither aristocrats nor the very poor were constrained by the same realities, it would seem.) The "other man," in fiction but no doubt in life too, typically deserted the flighty woman later on. This was the inevitable fictional outcome, given the moral aims of Victorian novelists and the expectations of the audience. It was therefore integral to the Biographer's conception of the situation that Mary Ellen, who was known to have gone to Capri, must have eloped there, and it was also likely that her solitary return was owing to desertion by her lover. The figure of the guilty, repentant, and doomed wife emerges from the biographical tradition to form our view of Madam in *Modern Love*, and, by extension, our idea of what the facts must have been.

The actual circumstances were somewhat different. It appears that Mary Ellen simply left George, intending to live by her writing and on a small private income. Her involvement with Henry was not necessarily even related to her separation from George.

Certain other aspects of her mad "elopement" remain distorted, or at least mysterious; for instance, the custody and whereabouts of Arthur. Meredith's earliest biographer, Stewart Ellis, reports that Mary Ellen did not desert him, but left him with Lady Nicolls, the mother of her first husband. This detail is repeated by at least two subsequent biographers, Sassoon and Clodd. But Lionel Stevenson, "believing it unlikely," left it out of his "definitive" biography of Meredith. He felt it unlikely, no doubt, that a respectable Lady Anybody would babysit while her former daughter-in-law ran off on an adulterous impulse. Such, however, seems to have been the case, quite as Meredith's Cousin Stewart reported. It is thought to be the case, too, by descendants of the Nicolls, who point out that while General Sir Edward and Lady Nicolls would never have approved of adultery, they were always most fond of Mary Ellen, and, of course, of their own granddaughter Edith, who stayed with them often. They were quite fond of Edith's little half-brother Arthur, too, and enjoyed his frequent visits, and need not necessarily have known what Mary Ellen was up to.

This is a matter of some, if slight, importance as an example of ways in which biographical tradition subtly changes. The idea that Mary Ellen deserted her little boy has earned for her much undeserved opprobrium, and reinforced George's pose of rectitude; and *these* attitudes, as I have argued earlier, greatly influence our interpretation of George's writing, whether we mean them to or not. My version of how George came by Arthur (pages 136–7 above) is merely conjecture.

33. The biographical tradition must again be questioned about the place of Mary Ellen's death. It is traditional that Mary Ellen lived in Grotto Cottage, but Grotto Cottage is too tiny to contain her ménage, which seems to have included at least Harold, his nurse, and a maid; it is possible that she lived in another, larger cottage on the Oatlands grounds. It is also possible that Harold lived with Nurse Bennet nearby, not an unusual arrangement at the time. Grotto Cottage is, however, a poetically tiny and wretched place for a wicked heroine to expire.

34. George's books are full of erring wives, and recastings of the story, for instance, from *Richard Feverel:*

The outline of the baronet's story was by no means new. He had a wife, and he had a friend. His marriage was for love; his wife was a beauty; his friend was a sort of poet [read, "sort of painter"]. His wife had his whole heart, and his friend all his confidence. . . . A languishing, inexperienced woman, whose husband in mental and in moral stature is more than the ordinary height above her, and who, now that her first romantic admiration of his lofty bearing has worn off, and her fretful little refinements of taste and sentiment are not instinctively responded to, is thrown into no wholesome household collision with a fluent man, fluent in prose and rhyme. Lady Feverel, when she first entered on her duties at Raynham, was jealous of her husband's friend. By degrees she tolerated him. In time he touched his guitar in her chamber, and they played Rizzio and Mary together.

> "For I am not the first who found
> The name of Mary fatal!"

says a subsequent sentimental alliterative love-poem of Diaper's.

Such was the outline of the story. But the baronet could fill it up. He had opened his soul to these two. He had been noble Love to the one, and to the other perfect Friendship. He had bid them be brother and sister whom he loved, and live a Golden Age with him at Raynham. In fact, he had been prodigal of the excellence of his nature, which it is not good to be, and, like Timon, he became bankrupt, and fell upon bitterness.

The faithless lady was of no particular family; an orphan daughter

of an admiral who educated her on his half-pay, and her conduct struck
but at the man whose name she bore.

After five years of marriage, and twelve of friendship, Sir Austin
was left to his loneliness with nothing to ease his heart of love upon
save a little baby boy in a cradle. He forgave the man: he put him aside
as poor for his wrath. The woman he could not forgive; she had sinned
every way. Simple ingratitude to a benefactor was a pardonable trans-
gression, for he was not one to recount and crush the culprit under the
heap of his good deeds. But her he had raised to be his equal, and he
judged her as his equal. She had blackened the world's fair aspect
for him.

In these stories, George indulges in punitive fantasies. The errant Lady
Feverel, for instance, becomes a pitiful old crone, despised by her son:

Her heart had almost forgotten its maternal functions. She called him
Sir, till her bade her remember he was her son. Her voice sounded to
him like that of a broken-throated lamb, so painful and weak it was,
with the plaintive stop in the utterance. When he kissed her, her skin
was cold. Her thin hand fell out of his when his grasp relaxed. "Can
sin haunt one like this?" he asked, bitterly reproaching himself for the
shame she had caused him to endure, and a deep compassion filled
his breast.

And the lover became "prematurely aged, [an] oily little man; a poet
in bad circumstances; a decrepit butterfly chained to a disappointed
inkstand, [who] will not put strenuous energies to retain his ancient
paramour. . . ."

35. Will Meredith was George's son by the second marriage. Will
did not fare altogether well with his father either. Richard Le Gallienne,
Meredith's great admirer, describes a scene in which he met "Mr.
Meredith's beautiful young daughter, and his son, really a very modest
and wholesome young Englishman, whom he had a rather cruel way
of teasing and addressing as the 'Sagamore.' With a kingly wave of his
hand towards him he would say: 'Behold the Sagamore! Mark that
lofty brow! Stand in awe with me before the wisdom that sits there
enthroned . . .' and so he would proceed mercilessly to improvise on
the sublime serenity of Wise Youth, seated there so confidently at the

top of the world, till the poor tortured Sagamore would blush to the roots of his hair.''

36. Here are some of Peacock's recipes Edith printed in her book *Fancy Cookery:*

WATER SOUCHY

Ingredients
Fish, Perch or Flounders.
Fish Liquor.
Four Parsley plants, roots and leaves.
One teaspoonful of grated Horse-radish.
One teaspoonful of Shalot Vinegar.
One teaspoonful of Cayenne Sauce.
One teaspoonful of Walnut Ketchup.

Stew the fish slowly, in just enough fish liquor to cover them, with the parsley, the horse-radish and above sauces. When the fish are done, lay them in a deep dish, with a teaspoonful of chopped parsley; strain the liquor in which the fish were cooked over them, and serve, adding a little more fish liquor to them if there is not enough left after the cooking to cover them.

FILETS DE BOEUF AUX HUITRES

Ingredients
One pound of Fillet Steak.
One Spanish Onion.
Two pickled Walnuts.
Two tablespoonfuls of Mushroom Ketchup.
One dessertspoonful of Walnut Ketchup.
One teaspoonful of Worcester Sauce.
One dozen Oysters.
One ounce of Butter.
Half an ounce of Flour.

Mix the butter and flour together in a stewpan; peel and chop up the onion, cut up the walnuts, put them into the stewpan, also the ketchup and worcester sauce. Lay the steak on these and let it stew for an hour, turning it every twenty minutes; it must not boil. Just before serving, put in the oysters, bearded, with their liquor strained through a fine strainer.

MINCED VEAL

Ingredients
One pound Minced Veal.
One tablespoonful of Mushroom Ketchup.
The grated peel of half a Lemon.
One teaspoonful of Cayenne Sauce.
One blade of Mace.
Half pint of Stock.
Two dozen of Oysters.
Sippets of Toast.

Mince the veal and make it hot in the stock with the ketchup, cayenne sauce, lemon peel, and mace. When thoroughly hot, take out the mace; scald the oysters in their own liquor, taking off the beards; put the mince on a hot dish, the oysters in the centre and the sippets of toast round.

ATHENIAN EEL AND SAUCE

Ingredients
Half a pint of good Stock.
One tablespoonful of Mushroom Ketchup.
One tablespoonful of Onion Vinegar.
One mustardspoonful of Mustard.
One dessertspoonful of Shalot Vinegar.
One dessertspoonful of Anchovy Sauce.
One dessertspoonful of Worcester Sauce.
Marjoram and Parsley.

Mix these all well together in a stewpan, and when hot stir in a dessertspoonful of chopped sweet marjoram and a dessertspoonful of chopped parsley. Serve very hot in a sauce tureen; the eels, cut in pieces, to be baked, each piece to be rolled in oiled paper.

BREAM OR JOHN DORY PIE

Ingredients
Two pounds of Bream or John Dory.
Four Eggs (hard-boiled).
Two Shalots (chopped fine).
Two ounces of Butter.

Three ounces of Bread-crumbs.
Half a teaspoonful of Thyme and Marjoram.
One teaspoonful of chopped Parsley.
One teaspoonful of Anchovy Sauce.
One teaspoonful of Worcester Sauce.
Cayenne Pepper.
Salt.
One gill of Stock.

Cut the bream in slices. Mix the butter, breadcrumbs, shalot, and seasoning together, and make into small balls. Cut the eggs in quarters. Lay the bream in a pie-dish, and then a layer of egg and seasoning, balls, &c., and, if liked, some pieces of lobster. Cover with a crust of rough puff-paste, and bake in a moderate oven one hour and a half. Mix the Worcester and anchovy sauce with the stock, and pour into the pie, after it is baked. A glass of Sherry or Chablis may be added.

STEWED TROUT

Ingredients
One Trout.
Four Shalots.
One pint of Fish-Stock.
One ounce of Butter.
Two Cloves.
One teaspoonful of Salt.
A few grains of Cayenne.
One Carrot.
One Bay-leaf.
One tablespoonful of Basil and Thyme mixed.
A bunch of Parsley.

Chop up the shalots and carrot, put them in a stewpan with the butter and parsley; let them get hot, add the stock, cloves, herbs and seasoning; let all this simmer for one hour. Clean and wash the trout, tie round with broad tapes to prevent it breaking. Put the trout into a stewpan, strain the stock over it, add three glasses of port wine; let it simmer gently till the fish is cooked; it will take about half an hour. Take off the tapes carefully so as not to break the fish, reduce the stock it was cooked in, and pour over it. Hand a quartered lemon round with this dish.

SALMI OF COLD WILD DUCK

Ingredients

Wild Duck and the gravy left, or half pint of Stock.
Two glasses of Port Wine.
Four Shalots.
One ounce of Butter.
Half ounce of Flour.
The rind of one Orange.
The juice of one Lemon.
Half teaspoonful of Cayenne.
A sprig of Thyme.

Cut up the duck into neat pieces, and stew the trimmings of the duck in the gravy, with the Port wine, shalots, orange rind cut very thin, the lemon-juice, cayenne, and thyme, thicken with the butter and flour worked together. Stew this till reduced to half its quantity, then strain over the pieces of duck, warm all together without boiling, and serve.

---

37. Henry's correspondence with Holman Hunt, from 1865 to 1896, attests a long, cheerful friendship and reveals the appealing personality of Hunt. The letters are intermittent but suggest a continuing intimacy. In 1874 Hunt sends Henry a "New Civil Service" ticket which F. G. Stephens has told him Henry wants, and says, "When I can get past some bothering tasks I shall come and look you up."

An interesting letter of 1886 reflects on some sidelights of British art at the time. An exhibition of French paintings had been badly hung and the indignant French artists had looked to Hunt to support their complaints, but he has trouble feeling enthusiastic: "The impressionists whose works I saw in King St. two years ago seemed to me to be the kind of artists who make you declare that both Art and Nature are hideous and intollerable [sic] still of course they ought to have no reasonable grievance. A fool the name of Chesneau wrote to ask me to go and see the works: when I went . . . I could really scarcely believe that he was serious in speaking of them as deserving attention."

Hunt was at this time engaged in a public altercation, via newspaper correspondence, regarding the Royal Academy, which Hunt had always attacked as being too exclusive and unfair in keeping people out. Henry, one of those kept out, was vitally interested in this subject. Hunt writes to Henry that their side, the Independent, has this weakness that directly any one of the body [of independent artists] becomes really popular the R. A. will entice him over and then the public will say "As the strongest go the independent group is confessed to be the inferior exhibition." I am lugubrious because at the present time I see English honor so vitiated. Every one (with very few exceptions) acts for him self only — and when a glaring case of repudiation of all the pledges of a life time comes the world says "I don't blame him He did the best for himself." Nevertheless I think it wholesome to fight the cause even tho we lose for the time. I believe a great crash is coming on Europe and afterwards men will try to reconstitute society on a firm basis — and what we do now will stand as proof how corrupt matters were in Art.

And gossip. If you go to Egypt this year, 1886, "you will meet bridegroom and his bride, G. F. Watts and the lady who has adored him for twenty five years. The world gets funnier as it gets more tragic."

In January 1887,

the long tension I suffered with that Jerusalem canvas, and all the lamentable consequences sleeplessness and incessant vomitings have so racked my breathing tubes that nothing but balmy and soothing air and life could afford me the rest necessary to allow me to recuperate. The constant drain on my purse nearly maddened me. Even now great bills come in, and I have to pay them when under ordinary circumstances I might expect payments that would more than free me from the losses I have suffered. Don't say anything of this but I am teased out of my life by People saying "Oh I thought you were going to Egypt" as if I was doing them great wrong by not having kept my promise, and I don't want you to think that I act waywardly without the guidance of reason.

You will be amused to learn that _Wells_ has presented a great scheme of reform for the Academy to adopt, it was announced in last nights' Pall Mall Gazette, and the writer speaks of it as the great project which he inaugurated [_sic_] and he adds that he cannot repine at the great pains he unceasingly took to bring about this grand end. (I quote from memory but it is at least as strong as this.) I am too lazy at this moment to get the paper, but as far as I remember the plan is to have 150 or more outside members of the R.A. who shall have special claims upon space for exhibition, and they will have the first chance of election as A.R.A.'s. It is amusing and it goes some way to confirm me in a suspicion that *there is not much hope for England until it has met with tremendous trials and humiliation to shake the Almighty humbug out of it.*

And more gossip:

You will have heard of Watts's marriage, and of his honeymoon in Egypt. The gay deceiver had been making love to several ladies, and he never let them meet. One now is in the greatest distress, confined to her bed. She had courted him for years and she did not know of the existence of this rival.

> *Yours affectionately,*
> *W. Holman Hunt*

It is in 1894 that he writes after the scarf, which not Henry but another friend managed to procure for him, as he writes to Henry later. Henry is evidently involved in writing another book on ceramics, which prompts from Hunt the startling remark, "Your book, judging from your previous volume, cannot but be extremely precious and beautiful, yet I do begrudge the time it will take from you, which otherwise would be spent in poetic work." Perhaps to Hunt, painting and drawing is "poetic work." Hunt is, as usual, discouraged about the state of the world: "Half the rule of the world is in the hands of newspaper young graduates, who learn the views that will be thought smart and state these smartly. . . . Now the only hope is— . . . that the rebellious [emerging nations] will justify their independence by success. I have great admiration of heroism in war, yet I think the time has come for courage now to declare for its abolition by the union of all European states."

38. A few other letters to Henry.

> *The Grange*
> *North End Road*
> *Fulham S.W.*
> *Mar. 22:   1878*

Dear Mr. Wallis,

Edward says, will you put the enclosed information into fine language. I was very sorry to miss you on Wed: thinking you would be here at dinner I did not come down to see you till too late. Believe me,

> *very truly yours*
> *G. Burne-Jones*

May 17, 1865
Torvilla
Campden Hill

My dear Wallis

I was sorry to find that your friend Hotchkiss had called while I was out yesterday — his card has no address upon it so I have no means of writing to him. I shall be at home on Monday as also on Saturday. If I knew where he lived I would call and see his sketches and pictures and then I should be better able to decide how I could help him.

Yours ever sincerely
W. Holman Hunt

Penkill Cirvan [?]
Ayrshire
11 October 1889

My Dear Wallis

Perhaps you have heard that I have at last (after keeping it on all those years I have been invalided here at immense expense) sold the lease of my dear old Bellevue House at Chelsea, and am therefore clearing out all my old collections to deliver it up. . . .

How have you been this long time? I am rather better: my lungs seem quite safely well just at present, but general health bad, making me give up the hope of getting again to London, and I have got accustomed to the quiet life of the country and have a studio here where I am going to put all my pictures (my own and a few others I possess) but all my books must go to Sothebys. The time for that is not yet determined, but a Cat. will be got up by Mr. Mudge of the firm.

Give me a few words and believe me
Ever very sincerely yours
William Bell Scott

To my old friend Henry Wallis

Cairo
4 Feb 90

My dear Sir,

Tano [?] says that he is selling off and wants to clear his stock and take to travelling dealing in Europe. He now offers the fine Rameses II green brick, with double cartouche on top, & inscription all round, together with the poor one with trace of cartouche and broken, for

£20 together. He says he gave Faraj [?] £30. I told him I would write to you. If you want them send him the money, & tell him to deliver them to Dr. Grant's, & I will include them in a box of mine when I leave, so their cost of carriage would be only a few shillings. This would be your cheapest way to get them over.

He also has about 100 leaves of a fine old Koran, sheet 36 × 24 ins, thick paper, 9 lines & illuminated at bottom, also patch of illumination in margin: writing about 1½ inches high, very beautiful, red [summation?] etc. The illumination is in gold and blue. I am no judge of the age, but it is certainly not late, nor is the writing cunic [?] on the other hand. He wants £30, or £1 a leaf. Being imperfect a few leaves would be as good as the whole for the style and art. I have bought some stuff, but nothing in your way here.

Yours sincerely,
W. M. Flinders Petrie

Hotel Pellegrino
Bologna, Via Ugo Bassi, 7
1. 12. 1903

My dear Felix,

I posted a picture card yesterday at Venice, giving Florence address, so that you might know I was leaving Venice. Your letter, etc, of Friday had not arrived when I left. I gave directions for it to be forwarded to Florence (Messrs. C. Hon) [?] where you can write this week.

The weather has changed for the worse & it is very cold, foggy, & rains a deluge, it certainly cld not be worse in Russia, so I am leaving today for Florence. I shd have stayed 2 or 3 days but the Socialist Municipality has sealed up the Museum. My old Friend Frati (to whom I inscribed the Tile Vol:) was the head Librarian. He died about a couple of years ago & his place is supplied by a distributore, a messenger! The Socialists are giving places of trust to the lowest class. It is as if a messenger or Porter was appointed to the Chief Cashier post — or whatever is the highest office in the Bank. The Socialists here show themselves in their true colours. What wld the idiots in England who play at Socialism say? The Museum has been sealed up, for 15 months, when people who want to study expostulate they are laughed at by the Council.

Hope you are quite well.

Ever affectionately yours,
Henry Wallis

BRIEF LIVES

Alma-Tadema, Sir Lawrence, R.A. (1836–1912)
An Establishment painter, like Wallis interested in archaeology. Alma-Tadema is said to have known everybody.

Broughton de Gyfford, Baron (John Cam Hobhouse) (1786–1869)
Byron's early and good friend, and a lifelong friend of Peacock's. He became an important governmental official. Peacock's most intimate letters are to him.

Buchanan, Robert Williams (1841–1901)
English poet, best known for his ill-natured attacks — among them the well-known "The Fleshly School of Poetry" — on Rossetti and Swinburne.

Burne-Jones, Sir Edward Coley (1833–1898)
Artist, old friend of Wallis's, and associate of William Morris. His wife, Georgie, writes the note to Henry on page 219.

Chesney, Francis Rowdon (1789–1872)
British explorer in the Near East.

Clairmont, Claire (1798–1879)
The stepdaughter of William Godwin, and stepsister to Mary Shelley. She was "ruined" at the age of sixteen or so by Lord Byron, with immense satisfaction to her vanity, and bore him a daughter, Allegra, who died in childhood. Claire herself lived to be very old and worked as a governess in Russia.

Clarke, Edith Nicolls, M.B.E. (1844–1926)
Daughter of Mary Ellen, and eventually principal of the National Training School of Cookery. She was distinguished by being made a Member of the British Empire.

Daniel, Peter Austin (1828?–1917?)

Friend and collaborator of George Meredith on the *Monthly Observer,* and lifelong friend of Henry Wallis. Daniel, I believe, wanted in his youth to be an artist, but he worked as a clerk in the East India Company, instead.

Gilbert, Sir John (1817–1897)

A painter of historical subjects.

Hogg, Thomas Jefferson (1792–1862)

In his youth a friend of Shelley's; he became, in time, a respected judge, though he never became respectable, but rather chased women and did not believe in God. Good Victorians disapproved of him.

Hughes, Arthur (1832–1915)

British Pre-Raphaelite painter and lifelong friend of Henry Wallis.

Hunt, William Holman (1827–1910)

Noted British painter and lifelong friend of Henry Wallis. The injured picture mentioned in the text was his famous *Light of the World.*

Kingsley, Charles (1819–1875)

A "radical liberal" clergyman of the Church of England. Mary Ellen wrote an essay in praise of his *The Saint's Tragedy* for the *Monthly Observer.* Author of *Westward Ho, The Water Babies, Alton Locke,* and many other novels and stories.

L'Estrange, Thomas

An obscure Irish gentleman who interested himself in Peacock's affairs.

Love, Harriet

Cousin to Thomas Love Peacock on his mother's side. She gave helpful biographical details for the earliest memoirs of Peacock.

Meredith, Arthur (1853–1890)

The son of Mary Ellen and George Meredith.

Meredith, George (1828–1909)

Important English novelist and poet. He was known in his day for his "advanced" views on such matters as women's lot.

Meredith, Mary Ellen Peacock Nicolls (1821–1861)

An unfortunate but courageous woman.

Mill, James (1773–1836)
 Peacock's predecessor at India House; British political philosopher whom tradition has held Peacock did not like very much, which is apparently not true. They went on many long walks together, in any case.

Mill, John Stuart (1806–1873)
 British philosopher, author of On Liberty, and Peacock's successor at India House.

Milton, the first Mrs (d. 1652)
 Mary Powell, who ran away from John Milton a month after they were married. Evidently she did not like him, and could hardly be persuaded to come back again. She is said to have inspired Milton's pamphlets in favor of divorce. Ultimately, she died of childbearing, so her first impulse may have been correct.

Morris, William (1834–1896)
 The artist, printer, designer, poet, decorator, socialist reformer, inventor, and a dozen other things. He lived at a beautiful place called Kelmscott and really started the arts-and-crafts movement.

Nicolls, General Sir Edward, K.C.B. (1779–1865)
 "Fighting Nicolls," father of Edward Jr., and "the most distinguished officer" of which the Royal Marines can boast.

Nicolls, Lt. Edward (d. 1844)
 First husband of Mary Ellen and father of Edith.

Peacock, Edward Gryffydh (1825?–1867)
 Peacock's son and Mary Ellen's brother. Said to be a "wild" young man.

Peacock, Jane Gryffydh (1789–1851)
 Wife of Thomas Love Peacock and mother of Mary Ellen.

Peacock, Sarah (1754–1833)
 Mother to Thomas Love Peacock, and his great friend and "best critic."

Peacock, Thomas Love (1785–1866)
 English poet, novelist, and principal Examiner of the East India Company — or, important bureaucrat.

Petrie, Sir William Matthew Flinders (1853–1942)
> A great archaeologist, whose most notable feat was to preside over the diggings at Abydos.

Read, Sir Charles Hercules (1857–1929)
> Keeper of the Department of British Medieval Antiquities and Ethnography, old friend of Henry Wallis.

Rosewell, Mary Anne (1823?–1883)
> The adopted daughter of Thomas Love Peacock, known as "May."

Rossetti, Dante Gabriel (1828–1882)
> English poet and painter, one of the founders of Pre-Raphaelitism.

Rossetti, Elizabeth Siddal (d. 1862)
> She was the unhappy model and mistress of Dante Gabriel Rossetti, who married her after a "long engagement." She died shortly thereafter of an overdose of laudanum, and Rossetti, in his extravagant grief, buried his manuscript poems with her, so that in a few years he had to have her dug up again to get them back.

Rossetti, William Michael (1829–1919)
> Brother to Dante and Christina, William Michael was the writer and scholar and "straight" member of this otherwise eccentric family.

St. Croix, Marianne
> Nothing whatever is known about her, beyond her early attachment to T. L. Peacock, whom she decided not to marry. She was probably related to George and Mary Meredith's friend Hilary de St. Croix.

Scott, William Bell (1811–1890)
> A poet and painter and friend of Henry's.

Shelley, Harriet Westbrook (1795–1816)
> First wife to Mr. Shelley, and the one Tom Peacock always preferred. Harriet committed suicide by drowning after Mr. Shelley ran off with Miss Godwin. She was pregnant when she died, which allowed her detractors to circulate ugly rumors about her, in defense of Shelley's desertion of her. But a recent scholar, Mrs. Boas, has shown that the poor girl was probably pregnant—once again—by Shelley.

Shelley, Mary Godwin (1797–1851)

The author of *Frankenstein*. She was the second wife to Mr. Shelley, daughter of William Godwin and the great feminist Mary Wollstonecraft.

Shelley, Percy Bysshe (1792–1822)

Major English poet who tragically drowned.

Smith, Madeleine

The defendant in a famous murder trial in 1857. She was accused of giving her lover arsenic.

Stephens, Frederic George (1828–1907)

An early associate of the Pre-Raphaelite Brotherhood, and for forty years art critic of the *Atheneum*. His son Holly (Holman) was notably handsome, and a friend of Felix Wallis.

Swinburne, Algernon Charles (1837–1909)

British poet.

Wallis, Harold Felix (1858–1933)

Born Harold Meredith, because Mrs. Meredith was still married to Mr. Meredith at the time she bore him to Mr. Wallis. He grew up to have a successful career in banking.

Wallis, Henry (1830–1916)

Pre-Raphaelite painter, distinguished authority on Far Eastern ceramics, and the villain — or the hero — of this work.

Watts, George Frederic (1817–1904)

Painter and sculptor. In 1886, when he was almost seventy, he married a "friend and disciple," Miss Mary Fraser Taylor — which accounts for the amusement of his friends.

Wollstonecraft, Mary (Godwin) (1759–1797)

The author of *A Vindication of the Rights of Women,* the first major feminist work. Miss Wollstonecraft did not believe in marriage, but in the end did marry Mr. Godwin, the father of her child (Mary Shelley), for the sake of giving the child a name. She died just after, of childbed fever.

A LIST OF MANUSCRIPTS USED

Oxford, England. Bodleian Library. MS Don e. 79. Henry Wallis letters. MS Autog. C. 9. m. 143. Mary Shelley to Mary Ellen Meredith, letters. MS Eng. Misc. c. 435. Edith Nicolls from Cole and L'Estrange, letters. No. 73. *Translation of an Anapestic Ode to Christ: Matthew X, 34.*

London, England. British Museum. Add MS 38, 831. Papers presented by Henry Wallis of the St. Marks Committee. Add MS 38, 794, I. Letter from Robert Browning to Dante Gabriel Rossetti. Add MS 38, 763, 70 ff. Memo to Lord Bathhurst, 1822, from Edward Nicolls. Add MS 47225 ff., 1–175. Thomas Love Peacock to Lord Broughton letters. Ashley 5730. Thomas Jefferson Hogg to Thomas Love Peacock and Mary Ellen Meredith, letters.

Cambridge, Mass. Harvard University. Widener Library. *The Monthly Observer,* January–July, 1849.

San Marino, Calif. Huntington Library. Edward Nicolls to Thomas Clarkson letters.

New York City. Pforzheimer Library. P'ana 2. Memo by John Laird on Thomas Love Peacock and steam navigation. 497b MS. Receipts on scraps of paper. MS. *Science of Cookery.* ALS. Mary Ellen Meredith to Eddy, letters. ALS. Mary Ellen Meredith to Thomas Love Peacock, letters.

London, England. Victoria and Albert Museum. 86/BB/30 Henry Wallis. 38 letters to Albert Van de Put. Box IV, 86. S. Henry Wallis notebooks. Henry Wallis. Original drawings to *Nicolà du Urbino.*

Purley, England. Wallis Estate. Unpublished letters to Henry Wallis.

New Haven, Conn. Yale University. Beinecke Rare Books and Manuscript Library. George Meredith's manuscript notebooks. Mary Ellen Meredith's Commonplace Book.

SELECTED BIBLIOGRAPHY

Cameron, K. N., ed. *Shelley and his Circle.* Cambridge, Mass.: Harvard University Press, 1961.

Clarke, Edith Nicolls. *High-Class Cookery.* 7th ed. London: William Clowes & Son, 1897.

Cline, C. L. "The Betrothal of George Meredith to Marie Vulliamy," *Nineteenth Century Fiction* 16 (December 1961): 231–43.

————. *Letters of George Meredith.* 3 vols. Oxford: Clarendon Press, 1970.

Clodd, Edward. *Memories.* London: Chapman and Hall, 1916.

Constant, Benjamin. *Adolphe.* Translated by B. W. Tancock. Baltimore: Penguin, 1964.

Dawson, Carl. *His Fine Wit.* Berkeley: University of California Press, 1970.

Ellis, S. M. *George Meredith: His Life and Friends in Relation to His Work.* London: Grant Richards, 1919.

————. *The Letters and Memoirs of Sir William Hardman.* Second Series. London: Cecil Palmer, 1925.

Field, Col. C. *Britain's Sea-Soldiers.* Liverpool: Lyceum Press, 1924.

Forman, Maurice Buxton. *George Meredith and the "Monthly Observer."* Edinburgh, 1928.

Fredeman, William E. *Pre-Raphaelitism.* Cambridge: Harvard University Press, 1965.

Galland, René. *George Meredith: les cinquante premières années.* Paris: Les presses françaises, 1923.

Globe and Laurel (The Journal of the Royal Marines). January 1897.

Hornby, Sir Edmund. *Autobiography.* London: Constable, 1929.

Houghton, Walter. *The Victorian Frame of Mind.* New Haven: Yale University Press, 1957.

Jesse, F. Tennyson. *The Trial of Madeleine Smith*. Edinburgh: W. Hodge, 1928.

Jones, Frederick L., ed. *The Letters of Mary W. Shelley*. Norman: University of Oklahoma Press, 1947.

Le Gallienne, Richard. *George Meredith: Some Characteristics*. London: Elkin Matthews, 1890.

Lehman, R. C., ed. *Charles Dickens as Editor*. London: Smith, Elder, 1912.

Matz, B. W. "Some Unknown Poems of George Meredith." *TP's Weekly* (17 February 1911): 209–210.

Meredith, George. *The Poetical Works of George Meredith*. With some notes by G. M. Trevelyan. London: Constable, 1912.

Meredith, Mary Ellen. "Gastronomy and Civilisation." *Fraser's Magazine,* December 1851.

———. "Soyer's Modern Housewife, or Menagere." *Fraser's Magazine* 44 (August 1851): 199–209.

Oxford Dictionary of English Art. Ed. T. S. R. Boase. Oxford: Oxford University Press, 1959.

Peacock, Thomas Love. *Letters to Edward Hookham and Percy Bysshe Shelley* (with fragments of unpublished manuscripts). Ed. Richard Garnett. Boston: The Bibliophile Society, 1910.

Peacock, Thomas Love. *The Works of Thomas Love Peacock*. Ed. F. B. Brett-Smith and C. E. Jones. 10 vols. London: Constable, 1924–34.

———. *Works*. Ed. Henry Cole. 3 vols. London: Richard Bentley, 1875.

Rossetti, William Michael. *Some Reminiscences*. London: Brown and Langham, 1906.

Ruskin, John, M. A. *Notes on the Principal Pictures in the Royal Academy*. 1856. Pamphlet.

Sassoon, Siegfried. *Meredith*. London: Constable, 1948.

Scott, Winifred. *Jefferson Hogg*. London: Jonathan Cape, 1951.

Shorter, Clement. "Literary Letter." *Sphere* 64 (March 1916): 328.

Van Doren, Carl. *The Life of Thomas Love Peacock*. London: J. M. Dent, 1911.

Yonge, Charlotte M. *Heartsease: or the Brother's Wife*. London: Macmillan, 1847.

.

A Note About the Type

The text of this book was set in the film version
of Optima, a typeface designed by Hermann
Zapf from 1952–55 and issued in 1958. In
designing Optima, Zapf created a truly new type
form—a cross between the classic roman and a
sans-serif face. So delicate are the stresses and
balances in Optima that it rivals sans-serif faces
in clarity and freshness and old-style faces in
variety and interest.

The book was composed, printed, and bound by
Kingsport Press, Inc., Kingsport, Tennessee.
Typography and binding design by Betty Anderson.
Calligraphy and ornaments by Monica Moseley.